A H... Easter

Dale Marie Taylor

Narrativemagic Press, San Antonio, Tx 2019

Copyright © 2019 DM Taylor

All rights reserved.

ISBN:
ISBN-13: 978-1-7339050-9-1

All rights reserved. By payment of required fees, you have been granted the non-exclusive, non-transferable right to access and read the text of this book. No part of this text may be reproduced, transmitted, downloaded, decompiled, reverse engineered or stored in or introduced into any information storage and retrieval system, in any form or by any means, whether electronic or mechanical, now known on or hereafter invented, without express written permission of Narrativemagic LLC or DM Taylor. No part of this document may be reproduced or transmitted in any form or by any means, electronic, mechanical, photocopying, recording, or otherwise, without prior written permission of Narrativemagic LLC.

A Home for Easter is a work of fiction. Names, characters, places and incidents are products of the writer's imagination or have been used fictitiously and are not to be construed as real. Any resemblance to persons living or dead, actual events, places, incidents or organizations is coincidental.

DEDICATION

To my father, Joe, who asked me to write the story and his sister, Clara. Also, to Heber and Michael.

CONTENTS

CHAPTER ONE

Spring 1837

Easter Ward lay in bed twisting and turning as she tried to fight the images in her head. The dream was a recurring one. Shamans frequently took flight and shifted, but she was surprised that she had that ability. She was both a wolf and a bear. Her vision was far-reaching. Her shape continued to shift. She turned into the wolf first. The wolf was high on a mountaintop and saw a long line of her people walking in the elements. Some died of thirst; some died of hunger — so many walked the long distance.

Bodies littered the landscape; people fell and were buried by their people and the soldiers. It seemed to be happening in the future and quickly. She moaned and twisted in her covers, a heavy wool blanket that kept getting twisted around her midriff. She frowned, her brow furrowing as she fought the truth being revealed to her. Totem Bear came to her next, motioning in the opposite direction. What could she be trying to say? Easter jerked up, sitting straight up in her bed in the little room she shared with her sister. Beads of sweat glistened on her face. She breathed heavily as she tried to work out what the dream meant.

She reached for a bowl and poured water into it from the jug beside her bed. The little room was quiet with the soft breathing of her sister. Stars shown brightly outside the window of the little house near Red Clay Springs. She rose and walked to the window, allowing the breeze to cool her face. She thought she saw a wolf sitting some distance from the cabin. No need to shoo it away; it was there for her. It often sat outside the compound looking in. It was said that one of her kinswomen saved a wolf cub and that the cub never forgot the kindness. The wolf had something important to tell her. She only need listen. She wondered too if there were answers to the mystery of her brother's death. The family had land and a small gold mine in the place now called Georgia. But her brother, Connutsee, had been killed trying to hold the property. The mystery gnawed at her constantly. She remembered the many close moments with her brother — his having taught her to hunt and fish — and his handsome good looks. His long dark hair and his tall, muscled body mirrored that of her younger brothers. His was a loss that she still felt keenly.

The next morning, she walked to the well to draw water and hauled the bucket back to the cabin. She wore a long skirt, dyed with red berries, and a soft beige tunic. Her sister, Lucinda, was getting out of bed and pulled the covers over the crude mattress. It was time to get food ready and to work in the little garden they had planted. Easter was one of those fortunate women in the Wild Potato clan, keepers of the land, who had land; she used it to plant potatoes, corn, beans, wheat, and other crops that benefited not only the neighboring villages, but the travelers on their route west. She managed to hang on to her property because she had developed a reputation for supplying the travelers. She also had customers in larger communities where her workers took the crops to get a good price.

She had two blacks and a Cherokee working for her, but the three men rotated, going from farm to farm, helping others. A Cherokee who looked white came to her from time to time to ask for work, but there were laws against hiring a white man, so she did not obviously hire him. However, when he offered to do chores for her in exchange for food, she allowed him to do so. She hadn't seen the four men in some time. It was likely some of them had been taken by the soldiers and were headed west. The Treaty of New Echota had been signed in December 1835, giving the Cherokees two years to remove to Oklahoma. She knew this, and others knew this as well. So, it was possible that the men who helped work her farm had been pressed into service or forced to move west. Time had passed, and the U.S. government was getting more and more insistent. The soldiers were pressing everyone to move.

At their cabin, Easter and her sister Lucinda had chickens to feed and eggs to gather. The few cows were kept in a barn, away from predators, and turned out each morning. It was a clear, bright day in March. The planting was done, and the wait for the harvest would begin. A large barn sat to the west of her property. It was a tall structure made of rough-hewn boards. It was as wide as six cows placed end to end, and had space for her horses, mules, cows, goats, chickens and Lucinda's special birds. It had double doors in the front and one high window at the top. Her father and brother said they should not trust predators to climb in a low window. So, their only source of natural light in the barn was an opening high in the building. She silently thanked her father and brother, Connutsee, for building it for her. They had been natural carpenters.

Easter walked to the barn, did the milking and shooed the cows out to the pasture. She rarely needed to bother with the goats, but this morning, her helper Josiah was away, so she tended them too. Then she walked to the cabin. She poured water into a large bowl and waited while Lucinda washed her face. Then, Easter took her turn, washing and then slipping a clean tunic over her head.

"You dreamt again," Lucinda said as she went to the little cabinet to get out the cornmeal.

"I did."

"The same dream?"

"It was."

"It must mean that we should go west," Lucinda said. "West before it gets bad, before we're forced to go."

"No, Luce, I don't think it means that at all," Easter said. "I'm not sure where we're supposed to be, but I don't think we're supposed to go west."

"You might not want to go there, but that doesn't mean I don't," Lucinda said. "You won't listen to your spirit guide. If you won't, I will." They had had this argument countless times. If they wanted to have peace between them, it was best that Easter not let her sister know that she would be going in a different direction, toward Giles.

Just then, there was a knock at the door. Walking Bird opened the door and invited himself in. "I'm here to help you eat your morning meal," he said, grinning. Walking Bird was sweet on Lucinda and insisted on being there to remind her as often as possible. He was from a different clan and rode a distance to be with Lucinda. He had to ask the sisters' grandmother's permission to be with Lucinda, but their maternal grandmother, Amadahy, the only surviving matriarch in the family, was slow to give her consent. Walking Bird had invited Amadahy to his village to improve his chances of marrying Lucinda.

"If you really want to eat, Walking Bird, I suggest you go out and get more eggs," Easter said. Walking Bird made an about face and went to the chicken yard. He turned to see whether Lucinda was following. Lucinda wiped her hands on her skirt, grabbed a basket and followed Walking Bird to the barn where Easter and Lucinda kept birds.

"So have you given any more thought to my suggestion?" he asked, smiling at her as they entered the coop. Lucinda scrunched her nose and said nothing. She fussed over her special doves. Lucinda and Easter were two of the most beautiful women in the compound. Their long, dark hair and smooth, olive skin attracted much attention. Both women looked so much alike that people thought they were twins. The two women worked together and went most places together so if a man wanted to visit with one, he had to put up with the other.

At nearly 20 summers, Lucinda was unusual because she had not taken a man. Lucinda was interested in her birds, spending time with them, training them and getting them to fly from place to place. Most all of the seven clans of the Cherokee believed that doves and pigeons were messengers. But Lucinda had been using them literally as messengers. At first, Walking Bird was skeptical, but soon he enjoyed working with the creatures too. They tried to urge those missionaries who lived nearby not to kill the birds, but not everyone cared about such things. Lucinda was certain that training the birds to fly from Walking Bird's village to Lucinda's would be useful. They used the Cherokee alphabet developed in 1821 by Sequoyah to send simple messages to one another. Lucinda had learned the written language from one of the mission teachers. Mrs. Gambold at Spring Place taught them much more than they needed. She entertained them with knowledge and the ability to understand a much larger world. So the birds became a bit of an obsession for Lucinda, and later Walking Bird enjoyed them too.

Easter did not think much of this pastime. Though Lucinda explained that she thought it would have a purpose, Easter thought her sister was playing when she should have been helping with the chores. Easter had been married but was still young at 23 summers. However, the two women had seen much suffering, having lost their parents to flu just a few years ago. The surviving family believed they died of broken hearts after having had to relinquish some of their land in a Georgia Land Lottery. Settlers were coming west in large numbers, and the sisters' parents had lost part of their homestead and a great deal of their assets. The land lottery was so ridiculous that many of the settlers paid as little as $4 for a portion of land. This state of affairs worried Walking Bird. He wanted to get Lucinda away from the last remaining patch of land owned by her mother's family. Settlers saw it as having the potential for gold.

"I think I could get a better offer elsewhere," Lucinda teased, holding one of her doves close.

"Better than me?" Walking Bird looked at her as though she were insane. He wanted her to marry him and go east with him to what the whites called North Carolina. But Lucinda was not interested. Two young men were interested in her and had made no secret of it. Walking Bird wanted Lucinda to choose him. As a partner in her sister's farming business, Lucinda was not wealthy, but she had assets. She was also attractive, with a face that was smooth and soft and a long, sultry neck. This morning, she wore a red skirt like her sister's and a beige tunic over it. Walking Bird could see the curves under her tunic. The morning sun peeked over the hills. Birds began to chirp, flitting from tree to tree and landing on the rich soil in search of insects.

"Let's talk about it later, Walking Bird. It's too early to talk about going anywhere." She placed the dove back in its wooden cage with more than a dozen others. She walked out of the barn and turned to face Walking Bird.

"I don't want you to go just anyplace with me, Lucinda; I mean I do. I want you to decide whether you will marry me. Be with me." He looked around to see whether anyone was watching and pressed her against the barn. She could feel his muscles and hardness.

"Lucinda, say you'll come to me. I've worked to be sure we have someplace to live. I have the birds that we split so that they can fly to you. We can work together. We can have a family in a safe place. Just tell me you'll think on it." He nearly whispered the words. He had already pleaded with Lucinda's grandmother and felt that she was near to agreeing that Lucinda could come with him. Lucinda took a deep breath and pushed him away gently. He backed up, smiling at her.

His long, dark hair fell across his back. He wore thick pantaloons and an embroidered hunting shirt. His hair was shaved back from his forehead and one single scalp lock hung as a braid from the back of his head. From the scalp lock hung one eagle feather. He wore a dark scarlet blanket over one shoulder, which he used as both a blanket and a bed. "Lucinda, I've come from some distance to see you and to ask you to walk with me. I will wait for your decision, but many are pressing us off these lands. Your grandmother is going to agree because we have no

7

choice in this. You remember what happened after they took land where your parents lived?" Lucinda shivered as he paused in making his case. He did not want to remind her of the useless waste of her brother Connutsee's life. Connutsee had been trying to protect family property when he was killed in a fight between some Red Creeks and a white man.

"You will see that my way is the best. When you have decided, send one of our birds to me," he said. He walked toward her again and wrapped his arms around her. He held her closely so that she could feel his ardor. He lifted her chin and brushed her lips with his. "Say it will be so, Lucinda," he whispered. Walking Bird was tall and muscled; she could feel his strength under his thick wool shirt. Walking Bird could feel her softness but also her strength. She would make a good wife. After breakfast, he mounted his horse; he pointed it east and looked back at her. She wrapped her arms around herself. He smiled at her and rode away, stopping once to look at her again, and then riding hard to the east.

Easter listened as her former husband, John Hester, shared the news of the latest treaty negotiations between the Cherokee tribal government and the U.S. government. Things had not looked good for many years. Andrew Jackson at first appeared to be a friend to the Cherokees. Then the Indian Removal Bill was ratified in May 1830. The Creeks, Choctaws, Chickasaws and Cherokees were to sign treaties agreeing to remove west. Her parents had insisted that Easter would inherit land in this place the Europeans called Tennessee. But it didn't appear it would happen. Her paternal grandmother, Hialeah, told stories of the proposed state of Franklin, a plan by whites to push the Cherokees from their land. That was years ago. John

Hester was a witness to some of the treaty negotiations and was close to John Ross and some of the other leaders of the Cherokees. John's deeply tanned skin, broad, muscled shoulders and shining dark hair made him a favorite with the women. He and Arter Beasley were half brothers, grown close through years of association.

"We tried our best," John said, looking downcast. "But the Chickasaws and the Creeks signed removal treaties." He sighed and sat down in Easter's small house. His 6-foot frame seemed to make the little cottage much smaller. He wore dark trousers and a dark Western shirt, the garb of the white men he associated with daily in his efforts to help the Cherokee. His muscled arms strained against the small shirt. He wore his long, dark hair pulled back from his face. His strong jaw curved in long lines away from his ears, where he wore a long earring on one side and a feather on the other.

It did not escape Easter's notice that he was still as handsome as he had been when they promised to be with each other. She hadn't seen him in two years. The house was Spartan and utilitarian, with few belongings. Easter prided herself in keeping things neat and clean. She knew that her siblings found her obsession with cleanliness to be a flaw. They often made fun of her because of her little requests. She wanted them to wash their hands in warm water before they ate. She wanted them to take off their shoes before they entered her space. She wanted them to use a clean cloth to wash and to wash often. Sometimes it was too much to tolerate, and, in response, her closest family members chose to live elsewhere. Only her sister Lucinda and her youngest brother, Wahali, were able to put up with her obsessions. Add that that her peculiar habit of reading. She had traded with other women in the area for many books. Wahali could not understand it. Sometimes, the two sisters read together. No one he knew did this. But the women kept their passion for reading to themselves. But Wahali was on his own quest for helping people. Wahali's older brother, Degataga, decided to marry outside the Cherokee — in part to help the family, but also because his wife was one-of-a-kind.

Easter's parents had built the little home on rich farmland so that she and her sister and brother might have some security when their parents passed. Their father's Blue clan had land in the state that was called Franklin, in the territory called East Tennessee. However, their mother's Potato clan was from the west and owned land near Giles County but also in Georgia where the rumor of gold had prompted whites to drive out many Cherokees. Easter pushed thoughts of her struggles to the back of her mind when Sarah Armstrong arrived at her door with a white settler who needed help. The man had a large gash on his forehead. Sarah and one of the men from the village were helping the injured man to Easter's door.

Easter opened it and said little as the injured man was helped in. He bled through the rag Sarah had pressed to his head. John Hester helped him into the little cabin.

"What happened?" Easter asked.

"Benjamin was helping his brother cut down some timber when a tree struck him," Sarah said. "Can you take a look, Easter?" Easter knew that this was Sarah's polite way of saying please help the man. Easter set to work. She kept some hot water in the cabin. She fetched it, removed the rag and cleaned out the man's wound. He flinched. That was a good sign. He might have lost much blood, but he was still aware. Benjamin slumped in the chair as she worked

on him, so Easter asked John and the others to put
him on the floor. Benjamin was a large man, like her
brothers. He appeared to be more than 6 feet.
Wahali, who dropped in from time to time at Easter's
cabin, came to to observe. She had been teaching
him how to heal for years. They often went to the
woods together to collect herbs and bark for healing.

Easter's collection of dried herbs sat in various
clay jars in her cabin. She had recently gone to the
woods to refresh her collection of sassafras, skullcap,
wild yam, goldenseal, comfrey and other herbs and
roots. She quickly got the tincture she used to clean
wounds, a mixture of goldenseal and comfrey. When
she had cleaned the wound, she reached for the
yucca thread she'd collected from trade and
considered whether she should use a new thread that
she'd bought from a passing pioneer. She grabbed
the new thread, threaded her needle and began
sewing the man's wound, a gash of about 6 inches
that bled as she pinched it closed. Finally, she was
finished with the stitching of Benjamin's wound. She
wrapped his head with some of the clean bandages
she kept in a wooden box.

When Wahali, John and Easter decided that
Benjamin was well enough to return to his cabin, he
turned to her.

"I'll not forget this kindness, mistress," Benjamin
said, holding his hat tightly in one hand. He held out
a hand to her in the way of whites. He gently
squeezed her hand and smiled at her as he turned and
left with his friends.

As the sun went down, Easter's thoughts returned
to her efforts to find a new home. She had papers to
prove her ownership of land in Middle Tennessee,
but whether anyone would recognize her rights was
another matter. The land was settled as early as 1810.
It might be too late for her to try to recover family

land. Her maternal grandmother, Amadahy, had gone to North Carolina, with no interest in family land. Amadahy's family were friends of family of Chief John Ross. However, many Cherokees were beginning to see their independence being chipped away. Her family had been wealthy, owning land throughout Tennessee, Georgia and North Carolina. But now, that land was taken, and family members, like so many others, were pushed further and further away. Easter prepared a meal and called Lucinda inside.

CHAPTER TWO

Autumn 1837

"My advice is to move west. The soldiers are already forcing our people into camps and forcing them to go west to Oklahoma," John Hester said. "I would take you myself, but I am needed. This will go on for some time. It will be complicated and violent. Many people will die. Some are suffering and dying in the camps before they even begin the long walk west. I fear no one will be happy with this outcome." John's dark good looks were apparent even though he was exhausted. He had ridden from Georgia, where a Cherokee was to be hanged for murder. He was worried that one of her brothers might have been caught in this bloodthirsty push to get Cherokees out of the territory. He wondered if it was because the Cherokees had sided with the British during the Revolutionary War. But there were many other concessions after that. The tribe had lost half of its numbers to a smallpox epidemic in the 1700s. The trials seemed never-ending.

The aggression of the Georgia Guard as well as white settlers participating in the lottery for Cherokee land was causing a number of confrontations.

Cherokee people danced, sang and prayed, but to John the inevitable would come soon. There were many, many settlers with a hunger for land. Many had already settled in the area.

Much of the fight involving Georgia, the Cherokees and the U.S. had been in court. Since the fight was not apparent, some Cherokees deluded themselves into believing that all would be well, that they could keep their lands and the whites would retreat. Chief John Ross had employed an attorney to fight against the state of Georgia. When the Supreme Court ruled in favor of the Cherokee Nation, many in the nation were heartened, but warring factions later prevented leaders from agreeing on a treaty for removal.

When John married Easter, some years back, he came to her from the nearby Deer clan. Couples were not permitted to marry within their own clans. A Cherokee priest had put the ceremonial blankets around the couple, first blue then white. She gave him corn; he gave her venison. His mother and her mother and some of her brothers were there. The ceremony was followed by much dancing and celebration, eating and fun. Then John moved into her household. They had had one child, who had died in a flu epidemic. Now John knew it must have been caused by close contact with those outside the village. Still, his heart was broken. Easter moved his things outside the house they shared with others. But in her heart, Easter was unable to let him go completely; he knew that. She was indecisive. He always felt that she had let her mother talk her into putting his belongings outside the door.

When Easter had moved him out of her household, John moved back in with his mother's people. Not long after that, trouble intensified between the Cherokees and the whites, who wanted more land. His grandmother and grandfather told him stories of the whites near what was called Franklin. Those white men wanted to declare Franklin a state and expel the Cherokees. Although they didn't get their state, the whites got much of what they wanted. John's family and Easter's family were pushed from the area.

John's words echoed in Easter's mind. "Move west before more whites come. Before they force us off our lands. If you prepare to go before you are forced, you will be able to take some goods with you. If you wait to be forced, you may leave with nothing." She, like many of the other Cherokee women, was being displaced by this new way of life the Europeans brought. Many of the men and those able to climb the steep slopes were hiding in the mountains. Her oldest brother, Degataga, Stands Firm, had married a white woman to hold the family land in Georgia. But it wasn't enough. The idea that there was gold on their land was too much of a temptation for the Europeans.

During the time of the old ways, Cherokee women were leaders, well respected with matrilineal inheritance. The power came to a Cherokee woman. But the settlers brought their male view. So things changed. Women in the tribe still played an important role, but not such as it was before the settlers foisted their values on the Cherokees. Easter thought of the stories of Ghi-ga-u, or Beloved Woman of the Cherokees, who was able to speak for, vote for and act on behalf of the people at all the peace and war councils of the tribe. She had a regal presence and had stood up for many who needed her help. But that was many years ago. She had been given a Negro who had been captured and so was the first to own a slave. Easter didn't know whether she liked that about Ghi-ga-u. Some said Easter's mother's family was related to Ghi-ga-u. Still, it would do no good to look back. It was time to make plans to escape and survive.

Easter had been making baskets and clay pottery, saving some for the storage of food and seeds and selling some to anyone who passed the compound and seemed open to looking over her wares. She had worked hard to ensure the crop yielded well. She sold some of the excess to nearby villagers and to passing settlers.

She dried and preserved meat and saved much of it in tight clay jars. She saved seeds for planting, grains and dried corn. Her jewelry was not as sophisticated as she wanted, but it sold too. She prepared bean bread for John with some wild hog meat and sweet potatoes. He ate his fill, drank from the clean cool water she kept in a clay jar.

"How long will you be gone this time?" she asked, looking up at him. They had long been friends and at one time lovers; when they parted as friends, she knew he would always be her first love.

"The whites are asking for help rounding up the Seminoles," he said. "The pay is good."

"Surely you can't help them do this thing, John," she said, looking at him as though he had grown a second head. "They are Nvada dinlyoli, sun children. They follow the old ways. Don't help them do this thing."

"I don't want to do it," he said, sighing. "But it seems that the whites are determined to move all of us out of their way so they can have land. Some of us are getting money for the land, but most of it is not enough. They say the land to the west is barren and will not grow food, nor does it have plentiful game as it does here."

Easter turned and looked out the window, she thought about the disturbing dreams and visions she had been having. In one of her dreams, she began a long journey west and then turned into a bird and flew back. She could not go forward as a strong wind pushed her back.

It made her think of her brother, Mohe, who has full of anger. He had decided to confront people as much as he could. His anger was overflowing. She wondered whether he was staying out of trouble.

"Have you heard how Mohe is doing, John?" she asked, frowning at him but expressing hopefulness.. He sighed. He was reluctant to talk to her about her brother, who had his own ideas for how things should go.

"There are many young men who are angry and are trying to take matters into their own hands. However, I don't think Mohe will go too far in challenging those who might be a danger to him."

The sound of squawking chickens came from the yard. One of Easter's two dogs, Waya, barked a warning. Waya, part wolf with light colored eyes, came to the door and sniffed the air as though something was coming.

Ama, Easter's female dog, sat quietly at the barn door.

A woman shouted for her children to clean the mud from their feet. Easter turned back to look at John.

"John, can you bring Mohe to me so that he can make the trip west?"

John thought about the heated words he had exchanged with Mohe, who called all the men working with the U.S. government cowards. John didn't want to worry Easter, so he decided only to share the general nature of the discussion. But he felt that Mohe was headed for trouble.

"I have already had this discussion with him, Easter. He refuses to back down from those who have the power to destroy him. I will look for him again before I go, but the chances of finding him are not good."

"Can you bring him and then go with us?" she asked.

"And what then, Easter?" he said looking at her. She knew what he was suggesting. He wanted back in her bed, in her life. But she could not come to an agreement with him. She looked away into the distance, unwilling to make a permanent commitment.

"It's unlikely that I will come back this way soon," he said. "I plan to go far west in search of some place to settle. Arter wants to help take care of you?" He said it like a question, the idea hanging in the air between them. He let the notion settle on her for a moment. His brother had long been enamored of Easter. When she refused to recommit to him, John thought the next best thing would be for his brother to protect her. "I'm fed up with all of it." He made a slashing movement with his hand. Even as he said the words, he felt conflicting emotions. He knew he still loved Easter. He knew his heart still belonged to her. But he couldn't bring himself to admit it to her. He also preferred wide-open spaces — hunting and fishing — to farming.

"Will any of our people keep their land, John? Will you be able to bring Mohe to me?"

"No, maybe. Some of us may keep our lands. I don't know. We will lose much. All of this fighting. It's not something I want to be in the middle of any longer. I plan to go as far west as I can go. But first, I will bring Mohe to you, if I can."

"You will not shelter with us? Grandmother approves of you." He and Easter had an understanding that was approved by her grandmother. For sometime, they had been a married couple. But then, one day, Easter had put his clothes outside her door. That meant they were not a couple anymore. He had no hard feelings because she let him return to her occasionally, but Arter always lingered nearby.

"No, I want to forget this all. The whites are even robbing graves to steal the silver buried with our dead. It is not going to get any better." He rose from his chair and walked over to her, placing his arms around her. She turned around to face him.

"This makes me very sad," Easter said, placing her arms around him and hugging him to her. He stroked her hair and kissed her forehead. She had seen so much loss, her parents and then Connutsee. The times were violent, and Cherokee people were dying from disease and the stress of removal.

"The only way to overcome this time is to continue to live, to blend in where you can and to forget the struggles for land, Easter," he said. "We will not win this fight. Promise me you will find a safe place for you and Lucinda, maybe Wahali and Mohe too. Let Arter help you. Go to the old lands and hide in plain sight."

"What do you mean by that?"

"Remember that your mother's mother has land that reaches far. Go there with Arter. Don't think that you must cling to some notion of being Cherokee," he said. "You are a woman who can pass as any person she wants. All you need to do is act the part. Promise me you will do so and promise me you will let Arter help you." He was referring of course to her skin, which grew dark from working in the fields. Was he suggesting that Easter might be a mixed-blood Cherokee? No, she looked at his face. He looked sincere.

The idea brought thoughts of Awinta, Fawn, who was her father's child by the dark-skinned slave woman Inola. The woman had long since disappeared. Some say she was kidnapped; others said she died of injuries sustained in a raid. No one knew where or how Inola had been taken or whether she had been. Some said the woman had lost her mind and had walked into the woods never to be seen again. But the child, Awinta, had stayed with Easter's parents. She would be nearly eight summers now. Easter's mother allowed Awinta to stay in their home in Georgia, but Easter had no idea what had happened to the girl after Easter's parents died. Her conscience tugged at her at the thought of the girl wandering about. She was hardy and had survival skills, but she could easily have been taken by one of the settlers as a slave. Easter pushed that concern to the back of her mind and addressed John's suggestion. The whites frowned on two men with one woman, so she was confused. Just what did John mean by this suggestion that she allow Arter to care for her?

"You can't mean that you want me to be with Arter," she said. "The old ways are passing away. Boudinot and others have declared the ways of passing wealth from woman to woman invalid."

"They can say all they want in the hearing of the government, but you know that our ways can't be changed just because they say it. We've been living an uncertain existence since the Europeans came to this land. It's time to find other ways to live among them. We can live anywhere we want and still be who we are."

"I don't understand, John," Easter said. "There is nowhere for me to go."

"Yes, there is. You just need to find it," he said. "You have land. Arter has another brother, Nathan. They both look like you. Go with Arter."

John slept with Easter on her little straw mattress. They were quiet as they held each other close. John kissed her and loved her until she was too tired to stay awake. Her sister snored away on the pallet across the room. Easter hugged John to her, not wanting to let him go. John prepared to leave the next morning after a meal with the sisters. Easter packed his sacks with nuts, apples, corn and dried meat. He did not linger when it was time for him to go. He kissed both sisters and rode off on his sable mustang. Easter sighed as he disappeared. They had engaged in a ceremony for protection before John had left. They would have to trust in that. She looked at Lucinda.

"Little sister, John has promised to look for Mohe," she said. "If he can find him, Mohe may go with us when we leave here. Shall we have some more sleep or tend the animals?"

"I think I'll go back to bed," Lucinda said. Easter wondered whether Lucinda had slept with Walking Bird yet. If so, that might explain Lucinda's fatigue. But no, she had no other symptoms. She dismissed the thought and went to the barn to milk the cows and turn out the animals for grazing.

Already Easter's home and land were being challenged by the white settlers. Ezra Poe had been a thorn in her side for quite a while. He followed her and watched her, seeming to want to approach her, but then changed his mind. He was of medium height and build. He had grown muscular from riding for months since he'd been assigned to the guards. He wore his hair a little longer than was usual. He dressed in a dark cap and dark pantaloons. His gray wool shirt was threadbare under his coat. His long rifle was a possession he seemed to take great pride in maintaining. One day, Easter had seen him sitting on a stump polishing the rifle. He had been lingering for some time. He was talking to himself as though there was someone there with him. She looked around but saw no one. She frowned. One day, he had caught her out by the mill alone. She had brought her bow and arrow with her and had been hunting some in the woods near the mill. She made a show of pointing the arrow toward where he was hiding. He thought she didn't know he was there, but like her ancestors, Easter had a keen sense of hearing and smell. She could often smell a man before she saw him. Poe did not wash often.

Poe was part of the Georgia Guard, but he was allowed to travel outside his assigned area. The only thing keeping the settlers from seizing her land was its close proximity to the holdings of other whites, who had become part of her compound.

Grandmother Amadahy had already journeyed to the mountains where some of her family lived. The Georgia Guardsmen raided a few times, but they had no right to cross the border into Tennessee. Poe, though, came whenever he wanted. Easter wondered whether he had been keeping other guardsmen and whites away from her. She stood at the banks of the Red Clay waters and looked about to be certain she was alone. The last thing she wanted was to be caught by Poe when she was most vulnerable. She stripped down to bathe, keeping her knife strapped to her leg and staying within sight of her bow and arrow.

She had thought about this problem with the Europeans. John was right; things were not going to get better. The whites came in droves, their population never ceasing to grow. There were not enough women of her clan to go around; not many women of any kind survived harsh winters and rough living. The constant fighting didn't make things any better. Rogue guardsmen like Poe were apt to show up at anytime. It was an unsafe time for a woman, for anyone.

As Easter swam, she thought about the chores that needed to be accomplished if she was going to look for a new home. She had been meticulous in tending the fields, feeding and caring for the cows, chickens and goats. Her herb and vegetable garden yielded more than most. She smoked and dried meat from her hunting forays.

Her muscles ached from the heavy bushels of dried corn and the hay she'd stored in the barn. The water soothed her aches and pains. She had made two sales to settlers traveling west who were looking for corn and grain. She saved the coins she earned from the sale of her goods and kept them in a wooden box under the floor of her home. She wanted the money to be safe from those who would steal. She thought of those things and how she might help her two brothers, who were determined to do things their way.

Already, Wahali, Eagle, was somewhere in the deep woods, trying to prepare for the inevitable. She knew he would be gathering the herbs and roots that might be needed for a long trip west. Wahali had accepted the missionary education that some Cherokee grudgingly endured; he could read and write and had a voracious appetite for learning. He was versatile and wanted to go back east to learn Western medicine. For now, Wahali thought going west was the right thing to do. His paint horse followed him everywhere, carrying the precious pouches of dried herbs, roots and strips of meat. However, Mohe wanted to fight secretly and with stealth. Easter worried about them both.

Her older brother, Degataga, hoped his younger brothers would have some protection from the evil spirits that seemed so strong. He knew they would be caught up in the winds of the time. Those winds were strong and would be difficult to fight. He was deeply affected by the death of Connutsee, who had been trying to protect their property in Georgia. That family property included silver and gold mines. Now,

Degataga was doing what Connutsee had not been able to do. He had put the family's land in the name of his wife's brother, Charles, who, so far, was not interested in living in the area but accepted a portion of the profits from the land, whether from agriculture or mining. "Our brothers will do what they must," he said as he consoled Easter after the death of their parents. "The answer to surviving these times is to think," he said. "If we do that, we will do well."

Easter turned her brother's advice around in her head. Degataga and Wahali had gone their own ways. Lucinda would too, soon. Now, it was time for Easter to consider how to live. These times were chaotic. She was confused about what to do next. Her oldest brother urged her to think, but how was she to think about the confusion going on around them? The constant arrival of new people, the urgent push to move, the murders and the other hostilities … it was all overwhelming. Often she felt like she was in a never-ending fog. Where should she go? What could she do?

The missionaries who had come to their village to convert Cherokee people to Christianity taught them English and the ways of the English. Some had married and settled among them. But the lottery had begun, and land was being distributed to Georgia settlers who wanted the Cherokees to leave their ancestral lands. Poe was just one of many who knew that Easter had land legally bequeathed to her. Easter had the papers to prove it. But proving she had the rights to her land, even with the right papers, would be challenging. Just then, Easter heard the snap of a twig in the distance. She dove under the water, swimming from the shore.

She knew it was Arter. She smiled as she came up

for air and turned toward the noise. His tanned skin shone with the suggestion of health. His dark hair was pulled back with a leather tie. His leather hat sat back on his head. His hazel eyes looked at her intently. His prominent nose flared as he watched her. His broad shoulders and narrow hips, leading to strong thighs and muscled legs, suggested a power and a mystery about him. He held himself tensely. She knew that he looked at her with longing, but she was not ready to return his feelings. Her stomach knotted, and blood rushed through her body. He wanted her, but she wasn't certain she wanted to be enveloped in the strength of his passion. He smiled at her, but she pretended she didn't see.

Arter Beasley stood in the shadows of the trees near her, watching as Easter walked into the warm waters. As a missionary, he knew that things were deteriorating quickly. He had a different father than John Hester, but they shared the same mother. Their mother had gone east in an attempt to learn the ways of whites. When she was there, she met Arter's father. His mother left Arter in the East with his father and returned to her people, thinking that he would get a better education and have a better life. But soon, he was drawn to be near his mother's people. He became a missionary and traveled west to be with his mother's clan.

A few years ago, he had bought property within the Cherokee Nation, but because the state of Georgia had said no missionaries could remain there without a permit, he had to give it up. It didn't matter that he was part Cherokee. He could not prove it, and he looked as white as any of the other missionaries. Getting a permit was nearly impossible. If missionaries had no permit, they could be

sentenced to hard labor. That had happened to one
of his fellows, sent with him by the Christian
Benevolence Society. Even though it was getting
cooler, the waters were warm at these springs. Arter
removed his clothes — dark wool pantaloons and a
dark wool shirt — and entered the water with Easter.

"You know you should not be bathing here alone,
Easter," he said. She jumped and rose higher in the
water to see him near her. She was tense after hearing
him and saw him wading behind her. Her long dark
hair shone in the dim light. Her long, strong, arm
muscles glistened with water. She had strength that
made his body stir and his heart clench. He wanted
her not just because she was strong physically, but
because she had strength of spirit. Not many women
could do what she had done with her property when
war raged around her.

"It is my secret place," she said smiling. "And
what if the other missionaries knew that you had
followed me here? What then?" He smirked and
straightened his shoulders.

"They know that I want you to wife," he said.
"They will forgive an anticipation of vows. Have you
given my proposal more thought? Have you heard
from your grandmother?" He reached for her
shoulders and pulled her to him, kissing her first on
the forehead and then on the mouth. He ran a hand
up and down her back. She shivered. But he knew it
was not because of the cold.

"Yes, I have," she said, choosing to omit any
mention of her grandmother because it was her
decision. "But I don't think we can marry." She
smiled at him, but it wasn't an invitation. "Aren't you
worried that I may still belong to your brother?" she
asked him in a teasing voice. He sighed. He knew
that she was baiting him. The notion of polyandry
was strong among some women of the clan. But he

wasn't certain whether she was a firm believer for or against it. Two men with one woman made sense in this time as many women died early in life. He wasn't certain he could accept the idea, but if he could find a way into her heart, maybe he could convince her to warm to the idea of having him.

"As much as we hope circumstances will improve, it does not look good for any of us – missionaries and Cherokees," he said. "It doesn't matter what my brother wants. He left you years ago, and you put him out of your house. You're a free woman now and can chose me if you want." He let some moments pass before he spoke again. His yearning for Easter knew no end. He wanted her in every way he could think. But she continued to refuse him. His many days spent among the Cherokee made him sensitive to the values of the group. Though other women had given him a few second looks, most of them were back East and there weren't many women this far west who were hardy enough to endure the frontier. He realized that if he wanted Easter, he would need to be patient.

Many women died before they reached the rich fertile lands. Many died in childbirth, and some just could not endure the climate. The winters could be harsh — the summers hot and humid. The weather could change in an instant in the winter or spring. The demands of living took their toll on women. Not many ventured to come this far west, away from civilization and the luxuries it afforded. So any men who wanted to make a life and stake a claim for land this far west had to look for a woman who was hardy —and Easter was that. There were simply too few women like her. She had the strength of a large cat. She did not announce her power, but it was there.

Arter's family had come from Wales two generations ago. His people were devout Christians

27

who believed in kindness and service to humanity. His father was an educator, philosopher and scholar. Alun Beasley had encouraged his numerous children to find their own way in the world. He wasn't surprised when Arter's mother, Ahyoka, She Brought Happiness, came to him with Arter when he was but seven years old. Alun had been heavily involved with the Christian Benevolence Society. He had seen Ahyoka when she visited the East to assist her people. She was good with languages and came to the society to help orient would-be missionaries. He fell in love with her instantly. Their affair lasted two years; his first wife had died in childbirth. He had young children by his first wife and needed to remain in the East for their sake. But eventually, they all grew up. Alun knew that Ahyoka was pregnant with his child, Arter, and had decided to care for the two. But she returned to her people and took their son with her. Ahyoka brought Arter back to him when he was seven, saying that the boy had to learn the ways of white men.

When Arter came of age, his father knew that Arter would want to join his mother's people in some way. His older half-brother, Nathan, had gone West long before Arter had decided to go too. Alun helped them with frequent donations for their cause, to educate their people. For Arter, it was a calling to help his mother's people. His father had helped him contact the Christian Benevolent movement in Washington, which funded his initial efforts to help with Christianizing and educating the Indians.

Arter knew, as Easter did, that the massive populations arriving in the East and proliferating throughout these new lands, now well established after the revolution, would take over. It would not be long before things would change greatly. When he visited his father, he was always amazed at how the

Eastern cities had become more and more crowded. There seemed to be an urgent need for people to go where they could make a new life. He knew what was coming — a large wave of people. They had nowhere else to go but west.

Arter had been trying to get Easter to feel for him what he felt for her. He'd come to her home with flowers, with food, with trinkets. He and his half brother, John, had talked about sharing her. Ahoyka had had John with a previous Cherokee husband who had died in a raid. At first, Arter was shocked at John's attitude. But John seemed confident.

"I want you to take care of her," John said. "She needs another husband."

"I thought you loved her," Arter said.

"I do, and this does not mean I am abandoning her to you. I am simply letting you borrow her." John grinned. Arter frowned; he had grown up partly with his father's people, many of them devout Christians who would be appalled at John's attitude. Though Arter was part Cherokee, he looked like any other well-tanned white man. His mother's people had intermarried with people of European descent. Where Arter was dark, John was lightly tanned, darkened by the sun and pale when he got no sun. However, anyone who looked closely at the two men could see the family resemblance.

Arter didn't have much, but what he had, he offered to Easter. He buried that bias of Christians and accepted that this was a different way of life. Women didn't survive long on the frontier, and he feared that his brother John would return to claim Easter. He had no doubt that she could breed children and that she was more than adept at handling the work of a frontierswoman. He didn't dare give up the opportunity of being with her. He loved her, but making her realize that would be his challenge.

Easter's family was land rich, and she was the female who inherited. Even if there were disputes about the land, she knew where to settle, and that was the key to finding and keeping land. John had made certain she had the papers to prove it. In the end, though, it might not mean much, considering the way land was being grabbed by whites. It always seemed that she had plenty, and that when Arter chose a gift for her he had to make it something different than the goods she made for the travelers who stopped on their way west. His friends told him it was a good match, but it would include many trials.

Joseph Rhea, who with his cousin Matthew had tracked through Tennessee to make one of the state's first maps, told Arter it would be so. When Rhea had visited months ago, Arter and Easter had looked at Rhea's maps together. She had shown Rhea and Arter where her family owned land, as far west as Giles.

"It won't be long, my friend," Joe said, pointing at the map. "Settlers will take over this land. There are just too many of them, and their needs are many. You might as well settle here," Rhea said, pointing to the place on the map that Easter said was part of her family's holding. "The land is rich for growing, and the winters tolerable." Arter recalled the conversation as though it were yesterday. Conflicting talks with two men, one his brother, the other a friend, both urging him, in a way, to stake a claim on Easter.

"Did you buy some of this land that belonged to Easter's family?" Arter asked Rhea. "Wouldn't it be best to let the Cherokees have their land?"

"Like you, my friend, I must find a way to take care of my family. It is land that we seek; if we don't buy it, some other white will. It is land that is the key to prosperity; the government gives it to us. We need it to farm, to rear our children. It is not my doing that the land is being taken from the Cherokees. Besides, this small piece of land might be all that Easter will get of her family's land. I will hold it for her if it comes to that."

The conversation receded in Arter's memory as he watched Easter wash her long dark hair. She had firm, small breasts and rounded hips. He felt his body stir and struggled with himself not to touch her again. She splashed water at him and swam further away. He stroked through the water after her. The Christian Benevolent movement encouraged missionaries to be advocates of the Indians. Arter considered marrying Easter the best method of taking care of her. Easter had been one of the best students in her class. She could speak the Cherokee language as well as English, French and some Spanish. He knew that some of his friends thought he was only trying to marry her for his own good. The saying among some of the men was:

All I ask in this creation
Is a pretty little wife and a big plantation
Way up yonder in the Cherokee Nation.

He tried to discourage other white men who seemed to think the wealth of the Cherokees was something to capitalize on, but many of them had continued to marry across tribal lines. He couldn't blame them. Wasn't that what he wanted to do too? Only it wasn't for gold or anything like it. The gold, copper and silver mines were a strong attraction for many white men. It was considered a class leap by some and caused a good amount of tension, especially now that white settlers wanted the Cherokees and all other Indians to go west.

So Arter planned to encourage Easter to be with

him. They would sneak away and live on the land Easter said was hers that was free of this roiling tension. He had received a letter from his friend Joseph inviting him to settle on land in Giles County, Tennessee. That would be about 160 miles west of Red Clay through some harsh territory and the threat of Georgia Guardsmen, but he knew that he and Easter could make the trip by horse in about two weeks if they stayed off the main trails.

He had saved as much as he could to be certain they had provisions. Easter had horses and mules of her own and other possessions given to her by her mother. His own horses had been given to him by his brother, Nathan, who had ignored the call to missionary work and had settled on land north of his friend Joe Rhea in the neighboring county. Nathan even kept slaves. Arter shook his head, thinking about the shameful behavior. The two were as different as night and day. No amount of talking to Nathan about the evils of slavery did any good. Arter had decided that the two of them would not associate with one another. He knew that he still had a responsibility to his kin. That was something he would not discuss with his brother. Nor would he share the identity of his new wife — if he could get Easter to marry him.

Arter made a decision then and there. It was clear to him that Easter would not come to him willingly unless he pressed her to make a decision. She would need to feel a necessity. He knew that she was highly regarded, not only for the crafts she made, but for the food she grew and cooked and for her healing abilities. Her farming skills were envied. He'd seen her saying goodbye to John Hester and was jealous, but he knew that jealousy would be no use.

It was clear to him that he would have to use some strong persuasion. Cherokee women did not feel inclined to explain their lives to anyone as they had such independent circumstances as part of the social fabric of their clan.

They were considered the heads of their families. He considered that the only thing left to do was to convince her that he could be both an attentive lover and a good hunter and protector. There was no doubt that she would need him. He had been paying someone from Dutch Smith's outlaws to secretly guard Easter and her sister. Though Smith was an outlaw, he had connections and knew people who could get things done. He also had written to Joseph asking to buy some of the land that had been in Easter's family. There was an unbelievable draw for him to Easter. Did she feel the same way?

Arter saw her rise from the water and swam toward her; her back was to him. The soft clay squeezed between his toes as he rose behind her. He knew that she could hear him. He wrapped his arms around her and ran his hands over her. When he'd given her attention, he nudged her gently to the ground. He kissed her eagerly. Her eyes seemed to be saying she was searching for something. He hovered above her and looked down into her eyes as though asking permission. She breathed heavily but did not say anything. She was warm and soft. He could not contain himself. He listened for evidence that she returned his affections but heard nothing. He wanted to say, "Tell me you love me. Say you will marry me." But she was silent.

CHAPTER THREE

Spring 1837

Joseph Campbell Rhea opened the back door to the country store he and his partner, John McNabb, owned in Pulaski. The little store was one of the few along a trail that led to west. Many settlers stopped on their way. They needed maps and compasses, items for traveling that they lost along the way or did not realize they needed. Most of all, they craved direction. The maps Joe and John provided were unusually accurate. Joe had spent much of his early time riding through the territory with his cousin Matthew Rhea, charting the territory and surveying the land for the government and for the benefit of early settlers. Joe's first wife, Catherine, died a few years ago, and he had decided to move. Joe and Matthew were both large men, sturdy and capable of enduring many days in the elements. Their challenges were many. First there were the vestiges of native tribes that considered the land their own. Some attacked, but frequently the native people could be parlayed with for goods or information.

It was in this way that Joseph learned not only the language of those native people who lived in Sullivan County, Tennessee, where he grew up, but those who lived in other regions of the vast Tennessee area. He considered God's word the most important part of his journey. Each time he and Matthew encountered a group of natives — from the Chickasaw in West Tennessee, to the Shawnee and Yuchi to the east of the Chickasaw and then the Cherokee to the far east, where his father had settled with his family in the Sullivan County — he considered himself one with the people and the land. The Koassati, who lived in the southern part of Middle Tennessee, were the most interesting group, excelling in basketry and agriculture and supplementing their diet with hunting and fishing. When it was apparent that they would not hold their lands, the Koassati, a peaceful people, prepared to move to Alabama. Then, they moved again. It was in Tennessee that Joe Rhea met Icho, who was with her people, the Koassati. Joe and Matthew had covered almost half of what would be the southern part of the state of Tennessee when they stopped in Koassati territory and were invited into the village.

When he saw Icho, Joe was moved by her beauty and by her shy countenance. She was dressed in a colorful red and burgundy skirt, with a tunic that covered it. Her small, pear-shaped face was smooth. She had bright, hazel eyes and a full mouth. Her black hair shone like the waters of a lake on a sunny day. She was simply breathtaking. She glanced at him as she walked by with three women, who carried baskets of food. Her tentative smile and the dimple in her cheek sent a shaft of warmth through him. He was dressed in the typical surveyors' garb, rough pantaloons and a wool shirt. Suddenly, he thought how he would like to look better. He smoothed his hair and returned her smile. He knew that it was dangerous to look at a single woman, but you could never tell.

Matthew stood beside him, watching his reaction

to Icho. "Don't count on having her come to you tonight," he said. "I hear she's highly sought, and she's a widow."

"I'd like to make her acquaintance, but it's too soon after Catherine." The two let it rest there and walked to the roundhouse where the tribe gathered. Matthew, tall, with sandy colored hair and broad shoulders, looked at Joe askance and shook his head. His cousin never had problems attracting the attention of the ladies.

The men smoked and shared news of the presence of other whites and of game. Joe and Matthew were given a space to sleep in one of the log cabins, and they settled down for the night. Joe could not sleep, tossing and turning as he watched the night sky, so full of bright stars, out of the small window. It was a warm night. He went out to see whether a bit of fresh air would clear his head and help him sleep. It was then that he saw Icho, near the lake, throwing pebbles into the water. She turned when she saw him. They'd talked for some time before they succumbed to the attraction they felt.

When Joseph realized he had to have her as a part of his life, he returned for her after the surveying was finished. She changed her name and married him without anyone questioning his choice or her identity. However, a year after the wedding, Icho died in childbirth. He was determined not to fall in love again, but somehow, life seemed to have other ideas. When he met Susan, the time for mourning had passed. He needed someone to care for his three children that he had had with Catherine and Icho. Susan was sweet and beautiful, a god-fearing woman who seemed happy to live in this rough place, where the weather could change in an instant and fights over land made life challenging.

Joe met Arter Beasley on one of those treks

through the wilds when it was not unusual but certainly heartening to see another soul in the wilderness. He and Matthew were defending themselves from a bear that had wandered across their path when Arter saw them. Arter was able to distract the bear long enough for the two cousins to escape. The bear headed in a different direction, and as it trotted off, Joe and Matthew invited Arter to share their meager camp.

"Good day to you, sir. Thank you for help with the creature," Mathew said. "What brings you to this area?" The men walked a short distance to their campsite.

"I'm following in the footsteps of my countryman, Evan Jones, who wishes to help teach the Indians," Arter said. "He and others of my Welsh countrymen have helped to find connections between the native peoples and the Welsh. I'm just one more who has come to help." Arter kept his actual identity hidden; no need for these men to know that he was part Cherokee.

"That's a high calling, sir," said Joseph. "How do you know the Indians want to become Christians?"

"We don't," Arter said, looking to the ground. "We don't force anyone who doesn't want to embrace Christianity." Arter knew this was not entirely true, but he was not going to argue.

Ezra Poe had returned again and again to Easter's homestead, waiting for the damn missionary to leave. Poe was on horseback and kept his distance. The governor of Georgia and the Tennessee people were scrambling to make order out of chaos. Brigadier General John Wool had been ordered to remove the Cherokees, but many of them were resisting. Wool had been forced to drive them into camps. Poe knew if he only waited, he could have all he wanted, the land that the Cherokee woman, Easter, claimed was hers and the woman too. But someone was always near her. He realized that he would need to wait until he could get her alone. He had to claim her and all she had without making anyone suspicious. It would only take a little patience.

He had watched as Arter Beasley claimed the woman. Arter was a big man and, though he was a missionary, he was known for his fighting abilities. Poe only needed to get Arter in a vulnerable position to steal the prize. It was said that the woman's family owned a gold mine in Georgia. Poe would force her to lead him to it and find a way to keep her as his own. She was a beautiful woman, and hearty women were hard to come by.

Poe's first woman died of dysentery, and his second died of injuries and some kind of consumption. She wasn't hearty enough. So he knocked her around a bit. She should have been able to take it; if she were a real woman, she would take anything he gave her. But that last one was weak. He needed a strong woman, one who could give him children and warm his bed. The men in the territory were fighting over any woman they could get. Some of them were stealing the native women and passing them off as white women. It didn't take much. He grinned. Poe would make this woman into what he wanted and get the gold too. He turned his horse away to wait for the right time.

*

It took time for John Hester to find Mohe, but find him he did. He heard that Mohe was at a makeshift jail near Spring Place, a Moravian mission that had been approved by the Cherokees for teaching them the "civilized arts." The Moravians were mostly Methodists, Baptists or Presbyterians who had varying views on how to civilize the Cherokees. But because the Creek Red Sticks had been defeated so soundly during the War of 1812, the Cherokees were making an attempt to assimilate. However, that was not always the case. Many young men were close to the Moravian missionaries, but many were not. Mohe was one of those who resisted the Moravians and anyone who purported to embrace the inevitable European tide. John shook his head as he recalled how much Mohe was like his father, Enorle, Black Fox. Enorle was certain that fighting the whites was the only way to survive. However, in the end, Enorle was defeated. Some of his land was taken. He died from fever. No one really understood it. Later Enorle's wife, Sitting Deer, succumbed to the fever too. So when John walked up to the little ramshackle jail, tucked away from the town, it was with foreboding. Two rough-looking white men stood with rifles. They appeared to be holding young men under arrest.

John left his horse quite a distance away, tied up in the woods. He always carried a few coins with him to bribe guards and to get information. He had a few in his pocket and left the others with his horse. He carried a small flask of whiskey as well. That always made for good negotiations. John walked to the little shack, taking off his felt hat and holding it in his hands deferentially. It would not do to look threatening. These men were looking for an excuse to do violence to any Cherokee who challenged them. He could see it in their eyes. One of them looked like a veteran of Indian wars. He probably had tokens of his long-ago battles in his leather bag; he wore tattered dark work pantaloons, a leather shirt and a black leather hat. The other man wore a leather shirt, pantaloons and a dirty cloth hat. They both carried long rifles: one had a Hawken and the other a Hall. Both weapons could put a large hole through any man. John approached them cautiously. One spit on the ground and raised his chin to look him in the eye. John was taller than both men but hunched his shoulders to make himself look less intimidating.

"Good afternoon," John said. Neither man spoke, but both looked at him with hostility. John cleared his throat. "Hello," he paused to allow them to process his voice and the quality of his English. "I'm looking for a young Cherokee man who is about," John had put his hand out to show Mohe's height when both men began to laugh hysterically. They looked at each other and then at him.

"And so there are just a million of you indjuns around here," said the shorter man with the leather hat. "What makes you think we know or care where one of them is?" John shifted from one foot to another, feeling as though he should run, but knowing that if he did, these two might shoot him in the back for the fun of it.

"Sorry to trouble you, sir," John said. "I'm looking for my sister's boy. He run off with the family gold, and we want to get it back." That got their attention.

"Gold, you say," leather hat said, grinning and pulling on his beard. John nodded.

"Well, now you're talking. We can let you look in the jail to see whether he's in there, but we got to warn you, it ain't a pretty sight," cloth hat said. Both men guffawed again, slapping their legs and spitting.

"If'n we let you take a look, do you have that family gold on you?"

"No, sir," John said. "The guards took it all away, but I do have a little silver." Both men looked at him and grabbed John roughly by the arm. John quickly produced the pouch with the coins in it. They let him go when they saw it, their eyes getting big and round with greed.

"Let's see what you got," said cloth hat. John gave them a pouch with the little silver he had on him and waited to see what they would do. They snickered and waved him over to the jail door.

There, hanging from a beam in the center of the room were two Cherokees. One of them was Mohe. John's heart sank. How would he tell Easter? She would blame him. She expected him to bring her brother home alive. But even harder might be getting the body. He knew this would take some more negotiation.

"Can I take that one with me?" he asked, gesturing to the right side of the room toward Mohe's body. "It's not my sister's boy, but a friend's boy."

Leather hat clinked the few coins John had given them.

"Well, now, that depends," Leather hat said. "He supposed to be kept hanging there as an example to all of y'all to stay in your places." He smirked at his friend and rubbed his stomach then his beard. "But what else you got that we might be interested in?"

"How about some whiskey?" John asked.

When John and his party rode to Easter's house, she wasn't there. He could see her in the distance working in the fields. Her brothers, Degataga and Wahail, got off their horses and loosened the body from its moorings on the mule that trailed John's horse. Both Degataga and Wahail wore dark pantaloons and dark wool shirts. They wore their hair short. A young girl sat on a pony, stoically considering her surroundings. She had dark skin and large doe eyes. The young girl wore a brown tunic that came well below her knees and brown pantaloons. John hoped Easter would not be offended that he'd brought the girl to her. John had been told that the girl was a relation to Easter. He'd found her near the house where Easter's parents had lived in Spring Place. He'd brought her along in hopes that Easter might find some solace in the girl. John, still seated on his horse, watched Easter in the fields. Her brothers tried to show no emotion as they looked into the distance where she worked. John nodded to them, indicating that he would bring Easter in. The young girl, Awinta, slid off her pony and led it into the barn, knowing what to do with not only her horse but those of her half brothers.

Easter was as hard a worker as any woman John had ever met. He didn't know where she got her energy, but she was certainly a healthy one. It pained him that he had to give her more bad news. He had been the one to tell her and her oldest brother, Degataga, Stands Firm, that their parents had died in early 1832. The Treaty of New Echota had been foisted upon the Cherokee. Elias Boudinot, John Ridge and Major Ridge were involved in the negotiations, but things did not turn out as most Cherokees had hoped. Under the treaty, Cherokees were to remove from their lands to Oklahoma in exchange for $5 million. John shook his head as he thought about it. He had been there when Boudinot and the Ridges, Andrew Ross, James Starr, Stand Watie and others had signed the treaty. There were a few hundred other Cherokee at the signing of the treaty. How could so few possibly agree for the entire nation? The U.S. government considered the agreement binding, and the process of removal began. John remembered the shock of many of the Cherokees as they realized what had happened. Easter's parents were among them. They tried to resist the push of the U.S. government, but their efforts left them with few resources. John sighed as he thought of the circumstances. He had no parents or family left, but he admired Easter for doing what she could to hold together those she had left to her. It saddened him to give her more bad news.

After he'd taken Mohe's body, he'd ridden into Spring Place for a shaman and to get help from some other Cherokees he knew who could help him gather Easter's family, the Wards. There was no way to get a message to them otherwise. His friend, Dutch Smith, and some others who rode with him, helped him round up the family and prepare for the ride to Easter's place in Red Clay. Dutch was wanted by the law for killing a U.S. deputy marshal, but he was always successful at hiding and evading authorities.

Usually John heard news first because he traveled about so often. Dutch helped him send a rider to Easter's brother, Degataga, and to her youngest brother, Wahali. Both had quickly found their way to John when they heard the news about their brother Mohe. While John waited for them to arrive, he'd discovered the girl, Awinta, near Easter's parents' home in Spring Place. The girl had been cared for by someone but had a blank look about her as though she'd seen too much in her young years. Easter's brothers worked hard to contain their anger and grief. The tribal shaman had come as well. He'd helped them prepare the body. It had been abused and had been hanging in the shack they called a jail for a while. They were all with him to help Easter send her brother to the good place.

A HOME FOR EASTER

45

Dale Marie Taylor

CHAPTER FOUR

Summer 1837

Easter knew when she saw the look on John's face that nothing good was about to happen. He'd tied up his horse some distance away and walked softly to her. He looked into her eyes and saw the tears forming. He put his arms around her and hugged her tightly to him. She shook with her sobs. Soon, though, she recovered herself and stood there in his arms.

"I had a dream last night that he was speaking to me," Easter said. "Was it a dream, John?" He said nothing as he continued to hold her. She breathed deeply and rested her head on his shoulder. She was tall for a woman and had little trouble resting there. He held her firmly. "It was so real. He said he wanted me to find a place for those of us who survived to live in peace. What did they do to him?"

"He did not suffer, Easter," he said. Though he could not say this for certain, as he helped the shaman with the body, he did not see evidence of torture. The young man had simply been hanged. If there was evidence of torture, it had not been obvious, and John didn't want to look for it. So he was telling her the truth.

"How will we get word to Grandmother

Amadahy?" she asked.

"It's too dangerous for her to travel a long distance through mountainous territory. She will be with us in spirit. I'm certain she knows by now. I sent a rider to her village in North Carolina. She will know by now."

Easter looked into the distance and squinted as she noticed her brothers and Lucinda waiting for her. A child had come out of the barn and was heading toward her brothers and sister.

"You brought my other brothers," she said. "How did you?"

"Shh," he said. "Dutch helped me." She huffed. She remembered Dutch as tall and proud. He'd stood up for Cherokees time and again. His dark skin was tanned by the outdoors. He dressed in traditional garb, made from skins, rather than Western clothing and had been known to take scalps. Dutch had a wide grin with bright white teeth.

"That flirt," she said, remembering times Dutch had ridden by and stopped to chat with her, trying to tempt her to ride off with him. "Still, I hope you thanked him for me."

"No need," he said. "You know Dutch is a good friend and would do anything for you." She smiled weakly and sighed. The grief was overwhelming. She fought down her tears and her sense of loss.

"I have work to do to get Mohe ready," she said. "I must get to it." He led her to his horse and lifted her on it, then hopped up behind her and rode to the little cabin Easter shared with her sister Lucinda. When Easter arrived at the cabin, Lucinda had installed Awinta on a straw mattress. The women prepared a light meal for the family and the shaman. Easter dug through a chest she'd kept with Mohe's belongings in it. She picked out all of his favorite items — some shells he'd kept, a favorite bowl, a pipe he'd found. She smiled as she fingered it. He'd tried to smoke once and had coughed so hard he'd nearly choked. She placed the treasures he'd collected into a small bag to take with her to the burial site.

She walked out on the porch and was about to call Lucinda when Arter Beasley arrived with one of the villagers. They both offered their sympathies, Arter doing so more demonstratively. Easter thanked them and waved Lucinda over as she announced that there would be soup for the travelers after the ceremonial cleansing.

John had been helping Wahali and Degataga in the barn. Easter noticed the tense look on John's face when he saw Arter. She shook her head at the jealousy the two men felt. Still, they were polite to one another. John walked up to Arter and gave him a slap on the back. Arter staggered a bit and grinned, doing to same to John.

Easter's friend Sarah Armstrong, the daughter of missionaries, and a few of the Cherokee women from the neighboring village arrived. Sarah had had a crush on Mohe and appeared to have been crying. She was engaged to marry another now. Easter wondered how deeply Sarah felt for her betrothed.

Meanwhile, Wahali and Degataga had gone to the burial site some distance from the house and had dug a shallow pit for Mohe's body. It was the Cherokee belief that the body should be allowed to go back to the elements. After Wahali and Degataga had gathered all of the tools needed for burial, they began helping the shaman with the preparations. The shaman prayed and chanted for the safe delivery of Mohe to a good place. The family had gathered wood to cover the body. They placed the body in a wagon and gathered stones to cover the grave.

Easter and Lucinda walked close to the wagon. Wahali and Degataga drove the wagon as they took

Mohe's body to the burial area, where Easter's parents had been buried. The men laid Mohe's body on a flat rock, and the women cleaned his body and oiled it with lavender. As the body needed to be laid to rest soon, the shaman held the ceremony immediately. After the women mourned, and the shaman said prayers, Wahali and Degataga lifted the body into the shallow pit. The shaman then ordered the mourners to the river for ceremonial cleansing where they were all to immerse themselves seven times, facing east and west. Following that, they burned their clothing and changed into new clothes. They did so as the shaman said purifying prayers. The shaman then gave them two gifts, tobacco to enlighten them and ceremonial beads to comfort them.

After the cleansing, the shaman entered the Ward home and cleansed it with smoke and tea. He had the family drink the tea and wash with it. The Wards were to mourn for seven days. On the fifth day, the shaman killed a bird and threw part of it in the fire to determine whether the family would be safe, particularly the men. It was determined that they would be. After the seven-day cleansing of the house and the family, the shaman announced that the family was again part of the Red Clay Cherokee. None of them was permitted to express anger, but Easter could tell by the tense looks on her brothers' faces that they were indeed hiding anger, and not very well.

The ceremony was finally over, and Easter felt that it was right for her to move away from this place. It was time for change.

A few days after the ceremony was complete, Degataga stopped Easter as she crossed to the well to get water. He and Wahali were lingering to be certain that Easter and Lucinda were prepared for the winter and had plans for the coming year. They hunted and fished and handed over their game to Easter for drying. Easter urged them to stop at some point as the amount of meat and fish they had preserved was becoming too much to carry wherever they decided to go. It would not do to attract the attention of wild predators on a long journey. Degataga's wife, Ruth, had many times invited Easter and Lucinda to stay with them. The two sisters had visited Degataga and Ruth in Coosawattee Village, near where their parents had lost their home, but never stayed long. Degataga wished his sisters would consider moving in with them.

Ruth's parents had been missionaries and had died, leaving her with their home and some of their worldly goods. Her brother, Charles, was a businessman and did not embrace the missionary way of life. He had wanted her to have their parents' home. The villagers made an effort to stay out of the way of the Georgia Guard, but it was not always possible. Degataga had taken what wealth his parents had in gold and silver and hidden it away.

Many of his people had been gathered together and forced into camps in preparation for the long trip to Oklahoma. He had decided to become a citizen of the U.S. and of Georgia to protect Ruth. They were unpopular among the whites and the Cherokees, but he had no other choice. He was certain that Ruth was pregnant. He would not force her to make the long trip to Oklahoma. He would lose her and the child she carried. So he had done the unthinkable; he had become a U.S. citizen and had hidden his papers carefully along with his assets. Still, it was a difficult time for everyone. Pandemonium seemed to reign as General Wool had been sent to gather up the Cherokees for the long forced trip west. Those who could afford to ride did, but many people walked.

Wahali wanted to go on this trip. It was insanity. But Wahali was deeply invested in his Cherokee ancestry and wanted to travel with those being removed to Oklahoma. Wahali walked up to where Degataga stood with Easter, trying to ease his way into a discussion about their future.

"Easter has plans to move west, Wahali," Degataga said. "She invites you to join her, along with Arter and the little girl." Easter looked between the two men and sighed.

"We've been through this before," she said. "It's better if you go with me, Wahali. There is family land in the place the whites call Giles. We can make a home there."

"I have plans of my own," Wahali said. "I will be a great healer, and my people need me on this journey."

"The numbers of Cherokee being forced to march are more than you could imagine," Easter said.

"That doesn't matter," Wahali said. "I will carry what I can in pouches on my body and on my horse. I will offer what healing I can to those who need it. You will know when I get there. You will feel it." Wahali looked at Easter knowing that she understood. The two had long had a connection. When she flew in the spirit world, she often saw an Eagle, certain evidence that Wahali was about.

"It's clear that you feel you have a purpose for going, Wahali," Degataga said. "Ruth and I will say prayers for you."

"Prayers in the white man's Christian religion, brother?" Wahali said, sneering at his older brother. "Say prayers in the old way, and I will feel them and will be protected."

"We will pray before you leave, Wahali," Easter said, "and I will prepare as many compact potions and much dried meat, nuts and corn as I can for you."

"Try to avoid the camps," Degataga said, letting Wahali's snide remark pass. "Stay in the woods and off the trails until you see a group traveling the way you want to go. This will help you."

"But I have seen in a dream the devastation that our people are already enduring," Easter said. "They are being gathered together and forced into camps. Lucinda and I have been fortunate in that we have been overlooked for some reason." She stopped and considered Ezra Poe, who certainly had something to do with keeping her and Lucinda out of the roundup of so many of her people. She supposed Arter might be helping as well. It helped, too, that she and Lucinda provided a service and dressed in western clothes at times. Lucinda helped Easter prepare nourishment for Wahali and for Degataga's return trip to Coosawattee. When they saw both men off, the sisters struggled to maintain calm. They knew that they too would need to leave and soon.

CHAPTER FIVE

Fall 1837

Walking Bird strapped more food and tools to the
small pony he had gotten from his brother. He had
asked Lucinda if she would be his wife, and she'd
agreed. Her grandmother had agreed as well. He felt
excited and satisfied. He had received the small dove
she'd sent to his village. The thing was amazing; as
Lucinda had said, the birds return to where they
think home or their mate is. Her birds thought his
coop was their home. She added an incentive for her
female bird to arrive in the Qualla village by leaving
her male mate with Walking Bird. He grinned as he
fingered the small parchment that had her words on
it: "I am ready." This was good news. However, he
also felt uneasy. Would he be able to protect her with
the unrest around them? Would he be able to safely
get her to the mountains of North Carolina, avoiding
the soldiers who were searching everywhere for
Cherokees to force them on the trail west. He had
paperwork proving that he was a citizen of North
Carolina and part of the group of Cherokees
remaining there, but he knew that the papers meant
little. It would take only one wild zealot to force him

and Lucinda west.

This made him nervous. Walking Bird felt certain that the time to flee was now. It was just a matter of fact: the whites encroached; the Cherokees left. He would need to tread carefully to keep Lucinda well. Now, their only obstacle was getting her sister, Easter, to accept the news. There were few of his group left. Most people had moved to the mountains in North Carolina. Now, he was determined to take Lucinda where she would be safe. This had to be the right thing to do. There was no way to claim any land; the whites had their papers and their paper money. Part of his family belonged to the eastern band of the Cherokee, so he and some relatives had decided to go there. As part of a legal effort by William Holland Thomas, it appeared the Eastern Band would be able to remain in North Carolina. Walking Bird was hopeful.

Chief Ynaguska was smart and had arranged for Thomas, an attorney, to defend the Eastern Band. Thomas was able to purchase land near Qualla. It was not the best of arrangements, but Walking Bird would be going to Wolf Town to help keep Lucinda safe. There, if things went as he planned, he and Lucinda would be able to rear their children and live in peace. Lucinda's grandmother was already in Wolf Town. It was a matter of time before more Cherokee would make their way to the Eastern Band. But there wasn't room for everyone. Walking Bird felt it best for him to establish himself and his family now. The treaty of New Echota appeared not to be working. Chief John Ross would not get the money asked for by Cherokees.

Indignities were heaped upon Chief John Ross and others involved in the negotiation of the treaty. Walking Bird could see no good outcome for any of it. Georgia lottery winners were grabbing land left and right. Cherokees were ordered to leave. Though some of the members of the western group persisted in staying on their land, it seemed hopeless to Walking Bird. He had heard rumors that Lucinda's brother might be one of the Cherokee who had been hanged in a jail where Ross had been arrested. But Walking Bird did not want to travel there to investigate. He wanted to get Lucinda as far away from the chaos as possible. She might be having his child. He wanted her safe and for his child to be far removed from harm. So, he pretended that everything was fine when he spoke to Easter.

He looked up to the sky, which was turning dark. He had to ride hard to return to Red Clay for Lucinda. It would be a good day to begin. He heard crows in the distance and saw a cardinal flit by. The crows cawed at one another. One flew west, toward Red Clay.

The wind whistled through the trees that were turning the beautiful colors of the fall. Orange, yellow and red leaves mixed together to make a vibrant canvas. The grass was mostly brown and yellow, dotted with the evidence of the earth's change. The air was crisp and cool. He breathed deeply. This would be a quick trip. He had packed all the food he needed along with a pony for Lucinda. He knew where to find the best water. He mounted his horse and headed for Lucinda.

Easter was not fooled by Walking Bird's rush to leave for the North Carolina hills. She helped her sister prepare for the trip. She wrapped corn and dried meat for her sister. She prepared leather containers of water and parcels of dried greens. She gave her sister seed for growing food when they arrived in the Qualla territory. Having been given

Amadahy's permission, they had an informal
wedding ceremony to acknowledge the union of the
couple. It was brief but heartfelt.

"We will see one another again, sister," Easter said
as she hugged Lucinda. "This will not last forever.
You will talk to me on the wind, too." Lucinda, not
one to get too emotional, nodded at her sister and
hugged back. She knew what Easter meant. There
was an undeniable tie between the two. Sometimes, it
seemed they were able to talk to one another or feel
one another from a distance. It was that strong
connection between them that made Lucinda feel a
calmness in her decision to go with Walking Bird.
She knew that he was anxious for her to go quickly.

Lucinda was worried about leaving her sister at
their cottage. But one of their brothers would come
along, and Easter's friend, Sarah Armstrong, whose
family owned land in the area, was always willing to
help. Sarah wanted to be a missionary, but her
betrothed wanted to go to Texas to help fight against
Mexico. Still, Lucinda felt this was the right thing to
do. She loved Walking Bird, and there was no telling
how long it would be before the lottery took the
farm that she and Easter had enjoyed for so long.
Their parents had worked hard to make it
prosperous, but little by little, the land had been
whittled away by settlers claiming parts of it in the
lottery. So, this was the right thing to do.

"You'll be fine," Lucinda said to her sister. "I feel
it here," she said, placing a hand on her chest and
one on her head. "It will be good for us to find other
fertile land for our seed. Our brothers will join us
when they are able. Meanwhile, we must prepare for
the children who are coming."

Lucinda knew that she would have Walking Bird's
baby. Every time they saw each other, they kissed
and held each other. She knew that their first child

was on the way. "I will get word to you when we are safely there and when the child has come," Lucinda said, smiling. "I will name her after you."

Walking Bird grunted. He wanted a boy but would be happy for a healthy baby, no matter its sex. Still, he felt it necessary to not worry the women with their assumptions about the baby.

Walking Bird waited patiently for the women to whisper more words of prayer and endearment to one another. They sat a distance from the horse and invited him to pray with them.

Easter motioned to the east, west, south and north, for the fire, wind, water and earth. She prayed for her sister and other siblings and for Walking Bird and the protection of all Cherokees and for the cessation of hostilities, for the hope that some day all humans would come to respect and love one another. The women chanted the words again and again, used the sacred smoke and drank from their special brew. When they finished their prayers they rose from the earth, brushed at their skirts, and hugged one another again. Lucinda gave Easter her prized female doves so that she could send messages. Lucinda had been teaching Easter how to tie a message to the bird's leg and to let her fly. Lucinda reminded Easter once more how to care for them. Easter gave Lucinda a crystal for energy and insight.

"Be certain to keep the doves out of bad wind," Lucinda said, handing Easter a bag of the special seeds and berries her birds liked. Easter stood back so that Walking Bird could lift Lucinda to the back of the strong pony he'd brought for the journey. With no more fuss, Walking Bird and Lucinda turned northeast toward North Carolina and the Eastern Band of the Cherokee.

CHAPTER SIX

Autumn 1837

Easter walked through the acres where she had planted winter vegetables. She had gathered as many burlap sacks and barrels as she could so she could take vegetables with her on the long trek to Giles. That morning, she dug up sweet potatoes. Awinta had helped as much as possible for a young girl. The girl was willing to do anything she was told and seemed grateful to have a place to stay, even if it seemed temporary. The corn had long been stored in the barn after it ripened during the warmer months. Easter had been fighting animals to keep the corn from being eaten. She had spent time shucking and scraping some of the corn for use as cornmeal later. Most of the dried ears were shelled and bagged.

Her brothers, Wahali and Degataga, had long left but had spent time helping her prepare for removal. Easter shared some of Lucinda's precious birds with them and showed them how to care for them. Both men scoffed at the idea but eventually accepted that the doves provided a way to share information with family. Wahali was determined to be a healer, to follow the people going west and to help them on their journey. Degataga was committed to his wife, who was soon to have a child. They regretted Mohe's death and also the loss of their older brother, Connutsee.

Neither they nor Easter knew exactly what they would do. Easter stood and stretched as she placed more potatoes in the barrel Arter had left for her. If she wanted to survive the removal, she would need to plan. Taking 8-year-old Awinta with her wasn't part of her plan, but the girl was family. Awinta rarely made any trouble and helped with the chores. Awinta seemed to know that she was part of a bigger plan and moved quietly among the adults, speaking softly. Arter visited frequently now and seemed to think she had agreed to remove to someplace safe. He'd talked and talked about his friend, Joseph. Sweat dripped from her back as she continued to harvest the crops for use in the new territory. She sat on a log and took a deep breath. Her thoughts returned to her conversation with Arter.

"We need to go before it's too late to make a better decision than those who are being forced to remove," Arter said. "If we wait too long, who knows what will happen."

"I understand that, Arter," Easter said. "I have been preparing for this. I have known that we would not be able to hold this land. It is too rich." She thought about the many days that her father and mother and brothers had worked the land, enriching it, rotating the crops and caring for it. They even had a small area where they planted seedlings. Their crops had been so plentiful and so well tended that they were able to trade and to receive coins and other goods for their stores of corn, beans, potatoes and other food. Their father had planted walnut trees early in his life with her mother. Those trees had been tended by her parents, and Easter and her siblings had enjoyed a rich harvest from them.

Easter had long stored the walnuts in the barn to prepare for the trip to Giles. But there was only so much she could do. Elizur and Lewis, two workers she had employed on the farm, had helped harvest as much as possible before they were called away to help an uncle with problems in Georgia. She had not seen them for days. But she knew, and so did they, that time was long past for them to sell the farm and to hope that they could get something for it. Many of the farms were being stolen, simply taken by the state government for settlers. But Sarah's fiancé was willing to pay a fair price for the Ward farm. Easter wiped sweat from her forehead and continued to place potatoes in the barrel. She had harvested all she could and was wrapping up the last few preparations for the trip west. She stopped at the well and pumped cool water from it into a bucket and then used a ladle to drink. She went inside and began to prepare food for the later part of the day. Just then, there was a knock on the door.

"Door's open," she shouted.

"Hello, friend," Sarah said, peeping into the large room that served as both kitchen and living area for the Ward family. "I thought you would be winding up your chores about now."

"Come in, Sarah," Easter said. "I was just preparing some cornbread and tea. Care to join me?"

"I never turn down a cup of tea," Sarah said, sitting at the table in the clean and well-kept room. Curtains hung at the windows, and cups, plates and eating utensils sat on a shelf above the small stove that Easter used for cooking. Sarah's red and white gingham dress hugged her figure and spread out at her hips in graceful folds as she sat at the table.

Easter always felt underdressed when Sarah was about, but the two had different lifestyles. Easter was a farmer and lived the life of a Cherokee woman who planted the seed and harvested the crops while her brothers hunted and fished. Easter's serviceable brown, wool dress was understated and sparsely embroidered with red and blue images of wildlife and flowers. Easter put water on the boil and picked up the pot to pour hot water over chicory leaves. She picked the chicory from the nearby woods and dried the mature leaves. She did the same for dandelion and sage but grew peppermint near the well.

When the weather was good, she enjoyed walking through the woods to find various plants that she used for medicine or for food. Her supply of honey was dwindling, but ample enough for tea with a favorite friend. Sarah and Easter exchanged books they liked reading. Their favorites were by Jane Austen — *Pride and Prejudice* and *Mansfield Park*. They had also enjoyed Amelia Simmons's *American Cookery*, which had delicious recipes for pumpkin and gingerbread. They'd whispered about Mary Wollstonecraft Shelley's *Frankenstein* and laughed together about *The Legend of Sleepy Hollow* by Washington Irving. The books were passed about by various owners; the books were stained, dog-eared and barely holding together. But occasionally, the women were able to find fresh copies to pass on to one another.

Both women savored the rich taste of the chicory with the sweetness of the honey. Easter served the cornbread with a bit of chicken. They made small talk about one of the books they were reading, *Sense and Sensibility* by Austen. They sat there for a while enjoying the quiet of the day and hoping not to be disturbed. Finally, Sarah sighed and sipped from the cup of quickly cooling tea.

"I came to tell you what Henry is offering for your farm, Easter," she said. "He has prepared all of the paperwork for it. We hope that it will be what you want." Sarah took the rolled parchment from a pocket in her dress and pushed it toward Easter. Easter smiled and nodded her head in agreement. Sarah handed Easter a pouch of coins. Easter signed the two copies of paper and handed one back to Sarah.

Easter looked out the window to the fields where her family had worked for years. It had belonged to her grandparents and to her parents, passed down from one woman to the next as a means of providing for the family and a means of sheltering generations of children. There were stories about struggles to keep the land, but most of all, there was a sense of belonging. She was reluctant to give that up. She felt guilty that it would fall to her to pass the land to someone outside the family. But she consoled herself with the idea that Sarah was like a sister. She could be certain that the land would be treated well, even if she could not do it herself. Sarah had spent many days visiting Easter, sometimes following her around as Easter did her chores, sometimes helping with simple tasks.

It felt like a burden to be the one to make the decision to let go of this parcel of the family's land. However, if she had to pass on the land to someone, it seemed right for her to pass it on to her friend, Sarah, and her betrothed, Henry Adair. Easter was not getting what the land was truly worth, but at least the land would be in the hands of someone who would care for it. Henry was keen to use the land for what was best for it. He had studied agriculture and asked questions of Easter and her sister. He walked the land frequently and was seen by many of the other settlers as having a claim to the land.

Now, he was making good on that understanding. He bought the property. Easter knew she should feel relieved and maybe even happy about this, but instead she had mixed feelings. She knew that there were many other Cherokee farmers who were not going to get anything for their land. They would be forced off of it and not have anything to show for the years of toil. But she was fortunate that her friendship with Sarah meant the family land would have someone who would care for it. Easter sighed wearily. Sarah reached across the table and took her hand.

"I know it's hard for you to get ready for something like this, Easter," she said softly. "But we want to help in this way. Maybe someday you can return to this land, maybe buy some of it back. We want to be the ones who will welcome you back if you want to come back." Easter smiled tenderly at her friend.

"Thank you, Sarah. It's important to me to hand the land to someone who will care for it. It's not just a sale for me. For me, it's a spiritual giving of the land to someone who will care for it and steward it properly. It's rich with possibility. I only hope you and Henry and your children will come to love it as I and my family have."

"We will," Sarah said. "And, Easter, I want you to know how sorry I am about Mohe. I know it is not your custom to dwell on the passing of a loved one, but there were others who loved him too." A tense silence passed between the two women. Easter knew that Sarah had cared deeply for Mohe, but Mohe was not Degataga. He would never have given up his Cherokee identity to be with Sarah. Easter sensed that Sarah knew this too.

Easter smiled at her friend and stood up to pour another cup of tea for the two of them. There was nothing more to say. Easter let the silence in the room and the warmth of their affection for one another relax the air between them. It was getting late, and the sun was sinking. The late fall was turning the trees beautiful orange and rust colors; the leaves had long since begun to provide a cushion on the various paths. Birds sang in the distance. It would be difficult to leave this beautiful land. Easter sighed. A journey was ahead of her.

"I know some other women who would like to help you if you think you'd care to have some help, Easter," Sarah said. "I know that you're very independent and don't often ask for help. In fact, we mostly come to you for help. I can't name the many times you've stitched or bandaged a wound or helped an upset stomach. Won't you let us return the favors and help you too?" Sarah asked. Easter nodded her head.

"I only do what comes natural," Easter said. "That would be very kind of you, Sarah. I could use a helping hand here and there to get ready for this trip."

"It's late in the year to set off on the trip," Sarah said. "If you'd like to stay with our family for a while and wait for the spring, you're welcome to do so."

"No, Arter and I want to get to Giles and get settled before the weather gets bad. I know we should have left earlier, but I wanted to get Lucinda off on her journey. It's lonely without her, but it's better this way. She will want to be settled for the arrival of her child." Sarah breathed deeply and smiled again.

"She's fortunate then," Sarah said. "She will have an easy time of it. You two women know more about giving birth, healing and such than anyone in the village. You won't have to worry about her. There's your grandmother, too. You girls are so fortunate. I know it doesn't seem like it, but you are." Sarah's own parents had died of cholera after they had arrived in the area. She and her young brother had been taken in by one of the missionary families, and Sarah thought that was where her future would be. But then she met Henry Adair, and her life had changed.

She wasn't certain what she would be doing now, how she would be doing things. One idea was clear to her though; she would be taking good care of Easter's land right alongside Henry. It was common for the Cherokee women to do the planting and harvesting, but Sarah hadn't been reared that way. Her parents were well-to-do merchants who had decided that they would like it better in the West. It was a well-kept family secret that her mother was Jewish. But her father had been a fervent Christian. When they met, her parents decided not to make an issue of their religious beliefs and to try to blend in with the many other settlers who were arriving in droves in the new western territories. It was difficult for them to witness the removal of a group of people who seemed content to live near beautiful rolling hills and wooded areas.

The next day, five women joined Sarah in the effort the help Easter prepare for her journey. Awinta joined in the carrying of items from the little house, baskets of dried corn, beans, potatoes and other vegetables. Awinta had little in the way of personal possessions and was placed in the wagon along with the goods. She wanted to walk, but Easter urged her to stay in the buckboard wagon for a while. Arter had arrived early with a large buckboard wagon, and Easter had a wagon of her own. Arter had backed his wagon up to the barn and was loading the barrels of potatoes and sacks of corn. Tall and broad shouldered, Arter attracted the attention of two of the single women in the group who arrived to help. He had taken off his shirt, and the taut muscles of his buttocks and back flexed as he lifted each heavy item.

The women fluttered their eyes and giggled when he smiled at them, hefting heavy bags of corn and barrels of carrots and potatoes into the wagons. Easter felt something twist in her heart when she saw the women admiring Arter's good looks. She stood for a moment watching the play of the sunlight on his head and shoulders. He was one good-looking man. But she had little time for such thoughts. She shrugged them off and went back to work. She made certain to place her treasures in a special wooden box that had a lid on it — her books, her clay pottery, her few pieces of fine eating utensils. Large and small pots went into a separate container. She had pulled up boards in the floor of the cabin to get the money she had saved in a squat clay pot, and put it in a safe place in the wagon.

Not long after the women arrived to help Easter, two missionary men arrived to assist Arter too. Before long, the men and the women had all of Easter's possessions loaded in the wagons and the horses and mules in their traces. Awinta stood and playfully called out the names of the horses and mules: "Keme the mule, Lulu the mule, Desa the horse, and Suzy the horse," she said. Keme and Lulu took the lead for Arter's wagon. Arter had tethered the mules and horses to his bigger wagon and let Easter drive her own wagon, thinking she better knew the disposition of her cattle. Two cows, Sallie and Daisy, were tied to the back of her wagon. Easter had given the third to Degataga to live on his farm. The cows complained at first but chewed and scuffed the earth as they waited. Easter had loaded wooden cages with her chickens inside the wagon, along with two pet cats who had made themselves useful at keeping rodents and other pests out of the barn.

She'd sewn together large leather covers for her goods and for the produce in Arter's wagon. She covered everything. Many settlers headed west in covered wagons, but Easter's were hardy farm wagons — there were no oiled canvas covers. So she had to compensate by covering her animals and goods with rough burlap and leather. Like Arter, she had four beasts — Hogan and Tom were her stubborn but strong mules. They led the way. Her horses, Kay and Mico, were as smart as they came. Kay and Mico were versatile animals who helped her with the farming chores and were bonded to her. She had raised and trained them herself. Easter felt certain, after her planning, that they would make the trip in a short amount of time if the weather held. Her dogs, Waya and Ama, waited in the shade of the wagon, while the people prepared everything. Two goats sat placidly. Two cats, one a kitten, Awinta had named Alice, the other a male cat she named Toka, mewed pitifully as the wagon was further packed with two trunks holding blankets, linens, dishes and other implements used for housekeeping.

Easter thanked the women who had arrived to help and gave each one a small jar of honey and a couple of bags of chicory and peppermint for making tea. They thanked her heartily, shared homespun wisdom about traveling with a heavy load of goods and waved goodbye as Arter and Easter pulled away from the house her parents had built and the land that she had cultivated with her hands and her heart. Something squeezed her chest as she left the farm. She refused to look back. Early that morning, before everyone arrived, she had said her prayers and said her goodbyes to the land, to the goods she had to leave behind. She could not take everything. She left much of the bounty for Sarah and her husband-to-be. Now it was time for Easter to look forward, not back. And so she did.

CHAPTER SEVEN

Late Autumn 1837

The wagons creaked and swayed as though they might break from the heavy burdens they carried. Easter's wagon was loaded with the many vegetables and other foods she'd harvested. She could not pack everything so she asked Sarah and Henry to distribute and sell what was left. She had long considered it best to avoid the major roads. They would need to avoid the soldiers who were looking for Cherokee, as well as bandits. This trip should take about two weeks. But it seemed that they were delayed time and again. There was the mud that bogged Arter's wagon; they had to get out and hitch both teams to his wagon to get it free. They spent time removing undergrowth and other debris from the side of the trail to make it possible for Easter's load to move around the thick muck.

Awinta helped carry sticks and other debris to the trail. She sat near Easter and said little for the first hours of the trip. Then, she noticed a red bird in the trees and pointed. Easter smiled at her.

"You like birds?" she asked the little girl. "They have special spirits. We believe that the red bird makes you quick to learn." Anwita smiled. "Do you like to learn?"

Awinta nodded.

"We had school when Doda said it was time to go,"
Awinta said. "We learned to say letters and to count
numbers. We pray much." Easter smiled.

"Yes, you went to a missionary school," Easter said.
"You must have been five years old." She guessed that
the girl probably knew very little beyond the basics of
numbers and the alphabet in English.

"What should I call you?" Anwita asked. Easter was
stunned that the question had not come up before now.
They had seen each other in passing many times. She had
sent Anwita on many errands and to do many chores, but
never had the girl addressed her. She supposed since they
were sisters, it would be best if she told Anwita.

"Did you know that we are blood sisters?" Easter
asked. Anwita shook her head violently, no.

"Doda said I have sisters and brothers but he did not
say who they are. Or maybe I can't remember."

"It is good to begin now as we intend to go," Easter
said. "We will be sisters." They rode for some time
quietly together. As they approached a marshy area, the
cows resisted their efforts to get them across the stream.
Arter whipped his team across the stream quickly, but
Easter's wagon faltered as the horses whinnied and shied
away from the running water. Easter drove them on, and
they were halfway across when one of the cows, Sallie,
tied to the back of her wagon, began to bellow and snort.
Easter kept shouting at the horses and mules and was
almost out of the muddy morass when one of her cows
seemed to scream in pain. She looked down and noticed
two snakes sliding away into the woods. They had bitten
one of her cows on her back leg. Sallie was holding her
back leg up. Easter snapped the reins harder on the
backs of the horses so that the load would be pulled up
and out of the soggy marsh.

"Arter!" she shouted. "We must stop. That clearing
ahead." He nodded and pulled his team and wagon to

the clearing as Easter struggled to get her wagon with the cows tied to it up the incline and to the clearing. Her two goats had been put in the wagon when she and Arter realized they'd be crossing several marshy streams. But the cows were suffering. They were upset and threatening to pull the wagon apart with their struggling. Something was not right. Easter pulled the wagon to the center of the clearing and got out to examine her cow. She had two in tow and both were good producers of milk. She tried to get near the one that bellowed and held her back leg up. It was clear that she'd been bitten by one of those snakes. Easter checked the other cow, Daisy, who seemed to be unaffected but her eyes were bulging.

"We need to stop here, Arter," she said. "This one, Sallie, is not doing good." It was rare for one of her cows to get bitten by a snake, but since they were traveling in some areas that were unfrequented by pioneers and by the soldiers, there would be dangers. Easter got out one of her herbs and mixed it with water. She attached the feeding pouch to the head of the struggling cow, who was now subdued, and looking a little calmer. Sallie began to suck greedily at the water from the leather bag.

When Sallie was finished, Easter attached a feedbag bag with a slightly different composition of herbs. Sallie was a little less enthusiastic, but never one to pass up a meal, she began to chew on the offering. Arter was examining the cow's back leg as Easter tried to hold Sallie's head in the grain bag. Awinta was busy gathering dried grass for the goats, who were butting the little girl with their heads. Arter began to unhitch the horses to take them down to the stream to drink.

He was careful to avoid areas that might hide snakes. The horses were skittish but drank thirstily. When he had watered them all, he gave them a loose lead and tied them to nearby trees. He did the same with the two cows. Awinta helped Easter get the goats to the stream and they were similarly tied and allowed to graze. The sounds of predators in the forest kept the goats nearby and the cows close to the wagons. Fortunately, the clearing was full of tall grasses. Though it was late in the year, the grass, some of it dried by the weather, offered plenty of nourishment. They would rest here a day or so.

Easter gathered as many pieces of dry wood as she could find on the periphery of the campsite and began to build a fire. She felt a prickling on the back of her neck and looked up in the dusk to see whether she could find the source of the uneasy feeling. Someone was watching them. She wondered if it could be Ezra Poe. She brought out the dried meat she'd set aside for the trip and the cornpones. She boiled water and motioned Arter and Awinta over to the fire. Awinta sat on the packed-down grass and quietly accepted the plate handed to her by Easter. When she finished her meal, Awinta yawned as though she were ready to sleep. Easter smiled at the girl and motioned to Arter to put her in the wagon on a pallet of blankets she had arranged. Arter came back and picked up his rifle, looking about as though he sensed someone or something was in the woods.

"We came far today, "Arter said, taking a bite of his cornpone. The crickets chirped and owls hooted nearby. A wolf howled in the distance. Arter tensed and put a hand on his rifle.

"It is not interested in us," Easter said, smirking. How could a man not know that this particular wolf was not a threat? The howling was at such a great distance that it was clear to Easter that the wolf had no plans to stalk her livestock, for now. She reconsidered her thoughts.

"But you are right to be cautious," she said. "There are some in the area who are being forced out of their hunting territory, just as the Cherokee are. So, the likelihood that they will look for opportunities to steal livestock is strong." Arter stared into the fire.

"We probably ought to hide our direction as often as

possible," he said. He pulled out the map that he had been given by Joseph Rhea and peered at it in the fading light. He pointed out the alternate trail that they would follow.

"This is not a trail known by settlers, generally," he said. "Rhea sketched this path for us when I told him we would be coming his way."

"And he expects you to bring me and all of this?" Easter gestured to the goods and the livestock.

"This is evidence of your wealth," Arter said, waving to the goods that they were taking with them. "He would expect nothing less. He knows who you are and has invited us to his land." Easter snorted.

"What?" Arter asked. He let some time pass before he spoke. "Easter, don't hold onto the idea that this family land will in any way be land that you will be able to claim. It belongs to Rhea and his neighbors. There is no way you can let it be known that you think you hold legal title to the land." He let her think on that for a moment.

"Why not?" she asked. "The Cherokee have gone to court to prove their rights time and again."

"Are they winning their cases, Easter?" She sat there looking into the distance. She heard the snap of wood in the woods and held her head erect. She looked around slowly as did Arter. Arter motioned to Easter to stay at the campfire and went to investigate. After some time, he returned.

"Nothing," he said. "I'll stay up and watch."

"Wake me when the moon is high above," she said. "I will watch next."

Arter nodded but planned to let her sleep.

She pulled herself up into the wagon, where the child, Awinta, was fast asleep. Easter pulled the covers over the little girl, and settled down near her. The nights were growing colder, so she hoped she had enough blankets and furs. She could feel the babe inside her stirring. Arter did not seem to notice. However, she tried not to draw attention to the growing child within her. She wanted no questions. When he had made a few passes around the campsite, Arter secured the other animals. He found a large boulder and rested against it to watch for predators, the human or animal kind. Soon, Easter, having rested some herself, insisted that he climb in the wagon to get some sleep as well. After a few hours rest, he woke and let Easter rest a little more. Easter dreamed the second time she slept. In her dream, someone had taken her, and she left a trail of crumbs to help Arter find her. When she woke, she said nothing of her dream but knew the time would come when she had to fight for her life. The certainty that she felt something more than friendship with Arter was dawning upon her. The sun was poking over the horizon when they prepared to continue their journey.

CHAPTER EIGHT
Winter 1837

It was near late afternoon the next day when Arter motioned for Easter to stop as they traveled down a fork in the road. Sallie, the cow, was feeling better. Most of the trail was narrow and some of it appeared to have not been used in years. Yet, Arter had received a map from Matthew Rhea that showed how to get to Pulaski without too much interference from other travelers. This was a trail that not many people knew, but it was treacherous. The area was hilly, rocky, full of brambles, fallen logs and rocks that had to be moved out of the way. Easter admired the way Arter stopped to get down from his wagon and without a word, pulled out an ax and chopped away at a log that had been too large to move. He'd taken off his tunic; although it was cold, he quickly worked up a sweat and had to wipe the perspiration from his face. Easter watched, mesmerized for a few minutes, the muscles in his back bunching and releasing as he swung the ax. Awinta stared up at her as she watched.

"He is your man?" Awinta asked.

"No," Easter said, realizing that she had lied to a

child about something so basic. She was not ready to talk about her feelings for Arter. Awinta seemed to have no reaction as she considered her sister's lie. She looked behind them as the goats struggled to get out of the wagon. The girl climbed to the back of the wagon and began to soothe the restless creatures. Easter, finally snapping out of her reverie, climbed from the wagon herself and busied herself tending to the cows and checking the chickens and cats. She helped Awinta get the goats out of the wagon to graze and relieve themselves. They were more like pets and very attached to Easter, so she did not worry much about them wandering.

All seemed well, but all of a sudden, she felt a tingling sensation at her neck. She looked about; someone was watching them. She watched carefully and thought she saw movement in the woods. But when she walked a step toward the place where she saw a shadow, it was gone. She shook her head. She must have seen the shadow of a bird. Waya, the youngest of her two dogs, growled, looking in the same direction that she'd sensed a presence. Ama ran in that direction. Easter motioned for Waya to stay. When there seemed to be nothing in the woods, Easter whistled for Ama to return. Arter paused and looked sharply when she whistled. Arter was surprised that she had the ability to call her dog in that way. Ama came trotting back.

Arter finished cutting up the fallen tree, and Easter hurried to help him move the wood out of the way. Many of the logs they had encountered were dry and easy to move, but this one was fresh and newly fallen. She looked at the trunk, and shivers raced up her spine. Again, she felt that tingling on her neck. She took a breath and looked at Arter to say something. He was looking at her.

"Ready to take a rest?" he asked. "It's getting

close to nightfall, and we want to find a safe place to camp. There should be a clearing ahead." She looked around and narrowed her eyes. Yes, she could feel it. Someone was watching them. But she didn't want to alarm Arter if it was just her imagination. Arter watched her intently and followed her eyes to the forest.

"What is it?" he asked.

"I don't know," she said. "It feels like. ... " She stopped herself, knowing that feelings were not really what Arter wanted to hear.

"Go ahead," he said. "You think someone is watching us? I agree. I felt that too."

"Yes," she said, relieved that he had picked up on not only her feelings, but his own too.

"There's not much we can do about it right now," he said looking around and hefting the ax in his hand. "We've been traveling all day, and the livestock need to be rested and watered. There's a stream ahead." He walked to her wagon and took out her Kentucky long rifle. He checked to be certain it was loaded and ready to fire. He was sure it would be in good order as Easter was a woman who kept such a weapon on hand.

Arter drove the wagon to a clearing that seemed smaller than their last campsite and helped Easter guide the horses that pulled her wagon to a V shape against the wind. He unhitched his team and tethered the horses and mules then unhitched hers. He led the first two mules to the stream and tethered them to a tree. It was growing cold, and the sky was darkening. The sky seemed to be heavy with snow. The water was shallow but clean for the animals. Then Arter returned for the second set of horses and mules. When he had both teams drinking and grazing he returned for Easter's two cows. The dogs, Waya and Ama, helped herd the animals to the water and then back to camp.

The dogs and cows drank greedily not far from the mules and horses. Arter met Easter halfway as she went to the stream with a wooden bucket for water for her goats and the smaller animals. She filled leather pouches for their own supplies and tied them to one of the horses to help with getting the water back to camp. Arter and the dogs returned a horse and the cows to the camp to find Easter had food prepared and was boiling water for a drink she insisted he imbibe. They fed Awinta and tended the goats and other animals. Then they had their own meal of cornpone and dried meat.

Arter looked about when he heard a noise in the woods. Waya let out a gruff woof and then, baring his teeth, a low growl.

"You think there might be a wolf stalking us?" Arter asked.

"More likely of the human variety," Easter said, not looking up from her meal. Arter sighed. He wished Easter would show more concern. There were women back East who might have swooned with anxiety by now, but Easter took threats in stride. He was grateful for her calm but wished he knew what would push her beyond reason. He shrugged, mentally.

"I'll take the first watch," Arter said. "No need for you to stay up. Get some rest."

"You've been working extra hard," Easter said. "Let me take the first watch."

"No, you get some rest," he said. She sighed, frustrated with his gallant behavior.

"I don't feel too much like resting right now," she said, feeling the tension of the unexplained noises in the woods. She looked about. The darkness in the woods felt thick and weighty. Someone was out there. Easter became aware of the knife she had strapped to her leg. Her brother, Connutsee, had taught her how to use it when she was as young as Awinta. He wanted her to be self-sufficient and to know those things that men knew. He wanted her to be able to hunt and also to defend herself. She thought of her brother's strong arms as he had pulled the knife again and again from the tree trunk they were using as a target. He wanted her throw to be accurate, so he'd made her practice until she got it right. It took a long time, but finally, she could throw the knife with some degree of accuracy. As she grew older, she learned to throw it with force.

Those thoughts and others returned as Easter sat with Arter at the little fire she'd built. She was wrapped in the western dress of the whites under her fur and leather coat. Her leggings were leather, and her feet were wrapped snugly in wool. On her head she wore a fur and leather hat that sat snuggly around her ears. She had mittens made of fur on the inside and leather on the outside — simple hide mittens that she'd fashioned for herself and for Awinta out of rabbit fur. She'd made certain Awinta was similarly attired before they departed. Arter had a similar hat and the leather and fur overcoat of men who traveled the hills.

She looked up from the fire to see Ama seeming to track something in the woods. She seemed torn over whether to stay near the camp or go off into the woods to investigate. Waya sat near Easter, unperturbed but alert and staring into the distance. Every now and then, he'd raise his nose to the air in the direction of the disturbance. Yes, someone or something was there. Easter thought it best to prepare for it. She made up her mind when Arter began to check both long rifles. Awinta was not sleeping yet, so Easter went to get the little girl and brought her around to the campfire.

"Awinta," Easter said. "You know what to do for the cattle if we should need to leave the camp?" Awinta nodded her head.

"Water them and keep them fed," Awinta said. "Build a fire to protect them from wild creatures."

"That's right," Easter said, smiling. "Awinta, there is someone in the woods who is tracking us. There might be trouble. We don't know what kind. If that happens and for some reason you are left to defend the camp alone, do you know how to use a knife?"

"Yes," Awinta said. "Doda taught me how to use a knife and so did Degataga."

"That's good," Easter said, regretting that she would need to trust such a young child to stay safe if something should happen. However, she had already guessed who might be out lurking in the woods. It was Ezra Poe.

Easter led the child back to the wagon, where she climbed up on the back of it and settled in with the goats. The goats kept the child warm as she snuggled down between them. It felt as though the temperature had dropped to freezing when the sun went down. Easter sensed snow would be coming. It was important to keep the pens covered with the doves, chickens and cats in them. She'd seen to their feeding and showed Awinta how to see to the welfare of all of the animals. Awinta seemed to know what was expected of her. It was likely the girl was expected to do such chores on her father's farm. This was not the type of child who was coddled and kept inside. Her life had always been one where she was expected to work.

Easter wished that she could have given the girl less of a burden from the beginning of her life, but she accepted the reality not only of Awinta's circumstances but of her own. The life of a woman or girl who lived on a farm was full of tasks. She would be expected from an early age to fulfill those tasks without complaint. Easter had shown Awinta how to make the simple corn patties and to use the dried meat sparingly. The child seemed to take in the information with ease. She'd been helping Easter feed the animals and watching her prepare the meals, so the girl knew what to do. Easter sighed as she hoped that there would be no need for Awinta to rely on herself and to protect the animals.

Easter went to the back of the wagon and dug through a leather satchel where she kept some extra weapons and tools. She tore pieces of fabric into strips and wrapped them under her arms and around her legs. If she had to fight for her life, she wanted to have a way to survive. She stuck another knife, enclosed in a leather casing, into her bodice. She strapped it to herself with the strips of fabric. She checked the Kentucky rifle that Arter had been working on. The weapon had only one shot, so Easter hoped that she would be able to make it count if that moment came. She gathered blankets and stepped into the wagon with Awinta.

"Going to take a rest anyway?" Arter asked. He looked up at the sky. It felt like snow, not just a light one, but a storm.

"I think we will have bad weather soon," Easter said. "I can feel it."

"It's early for snow, but not unlikely," Arter said. "It might be better for us to head to a cave I know of nearby. It looks like we will have bad weather for a while." He had traveled this area before, once with his brother and another time with Matthew Rhea. He knew there were caves in the area. It would be important to get to one that would offer shelter.

Easter nodded in agreement. The storm would delay their travels, but sheltering would be better than staying out in the biting wind and snow. The night was cold, but the animals were keeping things warm in the wagon. She'd covered the chickens' cages with tight leather. They were quiet and huddled together in the cold. The cats were curled into one another, and the goats were snuggled up to Awinta. Waya snuggled near Easter, and Ama curled up at the end of the wagon. Easter lay down among the barrels of dried corn and nuts and intended to keep watch, but soon was fast asleep.

The sound of ducks in the distance woke Easter. She wiped her face with a cloth and stepped out of the buckboard wagon. A dusting of snow covered the ground. She'd covered herself with a leather tarp and had done the same for the animals and Awinta, but the girl was not under it. Easter shook the snow from the leather tarp and used snow to freshen her face and hands. Awinta was out of the wagon and helping Arter with the horses, mules and cows near the stream.

They had watered the animals and brought the cattle, mules and horses to the wagons. Arter waved at her, nearly finished with strapping the horses and mules into their traces.

Easter looked around, apprehensively feeling that someone was nearby. As she stepped out of the wagon and onto the ground, she heard horse hooves. She picked up her Kentucky rifle but was too late. She was knocked in the head and swept up off the ground and over the side of a horse that turned quickly away from the wagon and into the woods. Waya, who'd been barking and growling, followed them in hot pursuit. Whoever had taken her turned and threw a knife at her dog. Easter heard Waya yelp, but the dog did not stop. He kept following. She heard Ama barking in the distance as the large stallion sped away.

Half-conscious and with the blood draining to her head, Easter knew Arter was saddling up one of the horses as her abductor kept putting distance between the camp and his large horse. She struggled to stay conscious and aware of where they were headed. Then she realized she had bits of material she could leave as a trail. She managed to tear off some of it without drawing the attention of the man who'd taken her. He had not taken the time to cover his tracks so she had no doubt that Arter would find her; that was her last thought as she drifted into unconsciousness.

CHAPTER NINE

Arter aimed the long rifle in the direction of the rider who had thrown Easter across his saddle. He cursed as he realized that it was too much of a risk. He could easily hit Easter instead. Arter took off his hat and slapped it against his leg, cursing his bad timing. Awinta stood looking at him fearfully. He looked around. He, Awinta and Ama had herded the cattle, horses and mules back to the camp to prepare for their continued trip. Ama barked and growled, running in the direction of the abductor. But Arter called Ama back before she could get too far. The dog seemed to sense that she was needed. He looked at the small girl. He had to leave quickly. Waya would follow Easter no matter where she went; he had no doubt of that.

He unhooked his stallion, Desa, from its traces and saddled up, grabbed a leather water pouch and his bag, which had a little dried meat in it. He'd left the other horse and mules in their traces, but tied Easter's wagon to his. The horses and mules should follow if Awinta had to drive them out of the coming storm. He covered the horses with a tarp and checked the traces. He led the cows to Easter's wagon and tied them to it. His wagon would have

one steady mule in the front and a mule and horse in
the back.

They could pull fine. He covered them with a
leather tarp. His hands shook as he considered his
task. He was reluctant to leave a child alone to
protect the cattle. The storm looked to be near, and
the weather was getting worse. The sky was dark and
gray with low clouds. A light coating of snow
covered the ground. He looked to the northwest. A
storm was coming. If Awinta was caught in it, she
might die. He had the reins of his horse in one hand.
He tied the horse to the wagon and bent down to
speak to Awinta, grabbing her by the shoulders. The
wind blew fiercely, obscuring his voice. He took the
map from his bag and then had the girl look with
him.

"Awinta," he said. "I must go find your sister."

"Will you bring her back from the bad man?" He
wondered how the girl knew that her sister had been
taken by a man who was "bad." He shrugged off the
thought. Easter had certain spiritual gifts; apparently,
her sister, Awinta did too.

"Yes," he said. "I will." He felt certain he would
find her; in his bones he knew Easter was capable
and strong, but something clenched his chest as he
considered how intensely he felt for her. Did he love
her? Yes. If he lost her, his life would never be the
same.

"Awinta," he said. "This is a picture of the place
we are in." He pointed to the map. "You see that the
snow is coming and may cause you and the animals
trouble. If things get too harsh, take the animals and
wagons, if you can, to this cave. There is one not far
from here. Take that road there." He pointed to the
right. The girl looked through the lightly falling
snow. "Continue on that road until it ends, and then
go to the left." He pointed in the opposite direction.

"When you see a large boulder, that will be near the cave. Take the hill up to it." He paused to look into her eyes. "Can you do that?" She nodded. "Don't be afraid. Ama will be with you, and the horses will do as you ask them. Can you drive the wagon?" She nodded.

"Doda taught me."

"I would take you, but I need to catch the man who has your sister," Arter said. "Do you understand?" The little girl nodded her head.

"If someone comes, look to see if they are with the ni a wi Bird clan or Potato Clan. Accept their help if they are. If they are not, try to hide." He paused, wondering if he was expecting too much of an 8-year-old. "If I take too long, head for the cave. We will come for you. Can you do that?"

"Yes," she said. "Will you return soon? Will Ama stay here with me?"

"Yes," he called Ama over. "Ama, you stay here with Awinta." The dog whined and barked, licking the little girl in the face. Awinta put her arms around the husky dog and shivered.

"I will take care of Ama and all of the cattle," she said. "Please bring my sister back." Tears formed in the child's eyes, and Arter's heart went out to her.

"You will be fine until I return. I'm leaving your sister's gun and one of my knives with you. The snow will make it difficult, but stay under the tarp and in the blankets with the goats until you hear someone coming. If a wildcat or other creature tries to get the animals, don't hesitate to use the rifle. Can you use it?" The girl nodded her head. He had his doubts, but there was no help for it. He had to leave before the trail went cold.

"Doda showed me how to put it on a log or perch, aim and fire."

"Your sister's long rifle is loaded," Arter said.

"There is plenty of food in the wagon and there is water nearby."

"Yes," she said. "One thing."

"What is it?" He was quickly losing patience; he had to begin searching for Easter.

"What do I call you?" she asked. Arter had been holding his breath and let out a puff of air that formed a small cloud of fog between them. He smiled, realizing that he had had very little to do with the little girl. He had never really thought of her as a niece or daughter, but it was clear that this event would change the way they saw each other.

"You may call me Uncle Arter," he said, not wanting to say that he and Easter might marry and that then he would adopt Awinta. But still, he was touched that she would ask. He gave the child a hug and helped her get the animals under a leather tarp they had rigged up.

As he looked back at the child, huddled down under the leather covering in the buckboard wagon, he looked to the west. He walked swiftly toward his horse, placed his left foot in the stirrup and hauled himself on the beast. The horse was the quickest and strongest of his own. He had a thick blanket and wore fur-lined gloves. His stallion had a warm blanket and saddle as well. He'd bought Desa from a trader in North Carolina. The horse was sure-footed and hardy. He let no one but Arter ride him. Arter gave one more look back at the girl and gave the stallion a nudge that sent him flying in the direction Easter had gone. He would need to trust in the good spirits of his mother's people to keep both Easter and Awinta safe.

As he took off after the rider who had Easter, Arter hoped the trail had not gone cold. The snow was falling harder. The cretin who'd stolen Easter had not done a thing to hide his tracks but the snow was quickly doing it for him. Still, riding double on a horse would leave an obvious trail. Arter rode quickly through the increasing snowfall. The air was sharp and clean. He rode until he could no longer see the trail. Then, he stopped, got off his horse and walked for a while trying to pick up any indication of the direction of the rider who had Easter.

Ezra Poe got off his horse and led it through a rocky outcropping. He had pulled Easter up and tied her hands to his saddle horn so she sat hunched over, her head resting on his horse's neck. He had no doubt that the man Easter had been riding with would be in pursuit. That was exactly what he was hoping. He would do away with his competition before the man could stake a real claim on Easter. He wanted what Easter's brother had — gold and silver, rich land — and he wanted Easter herself. He'd long waited for this opportunity to have her. He licked his lips thinking of how he would use her. She would never want another after she had Ezra. He grinned and slapped her. The woman was still out cold. After that slap, anyone would wake up. She seemed to be slipping off the horse, so he grabbed her by her neck, jumped back on the horse and held her in front of him.

He looked back at the trail from which he'd ridden. He'd driven his horse hard. There was a small cave ahead where he could hide until the worst of the storm was over. He rode to the cave and slid off his horse. He took Easter off the horse, found the cave entrance and led his horse inside. There was just enough room for the horse and two people. He took his blanket and saddle off the back of the horse and laid it on the ground. Then he laid Easter on it. She slumped there as though she had no life. He wondered if he had hit her too hard. Poe bent down to listen. He was relieved to hear her breathing and to sense a strong heartbeat. He regretted having to strike her on the head, but if he hadn't she would have struggled all the way.

Poe went to a nearby stream and watered his horse. He thought he heard a dog in the distance. Damn! If that dog of hers survived the knife he threw, it would lead the man straight to him. He decided he would let the dog find them and then kill it if he could.

Easter's head throbbed. She put a hand on her middle. She worried that the baby might have been hurt when she was taken. But she could feel it moving around. She heard Ezra Poe walking his horse onto the rough surface of the cave. The surface gave way to dirt a ways back, and the horse stood some distance away from the entrance to the cave. Not far from the entrance, a deep ravine stood like a gaping maw.

She slanted her eyes so that Poe could not see that she'd come around after that blow to the head. It took her a while to get her bearings. Poe bent to get something from his saddle and came to her side. He brushed the hair away from her face and took a look at the side of her head. It was then that he realized she was awake.

"It took you long enough," he said. Still weak from the long ride and the blow to her head, Easter opened her eyes and tried to speak, but no words came out. He spread another blanket on the rough surface of the cave floor and picked her up.

"I'm pleased to see you can't talk yet." He sat down with her in his lap. She struggled to get away from him, but was too weak to make much progress.

"Now, there," he said. "I like my women nice and compliant. You just lay there while I get my fill." She felt him brush at the hair where her head had a large knot. There was a bit of blood. He wiped it away with the edge of his shirt. He'd opened his overcoat and had her sitting between his legs. She tried desperately to clear her throat as he continued to pet her, whispering vile words. Her senses began to come back to her. Her arms were numb and so were her legs, but she was beginning to get some sensation back in them. She didn't want to let him know that she could use her limbs until she was fully functioning. To struggle but not to strike would do her no good, so she waited. He licked her face and fondled her and tried to position her so he could get a hand under her skirt. But just as he headed toward the knife she had hidden on her leg, she grabbed it quickly and stabbed his thigh.

He screamed, cursing at her, clutching at the wound and trying to grab the knife from her. She scrambled out of his grasp and tried to get up. Failing that, she crawled away. When she thought she was clear of him, she felt him grab her foot and pull her back. She let him drag her back and kicked with her other foot into his nether parts. He grunted and doubled over. She reached for the reins on the horse but it pulled back from her and moved about in a circle. She could not get it to go forward out of the cave. As she was trying to get control of the horse, Poe hobbled over to her and struck her so hard she fell to the ground in a heap. She fought the darkness that threatened to overcome her. She breathed heavily in the cold thin air. Outside, the storm was getting worse. The wind howled and the snow came down in buckets now. Arter would never find her.

Ezra tore the hem of her dress to wrap the fabric around the wound in his thigh and cursed a blue streak. He grabbed a leather pouch with water in it and took a long drink. He grabbed her by her hair this time and drug her across the rough cave floor and onto the blankets.

"You think that's going to stop us from getting to know each other?" he asked. "No, we're just getting started. When we get to town, you're going to marry me, and I'm gong to get that land your brother's sitting on. Now, where were we?" The wind continued to howl as he tied her hands and checked her over. She'd wrapped the other small knife in a great deal of fabric that was in her bodice. He had trouble finding it. When he did, he grinned and began tearing at the dress. She pushed at him to make him stop. Suddenly, a low growl sounded at the entrance of the cave.

"Waya," she said. "Go now. Find Arter."

"He ain't getting no one," Poe said, pointing his gun at the dog. Easter lunged at him, making him lose his aim. She kicked out at him again and he was about to subdue her when he felt himself being lifted and tossed against the hard cave wall.

There, as angry as a Cherokee could ever be, stood Arter.

"Like beating on women do you?"Arter asked. "Let's see how you do when you have someone your own size to tangle with." Arter stepped into him in one large leap and pounded Ezra in the face. Easter saw blood spurt from Ezra's nose as Arter continued to hit him. Ezra was able to get a few return punches in on Arter and the two men fought furiously as they did a war dance out of the cave and perilously close to the edge of a ravine. A jaw cracked as Arter drew back and hit Ezra again. Still, Ezra shook his head and struggled to strike back.

Ezra's horse, still equipped with Ezra's rifle scabbard, had reared and huffed out of the way of the two fighting men until it was out of the cave and standing in the falling snow. When Arter took a break to look back at Easter, Ezra lunged for his horse where his rifle was and aimed it at Arter. It took one quick throw of Arter's knife to stop Ezra. The knife landed in Ezra's shoulder. Blood spouted. The knife had hit an artery. Poe's eyes grew large with surprise; he grabbed the knife and pulled it free, but it took no time for him lose consciousness. He collapsed and rolled into the ravine. It was a long fall down, past boulders and craggy rock. Arter could not see him when he peered down into the ravine.

Arter heaved, breathing deeply as he turned to tend to Easter. He knelt beside her and gathered her in his arms. "I'm sorry," he said. "Sorry it took so long for me to get to you."

Easter felt the emotion of it all overwhelm her and tears rolled down her cheeks. She didn't cry often. No one saw the tears she shed after her parents died of the flu. When Connutsee died, she mourned him, but the tears were dried up. She kept telling herself that she would not let herself feel. If she didn't feel anything, she would not hurt. So she worked to cut off those emotions. But Arter was holding her so tenderly in his strong arms that she felt safe now. She knew then that it was more than friendship. She loved this man. He rocked her and looked at her head and face.

He cursed. "I'd kill him again if I could." She shook her head, overcome with emotion.

"Are you certain he's dead?" Easter asked.

"He is certainly mortally wounded," he said. "We don't have time to check. We have to get back to Awinta before the storm overwhelms her."

"Awinta," she said. Knowing she was asking about her sister, Arter shushed her.

"She's all right. I left her back at the wagons with

the animals. If we hurry, we can get back before the storm gets too strong." They both heard Waya whining. Easter tried to stand up but wobbled on her feet.

"Waya," she said, opening her arms to her dog. Waya wagged his tail and came to her, licking her face. She laughed and hugged him, and her heart swelled with gratitude. Both Waya and Arter had saved her life. "You're hurt," she said, examining the big dog's back leg. She looked at Waya's hind leg where he had been cut by the knife.

"I think this one must have thrown a knife at him as he was riding away with you," Arter said, pointing at the place where Ezra had rolled down the ravine. Easter tore off the hem of her dress and wrapped it around Waya's back leg. "I'm sorry he was hurt, but he followed you the whole way here. The blood from his wound made a good trail straight to this cave." Easter smiled at him and he hugged her to him. "Let's get back to the wagons."

"We'll have to move fast," Arter said. "There's no time for the body." Easter looked at him pensively. He knew she was asking with that look that he do something — not just leave the body here. He took his knife and wiped it on the cave floor. He walked to the ravine and looked down. He saw part of one of Poe's feet sticking out of some brush and rocks. Satisfied that Poe was not going to be harming anyone, Arter approached Ezra's stallion. He was able to sooth the horse and grab its reins. He led it into the cave.

"We'll make better time if we can ride two horses," he said. "We'll set this one free after we get back to camp." He spoke soothingly to the horse. "I'll ride this one, and you take my horse," he said. Easter immediately complied. He helped her get on his horse, lifting her with little effort.

"What about Waya?" she asked, looking down at him.

"I think he'll follow us back," he said.

"I don't want to take chances," she said. He shook his head at her coddling of the dog, but Arter scooped the dog up and handed him to her across the saddle of his stallion. The dog and the horse behaved well. Arter hefted himself up in the saddle of Ezra's horse and they rode through the biting wind and drifting snow. The darkening sky made it difficult to see.

CHAPTER TEN

Awinta snuggled down in the back of the wagon. The horses moved every now and then, shaking off the snow and stomping their feet. That made the wagon shake and shudder. The wind howled, and the snow got deeper. The cows, Sallie and Daisy, complained and tried to pull away from the wagon. Why did they keep doing that? It was too cold to go off on their own. Maybe they just wanted some water. Maybe they were hungry. Awinta got from under the tarp and looked for the feedbag and feed that Easter kept for the cows.

Awinta made sure each was half full and attached a bag to the head of each cow. She did the same for the horses and mules in hopes that they would settle down. Ama stood beside her as Awinta fed the animals. She wanted the animals to hurry so she could get out of the cold and back into the warmth of the wagon. She remembered that Arter had watered the animals and let them graze some this morning, but he had not added the special feed that

Easter liked to give them.

It seemed to be taking Uncle Arter a long time to get back. Would he find Easter? Would her sister be all right? Would Awinta be able to find the cave if she had to? She stomped her feet to warm them and clapped her fur-covered hands together.

The wagon shook again as the wind grew stronger. The snow fell in big fat chunks. Awinta stuck out her tongue and tasted the big snowflakes. She laughed as they fell into her mouth and into her eyes. She tried to look up at the sky. She rubbed the mules' noses, Keme and Lulu. Lulu snapped at her as was her habit, but Awinta knew to stay away from Lulu's mouth. She checked Kay and Mico, Easter's horses, and made certain they were covered. She tried to be certain the mules, Hogan and Tom, were covered too and eating from the feed bags, but Hogan kept shaking off the leather covering and did not care for the food. She exhaled in exasperation and checked the cows again.

Using the step at the back of Easter's wagon, she got back in. Ama hopped into the wagon with her. Awinta tried to relax, but she could not feel safe. She pulled the map out of her tunic pocket and tried to look at it. It was so dark she could barely see. The horses and mules stamped the ground as though they were impatient to move. She got out of the wagon and removed the feedbags from each of the horses, mules and cows. She dropped the feedbags back in the wagon and heaved a sigh, looking about her as though Uncle Arter and Easter would appear before her.

She decided it was time. The wind was blowing so hard, and the snow was getting deeper. If she didn't leave for the cave now, it would be too late. She might not be able to find it. Ama sat up and growled, poking her head out of the leather tarp that covered her, the chickens and goats.

"What is it, Ama?" Awinta said quietly. Ama looked intensely out of the back of the wagon. She looked out herself and saw movement. Was the bad man coming back? Was it a wolf or a wildcat? She couldn't tell. Maybe that's why the cattle were so restless. Maybe there was a wildcat in the woods. Ama's growl became louder. Ama jumped out of the wagon and began to bark and growl loudly as though she were warning something away. Awinta did not want to fire the long rifle. There was only one shot, and she might need it later. She dug around for Easter's bow and arrow. Doda had taught her to use it. Easter's was fashioned for a woman. Awinta threw off the tarp and aimed the arrow into the woods near where she saw the movement and let the arrow fly. She heard a swift movement after that. Something had run off.

"Come, Ama," she said to the dog. "We must leave this place." She tried to look at the map again, but the snow was coming down harder. She would need to leave now to find the cave. She scrambled up onto Easter's wagon and pushed the lever to unlock the wheels. Then she climbed down from Easter's wagon and climbed back up to Arter's wagon. She pulled the lever on that wagon, which was much harder to get free. But finally, the stubborn lever wrenched free and the horses and mules lurched forward. If Arter had not tied the reins to the wagon seat, she would not have been able to guide the animals. They were ready to move.

She struggled to get the thick leather reins from around the metal attached to the seat. She had to take off her mittens to get them undone. Having gotten the thick leather free, she held the reins tightly in her mouth and was almost pulled off the bench when Keme and Lulu lurched forward again. She dropped the reins out of her mouth and yelped as the leather straps seemed to be snaking away from her. They snapped at her cheek as they escaped. She jumped on them before they could escape completely and pulled with all of her might to get the horse and mules to obey her. She pulled the right strap far to the right and slapped all of the straps as hard as she could, shouting at the team. "Keme, Lulu, get up," she shouted. She was surprised when the animals shifted, stomped and stirred. Finally, the wagons began to move toward the road that Arter had said she should take to get to the cave.

The team moved laboriously through the deepening snow. Awinta looked back to see Ama at the back of Easter's wagon, keeping the cows protected and nipping them every now and then to keep them from pulling at the wagon. The tether that attached Easter's wagon to Arter's seemed flimsy, but Awinta could not worry about that. The cows were mooing, upset at the predator they sensed in the woods. The goats complained loudly. She wondered why they didn't seem to cry so much when Easter was there. Maybe they knew that Awinta didn't really know where she was going.

Awinta slapped the reins again, and the teams pulled the wagons through the snow on the winding road. It seemed to go on forever. She was having a difficult time seeing where the path was when she looked back to see that the other wagon was left behind. She pulled hard on the reins to stop the lead wagon. She tied the reins to a tree and ran back to the stranded wagon. Its team stamped in the snow and pulled without success. Awinta walked back to see that the front wheels had become mired in a rut.

Why didn't the wagon she was in stop? She wondered what to do. Seeing the muddy hole the wheels kept sliding in, she looked about for leaves, dry sticks and small rocks. She raced around, getting what she could from the side of the narrow road and from the woods. She didn't want to go too deep into the woods to gather material as whatever had been stalking them might be waiting for her. Her heart pounded furiously as she worked to gather debris. Finally, she seemed to have enough dry sticks, dry dirt and leaves to create some traction. She had seen Doda and Easter do this.

She pulled the reins of the horses leading the team. They seemed to hesitate, but after several efforts on her part to urge them ahead and Ama's barking and nipping at them, the team, led by Hogan and Tom, pulled the wagon over the muddy hole and lurched forward. Awinta drove the wagon to the lead wagon. Getting down, Awinta tied Easter's wagon again to the lead wagon, got back on Arter's wagon and continued down the road. When she got to the end of it, she saw that there was only one way to go — to the left. She pulled the reins to the left and leaned with all her might. The wagon scraped a tree as she turned the team. She thought she might have lost one of Easter's boxes in the jarring against a tree, but there was no time to get down to find it. She had to get to the cave.

Finally, she saw a large boulder at the end of this road and looked up the hill. There seemed to be an opening ahead. She wondered whether the team could get up the hill with the heavy load. Was it possible? Thinking that she would make the load in Easter's wagon lighter, she climbed up in Easter's wagon and lowered the chicken cage to the ground. She carried it up the hill till she got to the entrance of the cave.

She worried that there might be some occupants in the cave so she called Ama. Ama went into the cave and sniffed around. No one seemed to be there, so Awinta hauled the crate into the cave. Next, she brought the goats, and as many small items as she could carry from Easter's wagon. She rested as the snow got deeper. She realized, as the wind nearly blew her from a rock she'd perched on, that she would need to try to get each wagon up the hills separately. She untied Easter's wagon from Arter's wagon. She led the team with Arter's wagon ahead a bit and turned it toward the cave. Lulu snapped at her again but seemed eager to move. Awinta wrapped the reins around a large rock.

She walked back to Easter's wagon and perched on the bench. Like she'd heard the adults shout many times before, she said "Yah! Hogan, Tom," as loud as she could. But the sound did not seem to carry in the howling wind. She tried again and slapped the reins to the backs of the horses, and they moved up the hill slowly.

The heavy barrels slid to the back of the wagon. The wagon gate seemed to barely keep them in. The hill was not very steep; but it was a hill. As if they sensed that shelter was nearby, the horses and mules pulled the wagon straight into the deep cave. Awinta rested a moment, relieved that she'd been able to get one wagon into the cave. The ceiling of the cave was high and filled with sounds. She shivered, but this was better than the biting wind outside. Ama barked outside at the other team. The horse and mules neighed and stomped. She scrambled off the bench and left Easter's team in the cave. The horses and mules stood there obediently. She was amazed.

Awinta ran down the hill to the other team and climbed up on Uncle Arter's bench seat. She pulled hard to the right, and Lulu and Keme began the laborious climb up the hill. Ama growled at something in the woods, and the team seemed eager to get away from whatever it was.

The horse and mules were so nervous that they scrambled up the hill in a desperate effort to get to the safety of the cave. When Awinta got the other team inside, Ama came in the cave too. She sat guard at the entrance, while Awinta crawled into the back of the wagon, exhausted. After resting a minute, the little girl got up and put the cages and other goods back in Easter's wagon and herded the goats in too. Then she lay down and slept, covered in furs and blankets and snuggled up to the smelly goats.

CHAPTER ELEVEN

Arter stopped at the space where he'd left Awinta. The snow was deep, and the wind blew so hard it seemed the horses had trouble keeping on their feet. Easter looked at him through the large coat she wore. She was wrapped in cloth; only her eyes showing. Arter could see her eyes grow large through the fat snowflakes that were falling so fast and so hard that they had trouble seeing one another. Arter pulled his horse up as he tried to get a sense for where Awinta might have headed. He had given her directions to a large cave, but did she make it? Was she interrupted by beast or man? Waya had jumped off when they arrived in what he thought was the clearing where he'd left Awinta. He stood near the horses, shaking off the snow. If Arter's estimate was correct, the cave couldn't be too far from the clearing. Tall, naked trees surrounded them.

Easter sank in the saddle and leaned to one side as though she might fall. Arter grabbed the reins of her horse and caught her as she began to slide off. He shook her to bring her around, but she seemed insensate. The blow to her head must be making her drowsy. He grabbed her by the waist and pulled her onto the horse in front of him. He frowned as he noticed her waist was fuller than he expected. No time for that. He tied her horse's reins to his saddle, using one hand and his mouth. Waya barked up at him as he led the two horses through the deepening snow. The wind howled, and the snow fell even faster.

Waya barked and jumped about in front of the horses, as though leading them to the cave. It seemed that Arter had been turning the horses in circles. Finally, Arter made out the direction to which Waya seemed to be headed. Could the dog be leading him to the cave? He had to trust Waya's instincts and sense of smell. Arter pulled the horses' reins in the direction of Waya's short bark. It seemed there was only a wall of ice and snow. But as he came closer to the wooded area, the trees seemed to part and he could tell that, though the snow was deep, he was headed toward the cave.

Waya pranced up and down in front of the horses, nipping at them and running around to their backs, urging them forward. Arter thanked God for Waya, who was truly the Leaping Water that his name implied. It seemed miraculous to Arter that the dog was healthy enough to help though he had been injured earlier. The snow did not seem to hamper Waya's efforts. He did not tire in herding the horses through the snow, almost too deep now for both horse and dog. They trudged through slowly, the horses stumbling now and then but holding their own against the frigid temperatures and howling wind. Without Waya, they would have been lost.

Finally, after what seemed like hours, they arrived at the base of the hill that led to the cave. Arter gave

Poe's horse a final nudge with his knees, and the horse, as though it sensed food and shelter, bolted up the hill and into the cave.

Arter groaned as he slid off the horse and down its flanks, pulling Easter along with him. They landed with a thud on the hard floor of the cave, littered with rocks and dirt. The cave was so dim and their eyes so blinded by the snow that it took some time for Arter to make out the confines of the cave. He lay there with Easter on top of him. He wanted to save her from falling hard on the floor of the cave, given that she had been injured by Ezra Poe. He breathed deeply and looked under the horses. Both seemed as tired and weary as he was. The dogs played with one another, joyful in their reunion. There before him were the wagons that had Easter's goods. The mules and horses were still in the traces, but they were all safe and deep enough in the cave to be protected from the icy wind and snow. Arter sat up slowly and pulled Easter into his lap. She was unconscious. It was time to get her settled and to find out if the girl was safe.

Arter picked Easter up in his arms and laid her out of the way of the horses. He lit a fire to see, walked to the back of the wagon and saw Awinta, fast asleep, curled up with the goats. He smiled and shook his head. The girl had done it. If someone had told him that a young girl like Awinta, so small and delicate, could get two teams and two wagons to a cave in a snowstorm, he would have denied it. But here was the proof. The girl had followed his instructions and had found sanctuary for the beasts and for herself. He tucked the furs and blankets tightly over the girl. Arter heard howling wind and howling wolves in the distance. He looked anxiously at the opening of the cave. Had they borrowed the den of some other beasts? Too bad. They had nowhere else to go.

There would be no moving from this place until the storm let up and the wind died down. Arter reached for the bundle of furs and blankets that Easter had packed away and went about the business of wrapping her up. A pile of rocks seemed to have been tunneled at the side of the cave to make space for a fire. Someone else, probably someone ancient, had made a fire here before. So, Arter set himself that task next. The fire was nestled into the wall of the cave and created a good bit of warmth. Arter moved Easter near it and went to tend to the horses. He used the horses to maneuver the wagons to the side of the cave and placed the horses between them to make a sort of stall for them. If they felt protected, they might be less anxious with the wolves howling in the distance.

Arter unhooked the horses and mules from their traces and gathered enough snow outside the cave so that the horses and mules had something to drink. The dogs joined the horses and the other animals as he placed the snow in a small indentation in the rocky bottom of the cave. It was a good place for snow to melt and for the beasts to drink.

When Arter had finished, he searched the second wagon for hay that Easter had wisely stored in back. When she insisted on loading so much into the wagon, Arter thought she was creating more unnecessary work. The trip was taking longer than he thought, and Arter was glad Easter had brought all those supplies. Easter moaned as she turned toward the fire. Arter went to her and smoothed her hair from her face; her eyes opened slowly.

"How long?" she asked, her voice croaking with dryness. He put a finger over her mouth.

"Shh. Don't talk, Easter." He went to get a wooden cup from the back of her wagon and put snow in it. He held it over the fire so that it could melt and then held the cup to Easter's lips. This seemed to revive her, and she sat up, but immediately fell back against the cave wall. He checked her head wound and gave her some snow to put on it.

"Where is Awinta?" she asked, putting a hand to her head.

"She's in the back of one of the wagons with the goats," he said. Easter chuckled and lifted her head to see the two wagons had been made into stalls for the animals. She placed a protective hand on her abdomen; she knew the child was moving. Would she lose it? No time to fret over that, she thought.

"Waya and Ama?" she asked.

"Ama is in the wagon with Awinta. Waya, that fierce creature, is standing guard for now. He led us to the cave. The snow was so thick, I could not see. If it were not for Waya, herding the horses in this direction, we would not have made it."

Easter called Waya to her. The dog lay down beside Easter and put his head down to look at the wagons. Every now and then he raised his head up and stared at the entrance to the cave.

"What do you think he sees out there?" Easter asked.

"There is something out there that wants to get in," Arter said.

"Wolves?" she asked.

"No, they would not dare try the two dogs," he said. "We will see." He grabbed his rifle and held it near him as he pulled the furs over himself and Easter. He grabbed a bit of dried meat and gave it to Easter and ate some himself. He tore off a piece for Waya and Ama and fed them as well. Arter was so exhausted that he wanted to fall asleep himself, but something told him he had to stay vigilant. He propped himself up against the cave wall. His back hurt, and he used the jagged stone to press into his

115

sore muscles. Before he closed his eyes, he felt Waya and Ama tense and growl. He opened his eyes.

A large cat streaked by the wagons, and Ama and Waya gave chase. The cattle began a noisy complaint and stirred nervously, their eyes wide. The cougar carried a kill in her powerful jaws but gave no pause as she streaked past, disappearing into the dark depths of the cave. Arter sat up and called Ama and Waya back. The dogs barked for a while, their loud baying echoing through the cave. Arter eased himself from the furs that kept him warm with Easter. She had not moved, but he heard her moan as though asking what had happened. He whispered reassuring words to her and walked toward the back of the cave, weapon in hand. The cavern narrowed, deep and dark.

It was likely the cougar was trying to get to her kittens and would not make a return appearance. He wished there were a way out of the cave for the large cat. He didn't like the idea that Ama and Waya would have to guard both the back and front of the cave. The two dogs returned, excited about their chase. But Arter ordered them to guard the horses, cows and other livestock and went back to the furs where he tried to warm himself with Easter. It would be a long night and a long time, maybe a week, before he could dig them all out of this snowstorm.

The next morning, the wind was not any less fierce, but the snow was drifting down lighter, little tiny flurries landing among the large clumps of heavy snow. Arter grabbed a large bucket from the back of the wagon and scooped up some of the snow around the entrance of the cave. It was piled high. A wall of ice seemed to be blocking part of their exit. While it was very cold, that ice may have helped keep them from freezing. It covered part of the cave entrance but left a portion open. He could tell there would be little chance of a thaw.

Arter used the shovel to break a hole in the ice at the right side of the cave so he could get out to throw out the waste. It was difficult tunneling through the snow enough to dig a hole that could be used for the refuse. He would need to repeat this for the human waste, which they'd collect in a chamber pot. If they were out in the elements, there would be no need for a chamber pot, but things might get difficult if they were not careful. He fought the wind and drifts to get to the left side of the cave to collect snow for watering the animals and for the three humans. It took him several trips before he could rest and prepare for their breakfast.

The cows, horses and mules stamped their feet and stirred, restless for the chance to escape the cave. Arter would release Poe's horse later, when the poor creature might find some way to survive. The horses were restless — they probably smelled that big cat, Arter thought. It would take a while for them to calm down. He watered the animals and pulled more hay down from the wagons for them to eat. His heavy fur coat was wrapped around him with leather ties, keeping him warm against the freezing temperatures. He removed the crude leather gloves Easter had made so that he could better grip the shovel and other tools. Easter had insisted they all use the ragtag garments. They appeared crudely made but offered good protection from the biting wind and cold.

Again, Arter thought how wise Easter had been to insist that they bring so much — food, garments and implements for the animals and for the three of them. It had seemed more trouble than it was worth to drag along so much. The trip should not take so long, but human obstacles and weather were working against them. He sighed. The sky looked gray and dark as though the snow was not finished. It would take some time to get where they were going if this kept up. Still, the cave offered good temporary shelter.

Awinta was the first to stir. She climbed down from the wagon and began to help Arter feed and care for the animals. The cows, horses and mules were tethered to a line that Arter had tied between the wagons. The wagons made a good brace against the cold. Awinta pulled out the cows and brushed them with a wooden comb that Easter had stowed in the wagon. She did the same for the horses, standing on a wooden bucket she'd turned over so that she could reach them.

Easter began to stir soon after Awinta and Arter had finished tending the animals. Easter held her head and swayed a bit as though she were dizzy but got on with the business of making food for the three of them. She boiled water in a pot and then poured grains into the water, making a thick, hot mixture. She sweetened it with a bit of honey she kept in the wagon and, using a big wooden spoon, scooped up portions in a bowl for both Arter and Awinta, and then for herself.

"Is there a chance we can leave the cave today?" Easter asked. Arter shook his head.

"No chance," he said. "The snow drifts are getting deeper." Easter nodded and walked to the wagon to get dwarf ginseng and dogwood for tea. She got a small pot and dropped some of the mix into it, and then poured hot water over the concoction. She waited for the herbs to seep and then sweetened the tea with a bit of honey. She then poured each of them a cup of the brew. The hot tea would help keep them warm and fight off any cold that might try to settle on them, she thought. They all relaxed for a while after that, singing softly. When they'd finished their tea and morning breakfast, Easter gathered their dishes and cleaned them out then dipped them in boiling water Arter had brought. The meal would stay with them all day as there was little work to do in the confines of the cave.

"Awinta," Arter said. "I don't want you to explore the cave."

"But there is nowhere to walk," she complained.

"Last night, a large cat crept past the wagons," he said. Easter gasped.

"Ama and Waya gave chase," Easter said. "I knew they would."

"Yes, but it's likely the cat is feeding her kittens and is not looking for a fight. She might think about the chickens and goats if they were to get away from the wagons and into the back of the cave, but it's unlikely that she'll try to come this way again. If she had been able to get to her kittens another way, I'm certain she would have."

"Maybe her other entrance was covered by ice and snow," Easter said.

"I think that's possible," Arter said. "Meanwhile, I don't want either of you to go exploring in the cave without me. I'll carry my weapon if you decide you want to explore. There is no light back there, but there must be some areas that have a bit of light creeping through. We have a torch that can be used to light our way, but we don't want to use it too often.

"I will accompany you if you want to go, but we don't want to leave the cattle unguarded. One of us, me or Easter, will need to stay with the animals if we want to find out whether there are any other resources in the cave. There is a second weapon that Easter can use when she is watching the animals." Easter nodded, and Awinta looked to the back of the cave as though she were ready to explore.

"Let's rest awhile, and then we can see what is back there," Easter said. "I'll let Awinta go first," she said, knowing that the young girl was restless and eager to explore.

That night, as Easter and Arter snuggled together to ward off the cold, he touched his hand to her stomach. He looked at her with understanding and kissed her. He asked no questions but his kiss expressed his feelings. She returned his kiss, expressing the same love.

CHAPTER TWELVE
Fall 1837

Wahali, Easter's youngest brother, had shared with her his visions of what would happen during removal. But nothing prepared him for the dire circumstances the Cherokees experienced as they made their way north from Fort Cass, at Charleston, Tennessee, toward the Oklahoma territory that would be their new home. Though some Cherokee traveled with goods and some provisions, those ran low as the arduous journey continued across country, through rain, snow, wind and hail. Cases of dysentery and whooping cough were prevalent. Those who traveled in wagons and those who traveled on foot were affected equally by sickness and disease.

Wahali had prepared for the trip as well as he could, gathering many herbs and dried food stuffs that might help in the healing of his people. He carried them in separate pouches on the inside of his shirts and sewed others into the hem of his pantaloons. Over his pantaloons, he wore thin furs and strips of leather. He knew that he could not effectively help others unless he kept himself healthy.

He tried to prepare himself for the worst possible illness by feeding himself a regular bit of coneflower. He stored much of it in other pouches to provide to others who might need it along the way. He wrapped his feet in layers and strips of fur and leather, knowing that this would help him stay well, too. His horse, Sibu, a paint, was wrapped in one of Easter's blankets and covered as best Wahali could manage. He kept quiet as the soldiers ordered groups of people to move from the camp toward the trail. They were moving north across hills from the Chattanooga area and through places where others had traveled just north toward Nashville. However, the going was difficult.

The weather had been mild earlier, but it was growing colder as the trip progressed. The snow fell in patches, coating the rocky cliffs that skirted the road north toward Port Royal. The trees were bare of leaves and stood as large black skeletons heralding the coming hardships. Green spruce trees peeked out between the bare hardwoods. The sound of wagons and horses neighing as the procession moved slowly north created a sort of rhythm — the clanking of metal objects and bells, wagon wheels crunching over the rough terrain, the creaking of leather harnesses and traces. The cold weather obscured some of the smell of dung and unwashed bodies, but every now and then, the wind blew in the wrong direction.

Dogs skirted the wagons and worried the cows and horses as the travelers made their way on the narrow path. More than one thousand Principal People traveled this trail, unlike some of the other groups that had fewer people. This train of humans trekked over deep hills and through sweeping valleys. Occasionally, the travelers braved bodies of water and ice-laden streams. Their horses, mules and other livestock, bayed and mewled as the cold water assaulted their bodies.

Wahali befriended a medical doctor who had been assigned the task of looking after the Cherokees. Wahali had met Dr. Jason Roberts early in the trek, introduced himself and explained his interest in medicine. Jason initially had little use for Wahali, judging him to be too young to help and too uneducated to learn. However, he was soon proven wrong. As Jason stirred a pot of rabbit stew he'd prepared for the group that had gathered near him for the night's rest, he gave Wahali a second look as the young man silently dropped in root vegetables he'd gathered in the woods. The young man sat some ways back from the group of people who had gathered around the campfire. Thousands of people were making this trek west. Some were Cherokees who rode in wagons or fancy carriages. Others rode on horseback. But the great number of them walked. The old, the young, the sick, the dying — they were all gathered by the soldiers, forced into camps and marched west. It was cold out and growing colder.

Dr. Jason Roberts had been contracted by the government to help with the transportation and care of the Cherokees. He might as well have stayed back east for all the good it did. There were too many people and not enough help. The food and water supply was lacking. When the first stage of this journey began, he'd been optimistic. He'd traveled from Philadelphia by steamboat and stagecoach and reported to one of the many Army officers assigned

123

the task of transporting the Cherokees west. As he waited at Fort Cass with the Cherokee people, Jason realized how difficult the trip would be. Many people were already ill. There had been a terrible drought through the summer in some parts of the country.

As a result, the quality of water was not good. People in the camps suffered from dysentery. Jason had to caution people to boil what little water they could find before they drank it. But the diarrhea and illness, dehydration, cramps and general suffering were more than he could manage. It spread to the soldiers as well. No one was immune. But there were enough soldiers to herd the Cherokee people out in the fall as the weather began to cool. The people left in various stages. The largest number was herded out as Jason had just managed to get some of the people clean water, food and help. The rain began as they'd begun the march.

He hoped that people would try to catch what water they could in containers, but it was a cold, biting rain; most everyone was concentrating on staying warm. The sky darkened, and the clouds opened to let down a deluge. Now there was mud everywhere. But the people marched on. A couple with a young child came to him. The whooping cough affected not only the child but those around him who were not strong enough to fight off the effects. Jason took the child from his mother and gave him what nourishment he could. Jason was given one covered wagon by the army that could be used to nurse the sick. But there was little room. He wondered if putting the sick among the sick did more harm than good. He was sad to see that the child died in the night. The wailing and sobbing of his mother and her family tore at Jason's heart.

The child would not be the only casualty. As the trip continued, women, children and the elderly died of exposure, dehydration and lung ailments. He urged the soldiers to allow the people to stop often, but they kept the brutal pace, saying that the sooner the trip was over, the sooner the Cherokees could rest. It was during one of his efforts to help a woman who was overcome with fever and in a weakened condition that Jason saw Wahali. The young man had tried to talk to him, but Jason was just too busy to hear him. A soldier drove the wagon for Jason from time to time, but Jason often found himself driving the wagon. He knew he would need a permanent driver. He felt the back of the wagon shake a bit and looked back to see the young man dipping water from a bucket.

"Hey, you," he shouted. "Don't do that." The boy looked up at him and smirked.

"The water has been boiled and cooled," he said. "I know what I'm doing."

"Is that right?" Jason said. "And just who are you?"

"My name is Wahali," he said. "Or in your language, Eagle." Wahali smirked and continued to make his way around the people who were lying in the wagon. What he didn't tell the white doctor was that he had sprinkled a little of his herbs into the water. One old man opened his eyes and looked at him knowingly. He nodded at him and drank the brew down. Jason figured the help he was getting from the young man couldn't hurt, so he took a break from his own ministrations. Before long, he relaxed, feeling that Wahali was probably comforting to the patients — and that could not hurt. Even if a little water was all the boy could give them, what they needed most was fluid. The doctor separated the lung patients from those with dysentery. They were weakest, too weak to walk.

Jason did his best for them. When they stopped

that night to make camp, he took each one of his patients some of the soup that the boy, Eagle, had helped make. The soup was heartier than usual. The boy had dropped in some different herbs. The soup tasted rich with herbal flavors and vegetables, and the rabbit meat was a welcome addition. All who rested in the doctor's wagon had a good taste of it. Jason tried to arrange for each of the patients to have his or her own bowl. But the illness was so overwhelming that it was difficult to get people to care about such things. As the days of the trip wore on, Jason noticed that three of the people in the back of the wagon recovered, jumped out of the wagon and walked with the rest of the group.

Sadly, a man who had weakened from the lack of fluids also had a wracking cough. That man died not long after they made camp. Jason and the man's relatives had buried him in the woods.

CHAPTER THIRTEEN
Winter 1837

Wahali walked on the trail with his paint, Sibu. He had painted handprints and cross-like symbols on his horse to let the people know that he was a traditional medicine man. He paused at that thought. His sister Easter would frown at that. He did not have the approval of his family as a whole, but he knew that things were so broken between his family and the clan they were part of that it wouldn't matter. This was his chance to prove himself, not only to the European medicine man, but to his own people.

Wahali wanted to learn all he could from the white medicine man, but he knew that his method of helping his people was as good as that of Jason Roberts. The white doctor viewed Wahali with suspicion, but Wahali could see that the tinctures that Jason relied on were nearly used up.

The doctor was using the physics of his profession, a distillation of herbs and other substances, but did he know how to find more? Wahali guessed he did not. When Jason was preoccupied with a sick woman, Wahali climbed into the man's wagon and peeked into the white man's box of tools. There were several bottles with labels. Jason had come back sooner than Wahali expected and paused as he perused Wahali. Wahali was certain the white man thought he could not read. But Wahali and his brothers and sisters were all educated by the missionaries who'd set up schools in their villages and at the churches where they preached their religion. Wahali jumped down and rejoined the walking members of the trail.

The rain had begun to fall heavier as they trudged on the trail. That's when he saw her. She was tall for a young woman, almost as tall as him. She had long silky black hair and curves. She was covered up well. Someone cared for her and had provided her with enough furs, cloth and leather to keep her warm in the freezing weather. She walked alongside a horse of her own that pulled a travois. She was leading it behind a group of people who looked to be her family. A young boy sat on her horse's back. She'd wrapped leather around the legs of her pony, and it had a bright blanket on its back. The boy, who appeared to be no more than eight summers, was similarly wrapped in furs and had a blanket around him. She stopped for a moment to give the boy a drink and to check her horse.

Her soft leather boots came up to her knees and seemed to insulate her from the rain that was quickly changing to sleet and then snow. The wind blew swiftly, but the line of people did not stop. However, she stopped every now and then to check on the boy. As though she felt Wahali's eyes on her, she turned and stared at him. Their eyes locked. He felt warmth seep through his body. Her rich brown eyes glinted as she peered at him for a moment and then turned away. A wool scarf covered her face. Her long hair, blowing in the wind, trailed outside the scarf and down her back.

She was about 15 hands; by the white missionary's education, she would be just under six feet, slightly shorter than him. Wahali was stunned by that; not many women were that tall. She appeared to be strong too. She adjusted some packs that were hanging from her horse and stood behind it to push it forward through the muck. She took a drink herself. Then she handed the boy something nourishing and took a bite herself. She wore a bright red blanket wrapped around her, with decorative blue and white designs on it. There were hand shapes and swirls, odd crosses and designs that suggested that she might be a healer. He breathed deep. She gave him a quick look again and jumped atop the pony behind the boy to ride. She had done that from time to time throughout the long journey.

Wahali smiled. She was certainly flirting with him. She wanted to prove that she was healthy and superior. Her strength was apparent in the way she rode. She held the boy close to her as they rode. Wahali decided to mount his own pony, Sibu, and hopped on. He rode near her and turned his head to look at her. She peered straight ahead, not looking at him at all.

"It is said that a woman who is strong enough to mount a horse is strong enough to do many other things," he said, smiling at her. She turned her head and looked at him.

"And what does it say about a man who follows a woman who is strong?" she asked. He chuckled.

"It must mean that the two can work miracles together," he said.

"What kind of miracle did you have in mind?"

"How about the miracle of survival?" They rode together silently for a while. The wind picked up, and the snow began to fall faster. Still the woman rode on slowly with the paint struggling to lift its hooves in the snow. The temperature was rapidly falling and the snow dropped in heavy clumps. The darkening skies suggested that the day was near its end. They would soon make camp. But the soldiers ordered the people to continue moving. They were headed north through rough country, but the people kept trudging forward. More people stopped along the trail and could not continue. The soldiers did not stop to help them. From time to time, Wahali stopped to help as he could. He noticed that the woman did too. A fierce blast of wind hit them both, blowing the laden pouches that hung from his horse and slowing them as they attempted to move forward. He jumped off Sibu and led him forward. Though he walked, he was able to move as fast as her horse did because of the deepening snow.

"What are you called?" he shouted at her. She looked at him as though she did not hear. It very well could be that she could not hear as the wind's howling made a terrible noise. She also looked at him as though he were crazy. Wahali knew this was a strange time and place to make the acquaintance of a woman, but if he didn't try to befriend her, he could lose her in this long line of people. Some of them moved ahead, and some fell behind. If she fell behind for some reason because she tried to help someone, it would be difficult for him to find her. He had decided he wanted to keep her in his sights. She smiled at him and narrowed her eyes and made the sign for Hummingbird. His eyes widened as he realized that she used hand signs as the ancient tribes did.

"Hummingbird, Waleha?" he asked, signing back. She nodded. He made the sign for Eagle, pointing at himself.

She signed to him, not to talk. It was too cold and too windy. She signed that she was tired and that her

brother was cold. He was relieved to see that the boy
was her brother and not her child. He climbed back
on Sibu. Allowing Sibu to move forward by using his
thighs, he signed to her that he wanted to make camp
near her. She nodded and signed back that she would
be with her family members, pointing ahead. Soon,
the darkening sky made it impossible to move
forward, and the people headed for the protection of
the forest in hopes of finding shelter from the biting
winds. An elderly woman had fallen in the snow not
far from where Wahali was heading. He jumped off
his pony and helped her to mount Sibu while they
moved into the forest. The men began to clear space
in the increasingly heavy snow. Those who had heavy
cloth to build a shelter against the snow, did so.
Those who did not went about gathering wood to
build lean-tos and other rough shelters from bits of
wood and branches from trees. Some men helped
build fires; some sank in the snow to rest. After tying
Sibu to a tree, Wahali helped the old woman down
and guided her to her people. He nodded to them
and walked away to gather as much kindling as he
could find.

He helped Hummingbird to clear an area where a
fire could be built for the members of her family.
After getting a fire started, Wahali walked far from
the camp to find water. He took Sibu and
Hummingbird's pony, Coyote, to find a stream. The
water was frozen; he had to break through the ice
with a heavy stone. Sibu and Coyote drank deeply.
With that done, he brought the two ponies back to
camp and fashioned a shelter for them, which had a
small sloping hill to it. He cleared away snow from
the ground near where he tied them. When they had
their fill they could shelter in the pit. Some did not
care well for their horses. But he knew that Sibu
would eat snow if he had to and scuff under the

snow to find grass. He put the horses under a heavy blanket. It appeared that Hummingbird had prepared for the journey by bringing as much feed as she could manage for her horse. She hung some of it from the horse and dragged other bits on a travois. He supplemented their food by gathering some dry grass. It would help them continue the journey.

The women of Hummingbird's clan gathered around the fire and heated snow to make water, adding dried meat and root vegetables they had dug from the earth. Wahali smiled, thinking that they had the same wisdom as his sister. Some of the tribe did not understand how to live from the land. But he had the advantage of having brothers and sisters who taught him what to look for in the wild and how to find the most nourishing food. He went to gather some of that food for the pot the women stirred with a wooden spoon. When he returned with the fruits of his labor, the women nodded their appreciation and continued to stir the brew. Soon it was done, and they ladled out bowls of the rich soup. His body soaked up the delicious meal.

Jason listened to the chest of a young boy in another camp. He had pulled his wagon to the edge of the woods. The boy certainly had lung fever; his breathing was labored, and he was unable to move. Jason was certain the boy was not long for this world. This biting cold would not help. The child's parents had carried him as long as they could. Jason put the boy in his wagon, wedged between those who were suffering from similar maladies. It wasn't likely to help much, but that's all he could do. He checked the other patients and administered what little nourishment he could. A woman who traveled near his wagon had given him one of her chickens to make broth for his patients. She pulled the birds

along in a rickety wagon; some had been stolen from
her. Others she used herself and donated. The wind
whipped the wagon covering around, threatening to
tear it off its rattling supports. Jason looked up,
hearing a noise that wasn't that of the howling wind
or camp noises. There stood the young man who
called himself Wahali, Eagle. The boy's obvious
health radiated from him. His eyes roved over the
sick, seeming to make mental calculations for what
he could do and for whom.

Jason knew that if he stood in the young man's
way, Eagle would not try to help. So he inched back
toward the front of the wagon and sat on a little
stool. There was not much harm the young man
could do, as the suffering would likely not recover.
There would be no harm in letting Eagle do as he
saw fit. At that gesture, the young man entered the
wagon with a small bucket of hot water. Wahali
reached into the pouch hanging from his side and
sprinkled herbs into the hot water. Jason saw Wahali
look for drinking cups and pointed to the small
collection at the front of the wagon. Wahali gingerly
stepped through the small aisle to the front of the
wagon and poured the mixture into a wooden cup.
He began to give the mixture to the patients, lifting
their heads gingerly and urging them, in his language,
to drink. "Atistasti," he whispered. There was a
woman who appeared to be middle aged. She was
not yet old, but she had seen many summers. A
young boy coughed and wheezed. He was wrapped
in blankets and shivered. He seemed the worst, so
Wahali went to him next. A young girl lay away from
the others as though she slept, but Wahali could hear
her laboring to breathe; he gave her some to drink
next. As he moved from person to person, Jason
urged him to switch cups and dipped the used ones
in a bucket of hot water. He hung the cups back up

as Wahali used each one. As Wahali moved about the wagon, he noticed that Jason had a makeshift stove that had a vent poking out the side of the wagon. Jason motioned for Wahali to meet him outside. An old man, who sat in the front of the wagon, driving it for Jason, sat still and held the animals as Jason talked to Wahali.

"Thanks for that," Jason said.

"I'm not doing it for you," Wahali said. "It's for my people, who are suffering." Jason smiled.

"Yes, I can understand that. Still, any help is appreciated. What did you give them?"

"It's an ancient herb of my family," Wahali said. Jason's eyebrow shot up. Wahali smiled.

"Easy to find in the woods if you know where to look," Wahali said.

"If the patients in that wagon begin to improve, I'm going to be asking you to show me where you find this herb."

"How long have they been in your wagon?" Wahali asked.

"Some of them for more than three days. Others for just a day. As the weather worsens more come to me for help, but I have only so much room."

"What is that stove-like thing you have in the wagon?" Wahali asked, looking toward the device as they talked.

"You noticed that, did you?" Jason said. "My nephew made it for me. It's a miniature of a Pennsylvania Fireplace. It has vents in it so that it will breathe but it can warm. He made it so I can heat the small confines of the wagon while warming pots on the stovetop. The only problem is that I have to keep my sickest patients away from it as it can burn. However, that's not a problem. I have an enclosure around it to keep patients safe. Would you like to see it up close?" Wahali nodded and they climbed back into the wagon. Jason had put the heated water on top of the little stove, and it was creating steam that helped moisten the air inside the wagon. He'd closed the back of the wagon as much as he could and put a blanket over its small opening. He could tell that this would help the sickest of the patients to breathe in the harsh environment. Jason explained how the stove worked and let Wahali see the innards.

"Where can I get one of these?" Wahali asked Jason.

"You can't," Jason said. "I had it made especially for these circumstances. When I explained to my nephew, a smithy, what I'd be doing, he anticipated that I would need some way to boil water and heat food. It was with my needs in mind that he made it. However, I've used it to help my patients. I'll let you study it when we have a chance to cool it. That won't be for some time, though, I think."

Wahali nodded and explained his interest in medicine. He thought probably Jason would put him off and behave as though no mere "Indian" would be able to learn the methods for healing. But Jason surprised him.

"I will loan you my few books," Jason said, adding that he was unable to bring too many texts with him. "I'm certain you can learn more from them than from my telling you anything. I was counting on learning from you." Wahali's eyebrows shot up this time.

"From me?" Jason nodded and smiled.

"Medicine has a long path to trod," he said. "It's only by learning from one another that we advance." That sealed the friendship between the two men, and so Wahali's journey into the pursuit of medicine began.

The next days were long and arduous. The soldiers halted the procession for a day while the storm became less severe. Those who stuck near the few who had resources survived. Those who lost their bearings and wandered away from their family and friends struggled the most. It was a surprise that two soldiers showed up at Dr. Roberts's wagon. One listed on his horse as though he were about to fall off. His companion jumped off his horse and pulled the ailing man from his.

"Doc Roberts," the man shouted above the wind.

"Here," Jason said.

"You have to see to this man," Sergeant Davis said. "He began to get sick as we came to that pass up there." The man pointed to the steep dip in the earth. Wahali had been treating the sick for the last few days, and one of the men had left the wagon and rejoined his family. They had little room, but enough. The sick soldier appeared to be sweating with fever. Jason motioned to Wahali. Wahali left Sibu and the young boy he'd placed on his back for a moment. Sibu stayed where Wahali left him. The horse would not move unless Wahali told him to do so. As Wahali approached the sick soldier, who sagged in the arms of his fellow soldier, the man mumbled about not wanting a "damn injun" to touch him. Jason stepped up to the man.

"If you feel that way, you have no choice but to die, man," Jason said. "Wahali here is a practiced medicine man who knows what he's doing. He is also learning the ways of Western medicine. I can't stay with the wagon. I'm needed on the trail to tend to people as they traverse this rough terrain. If you don't want to be tended by my assistant, you will need to rejoin your troop. I have no time for sick bigots." *Assistant*, Wahali thought. That's a change.

The man, whose gray skin seemed to become more sickened, vomited. He sank into the snow, and his eyes rolled into the back of his head. Jason motioned for Wahali to help him carry the man to the back of the wagon, where they made room for him among the patients who were also struggling for life. Just then, a young boy came to Jason to say that a woman was in labor and having her baby. Sergeant Davis gave Wahali a nod of thanks and rode away. Jason grabbed his bag and untied his horse from the back of the wagon. He rode away to help bring a new life into this harsh landscape. He prayed that both the woman and the child were hardy and capable of surviving.

Wahali grabbed a blanket from the stack Jason kept at the front of the wagon and walked to the back where he and Jason and had put the soldier. The man was sweating and moaning. He seemed unaware that Wahali was wrapping him in the blanket and then forcing him to drink a little of the herbal mixture that was distinctly Wahali's. The man grimaced, but managed to get most of it down. He shivered as Wahali removed his weapons. The man grabbed Wahali's hand as if to say don't touch my weapons, but in weak acquiescence, seemed to lose consciousness again. Wahali moved the weapons out of the man's reach, unstrapping his sidearm and then his bayonet. Apparently, any other weapons were on the man's horse. He placed them in the compartment under the seat of Jason's wagon and then jumped down to tie the man's horse to the back of the wagon. An old Cherokee man drove the wagon for Jason when the doctor was making his rounds to the various camps. He was so quiet, wrapped in blankets and sitting stoically on the wagon, that Wahali wondered whether the man was aware of his surroundings. When the man turned to look at Wahali and nodded his head, Wahali knew. This was an old soul.

CHAPTER FOURTEEN

Hummingbird slipped down the side of her horse and let her brother, Dustu, ride alone for a while. The soldiers had kept the procession of people moving, though the snow blew viciously and the wind bit into the skin of the young and old. She had heard that they were headed toward Big Spring. Hummingbird was fortunate. Her mother and father both were doing well and walking ahead, along with her grandmother. Her grandfather had been among those who had tried to support Chief John Ross during the removal negotiations. Her grandmother's family had been land-wealthy, one of those with land and other resources.

Still, members of Hummingbird's family felt it necessary to go when the others headed for the place where land would be parceled for the clan. She wondered how they would get along once they arrived. She was 15 summers and had once had a suitor. But he had died of the flu . So many people had fallen due to disease that it was a wonder that there were people left to walk to the new land. Her mother turned around and looked at her as they trudged forward in the snow, which kept getting deeper. Humingbird's mother had always been a healthy woman, but this long trek was trying for her. Hummingbird's father worried about her mother and urged her repeatedly to get on the one other horse they'd brought for the trip. They'd had three when they left their compound, but one was taken by a soldier. There was nothing they could do about it.

Hummingbird stopped her pony. Her brother sat bowed over the horse's neck. He was tired, and she feared for his health. He was eight summers, and Hummingbird worried about his ability to endure the harsh weather. She kept assuring him that they would make it. She boiled his water and gave him the best morsels of food in her pouch. Whenever she could, she fed him broth made from fennel or goldenseal. She had wrapped his feet in layers of wool, skins and fur. He walked some, but mostly he rode Coyote.

Hummingbird's mother, Trahlyth, Cherokee Princess, trusted her to look after her little brother, knowing that Hummingbird had learned the secrets of healing. She also knew the secrets for staying well, especially in cold weather. Walk as often as you can to keep the blood flowing, rest whenever possible, drink only boiled water, some with herbs in it, eat the dried meat sparingly, dig for roots.

When Hummingbird stopped at night, she'd dig in the woods, looking for roots. Sometimes, she came up with nothing, as many others seemed to look for the roots of plants slept. Occasionally, she came upon nuts on the forest floor, a welcome and delicious surprise. She collected them as well and hid them in pouches in her clothing. As they walked, she'd crack them and feed some to her brother and eat some herself. She'd crack more and take them to her parents and grandmother. They had prepared as best they could for the long journey by drying meat and sewing it into the folds of their clothing. Her mother had brought two chickens in a cage that were placed on a travois and carried behind the remaining horse. Her mother placed dried vegetables in hidden places throughout the folds of one of the blankets attached to the travois.

The root vegetables Hummingbird was able to dig from the ground on the way made good stew. Sometimes, her father left the trail and was able to kill a rabbit or other game. Hummingbird preferred the root vegetables, but on this trip, no one could be picky. It was important to let the food nourish the body because each day was a challenge. The snow did not seem to let up at all. The long line of people were sometimes allowed to move to the sides of the path for those who were moving along at a quicker pace. Soon the path grew muddy and was difficult to traverse. Still, everyone walked on through the long day until finally dark arrived, and the families of women, children and men gathered in their respective groups and huddled together for warmth. Some had tents, some lean-tos, some slept wrapped in blankets.

Hummingbird marveled at the way people managed to survive the harsh weather. The cold was biting, and many people were unable to continue the long walk. Their limbs froze; they could not move their feet, and some dropped, exhausted. But those who were resourceful wrapped in wool and furs and kept their body well-nourished and moving. Too many layers caused a person to sweat, and getting wet was the way people grew sick and died.

Hummingbird helped her brother wrap but stay dry. This she did for her grandmother as well, wrapping her feet and hands but leaving room to keep her skin from sweating. When they stopped, she heated flat stones and wrapped them for warming hands and feet. Her parents, who had taught her this method for keeping warm in cold weather, helped each other wrap for the cold.

The nights were Hummingbird's favorite time. Her father always erected a small hut made from skins; Hummingbird, her brother, mother, and grandmother snuggled inside. Hummingbird's father waited until everyone was settled and then joined his wife in her blanket. The whole family stayed in the hut together. This was unusual for them all, for the home they'd left behind was a large wooden structure. Her mother and father had done well for them, having adopted the ways of the whites and used their skills to barter crops for goods.

Hummingbird's mother had brought wealth to her family; she had come to the marriage with several ponies. Her grandmother had given her mother gold stones. These her mother hid carefully and over the years used a few at a time to help the family buy land and other goods. As they were able to grow food, the family prospered. But long after a war in the late 1700s with the Tennessee militia, her grandfather died and the family settled into a well-maintained farming business in parts of Georgia.

Her grandfather urged the family to become farmers and to adapt to the changes that were forced upon them. So the family became one of many that prospered among farms and mills, shops and schools. Her grandfather thought it was a mistake for the Chickamauga Cherokee to ignore the call of war from the Creek in the early 1800s, but knew too that the days of winning against the Americans were over. Though the Principal People had their own tribal council, written constitution, written language and newspaper, the progress they had made was pushed back when removal negotiations failed. Hummingbird's grandmother thought it had something to do with the gold that was discovered by the whites on some of her family's land. It was also rumored that a young Cherokee boy traded some gold for a trinket to a white man. After that, word spread like wildfire. Her grandmother and her family did not consider the gold important, but apparently the whites put great stock in it. Grandmother said that's when everything began to change for the Cherokee.

But none of that was important now. They were forced off their land and herded with the other Cherokees and other true people toward the far West. Most were resigned to it. Hummingbird was too. She felt a sort of excitement about it. What would this new place be like? Would they be able to farm there? Would they be able to breed horses? They only had two now, a mare and a male pony.

Her thoughts drifted to Wahali. He reminded her of Kanua, who had made his presence known in her life while the unrest and uncertainty of their future concerned her parents. Her mother and grandmother accepted what her father and other relatives could not. Kanua was like her father. He railed against the unfairness of the removal plans. He came often to see her, bringing her beads and fruit, skins and other gifts. They spent time in the woods behind her parent's home. She remembered clearly the day he proposed that they stay together.

"Can you think of being with me for your lifetime?" he asked as he held a yellow flower to her face. He smiled at her and ran a gentle finger down her cheek. She smiled. The spring weather blew the fragrance of honeysuckle around them.

"Is it safe to make plans now?" she asked.

"Nothing will be as we want it to be," Kanua said. "We will need to make our plans to be together and move wherever the wind takes us. This is not something we will be able to change. But we can promise to make a life with each other." He put his arms around her and held her close. He smelled clean and fresh and earthy like the outdoors. She breathed deeply and thought how much she cared for him. But none of their plans came to be. He had gone to help a relative prepare for the removal when he encountered a group of Eastern travelers who had arrived to take his cousin's land. There was no fight in it. But the travelers were ill. It did not take long for Kanua to become ill, too. Within three days he had fever, and by the fourth day it was clear to his cousin that he would not recover. Eventually, Kanua's cousin also succumbed to influenza, and the settlers in the area buried them on his cousin's land.

It didn't take long for Hummingbird's thoughts to return to the here and now. Wahali's face replaced Kanua's, and she wondered whether Wahali was someone who had plans for his life too. So many people were overcome by the elements. The cold and the wind took lives as they wanted. But she would not grieve those who returned to the earth. There was so much grief and so much sadness it would overwhelm her if she dwelled on it.

She tried to help those who were outside her family when she could, but there was just not enough to go around. The people who walked the path ahead of them stripped the ground and the trees and the land of any resources they could find. She had to travel off the path and deep into the woods sometimes to find anything worth eating. But once she did, it was worth the hunt. Sometimes she used an ancient blow stick to kill a rabbit. Before the weather turned cold, many died from tainted drinking water. She wondered whether people stopped thought about the drinking water. It had to be boiled. Not everyone understood. She'd learned from her mother and a missionary woman who taught school near their village. Being careful and clean helped people survive. With that thought, she sighed and snuggled up to her grandmother, her little brother between them. It would be another long day tomorrow.

CHAPTER FIFTEEN

Morning did not seem to arrive the next day. The sky was gray and dark; no light seemed to penetrate the thick clouds. The hut, dug into the earth, was covered in snow. The fire, partly protected by a rocky overhang, was long out, but the embers were still warm. It was warm in their hut. Humingbird's father, Austenaco, was up and out, as was her mother. They were tending a cook fire to make sweet potatoes and other vegetables with some meat. They carried quite a few sweet potatoes in a sack on the horses.

When Wahali had taken the travois off their horses, he had hidden the food sacks high in a nearby tree so the animals of the woods would not be tempted. Wahali, who had made a lean-to near the horses, was now helping to get the horses back from a stream that was deep in the woods.

He cleared another patch of snow from an area where the horses could graze but still be tethered. But clearing an area was difficult because the snow was almost waist deep in places. It was important for the horses to get enough food; otherwise, they would not be able to continue the journey. Wahali made them his first priority each day. He checked their legs and hooves often. Without food, the horses would die in this cold. He gathered dried grass that he found in areas where the snow was less deep, and added that to what the horses were eating. He tied them to trees in areas where there seemed to be grass but also brush that they could consume. When they had exhausted one area, he moved them to another. As he moved the horses, he noticed that soldiers and travelers ahead of them were not stirring.

Everything was quiet. There were no soldiers shouting for the people to arise and trudge forth. They were not riding their horses up and down the line to make certain everyone was moving. Everything was quiet. The people had entered an area of steep hills. The hills were covered with snow. Hummingbird wrapped herself in the woolen scarves and other wool clothing and stepped out of the hut where her father had cleared a path.

She went to some bushes away from the camp and well away from the stream and took care of her needs. She pulled out a small lump of soap and washed her hands. She and her mother had made the soap before leaving home. They made it once a year and stored it in the barn. The ashes from their fires and the fat from the animals helped to make the soap. She liked to add the smell of lavender to her own lumps of soap. The soap reminded her how important it was to try to maintain some cleanliness on this journey. She washed and dried herself and stored the soap away in a little pouch. When she returned from her chores, she found her mother and grandmother working at a sweet potato stew. The smells were delicious. She added her own herbs to the pot and went to find Wahali.

She could see some movement through the trees. He seemed to be struggling with the horses. She went to him and helped take the horses back to her family's camp. When she secured the horses to the

frowns of her parents, she went back to where
Wahali stood. He signed to her that there was a wild
hog — stay back. She ran back to the camp and
grabbed her bow and arrows. Her father, alerted to
her sense of urgency, grabbed his large hunting knife
and joined her. When they arrived, Wahali was
standing a few yards from the wild hog. He had
struck it with his arrow, but it was still coming at
him. Hummingbird drew out an arrow and notched
it. She let it fly and the hog stumbled. Finally, the
animal went down. Wahali finished the hog.

Wahali and her father approached the hog and
were praying over it, thanking it for its life and
apologizing for having to take it. Wahali and her
father then got busy skinning the hog. They were
careful to clean their hands after they completed their
task. They carried the meat back to camp and
prepared a pit to cook and smoke it overnight. As the
hog smoked in the pit, the curious and hungry could
smell meat cooking and wandered near their camp.
When the meat was thoroughly cooked, Wahali and
Austenaco cut up the usable bits and dried some as
well. They took the usable food and animal fat and
shared some with others. Nothing was wasted. Bones
were used for soup.

They cut up well-cooked portions to share and to
freeze for later consumption. The meat would freeze
quickly. They thanked the Great Spirit for their good
fortune. It would be some time before they could use
the skin, but Hummingbird was good at finding a
purpose for it. When the animal's fat was separated
from its meat some in camp used the fat on their skin
to protect themselves from the bitter cold. When the
family had eaten and settled into their hut,
Hummingbird's father invited Wahali to bring his hut
closer to their own. It was then that Hummingbird
asked why they had not been roused by the soldiers

that morning.

"There has been an avalanche," her father said. "The snow fell from some hills onto the path and is blocking the way. The hills cannot be traversed yet. The snow is too deep, and the people are unable to clear the path. The snow is beginning again, so the soldiers will need to wait until the snow can be cleared some before we can move again."

"That is good news," her mother, Trahlyth, said. "The people need a rest. This is a difficult journey. It will give us a chance to fatten ourselves and our horses." Her father nodded.

"Tell us a story, mother," Hummingbird's brother said. Trahlyth smiled and they gathered around the fire in her parents' hut.

"The earth was made by a large vulture," her mother began. "It flapped its wings and made volcanoes. It flapped its wings again and made everything that you see here on earth: the trees, the birds, the animals. One day, woman said to man that there would need to be more people. The man hit the woman with a fish, and children were born." The story went on to explain the way the people had come to be, that women were prevented from having too many children and that the Great Spirit was a generous, all-powerful being. Every time Hummingbird's mother told the story, it changed. She made it different. Today, twin boys fought over their sister and the result was an epic flood that turned to snow. Hummingbird's brother asked whether the snow went away. Her mother always told the story so that whatever fear her brother had would always be eased by the telling of the story. They had another serving of the stew, and Hummingbird's father went out again to be certain the horses were covered. The sky rumbled with thunder and the snow fell with a vengeance. The family tucked into their makeshift hut, with Wahali's extended hut connecting to their hut and dug into the ground and snow. The flat stones Hummingbird collected helped keep them warm.

Jason Roberts received requests from two more Cherokees who had come to him for help but were not seriously ill. They were starving. He had some rations stored and had been attempting to use them wisely. But the doctor could tell that if these two did not get nourishment, they would become very ill. They had the markings. One appeared to have the beginning of chin cough; the other seemed to have lung fever. But both appeared to be strong enough to hang on if nourished. Jason wondered why they were not hunting or fishing like some of the other Cherokees. Many of them seemed to have more resources than he did, especially those like Wahali and his people. However, Jason realized that when someone is cold and disoriented, he might not use his faculties as they should.

These two, one an elderly man and the other, to his surprise, an elderly woman, huddled down near his wagon, which had been pulled into the trees by his driver, Tisyi. Tisyi seemed to know how to weather the elements and sat wrapped in wool and furs. He smoked a pipe from time to time and moved slowly but efficiently. When they pulled into the trees, Jason's driver found a copse of oak and low bushes that provided some protection from the wind and snow. Jason was grateful for this maneuver on Tisyi's part. Sometimes Jason thought the man was half asleep and not paying attention but realized later that he was very much aware of his surroundings and often anticipated the next need of the doctor and his patients. Jason wondered whether he could count on

Wahali to help him in the morning.

Jason climbed into the wagon and began to administer broth and herbal tinctures to his patients. Some remained asleep. He gathered wood from the forest and broke the small, dried branches into parts small enough to fit into his nephew's little stove. While the wind still whipped the wagon covering, it held, and Jason made room for the two new people and Tisyi. They hunkered down for a cold night.

When Jason woke the next morning, a soldier had ridden to his wagon to tell him that the pass ahead was blocked by snow from a avalanche. Since the snow was likely to keep falling, they would not be moving until they found a way around the pass or were able to clear it. The people were too weak to help in this biting wind and snow so they were to wait it out while the worst of the snow and wind continued. Jason went about feeding his patients and checking to be certain they were still alive. He didn't take that for granted anymore. Once he did and was surprised to learn that one of his patients had died in the night. So every morning he checked. This time, everyone was doing well. He noticed that since Wahali had begun making regular trips to his wagon to administer his tinctures and teas, his patients were surviving and one or two would soon be well enough to begin walking again.

He helped those who could walk tend to their needs. Then he managed to take care of his own needs and clean himself up. When he returned to the wagon, Wahali was standing outside with some meat for his pot. He grinned.

"Hello, young friend," Jason said. "What have you brought us today?"

"We killed a wild hog," Wahali said. "I did not want to take its life, but it was insisting on taking mine. We had a disagreement, and he went down."

"Were you injured, Wahali?" Jason asked, knowing that wild hogs could be dangerous and one had to be careful at preparing it.

"No, I got off a lucky shot," Wahali said.

"With a gun?" He knew the soldiers did not approve of the Cherokees having weapons so he wondered how Wahali had managed to kill such an animal. Some wild hogs could grow to 200 pounds or more. Wahali shook his head and pointed to his quiver, which carried a bow and arrow. He was using the crudest method available, but apparently the young man knew what he was doing. He had killed the animal. Though the meat was not like that of domestic animals, its fat would nourish his patients and protect their skin. Jason thanked Wahali and added a little of the meat to his pot along with some root vegetables that Wahali brought. His patients would be getting better soon. He smiled, thinking Wahali was a good friend.

The snow began to fall in ever-increasing layers as Wahali made his way into the forest to hunt for more tubers and nuts. He found much of what he wanted and was headed back to the camp of Hummingbird's people when he saw her headed his way. She was always coming after him. He could not understand the woman. She wanted to be with him, but it was too cold, and the weather was too bitter for her to be out. She should be inside her parents' hut. But he considered what she might be saying to him with her body language. She wanted a mate. Was he ready for that? Could he take care of her and learn everything he needed to learn to be a good doctor? Would she join him on his quest to get more education and to help those who needed it? He was thinking that when she approached him. He pulled her to him and hugged her to him. Their body heat seemed to seep through layers of their thick wool and fur clothing. They were in a small clearing in the deep woods under a large oak tree. The layers of leaves and branches covered them. Around them were other trees. The snow glistened off the branches of the trees. The trees moaned with the increasing weight of the snow, and they held each other tightly, allowing their bodies to warm one another.

"Are you planning to spend your life with someone, Hummingbird?" he asked.

"I was," she said.

"Was?"

"He is back home," she said. Wahali's spirits sank. He had dreamed of her last night, thinking that somehow they might make a life with one another. Maybe his dream of being with her was not meant to be. He sighed.

"Is he going to join you at the new land?" he asked.

"No, I don't think he ever will."

"Why?"

"Kanua died last year before preparations for removal were complete," she said.

"I'm sorry, Hummingbird," he said. "Two of my brothers also died. Both of them were making an effort to hold on to our land. Well, maybe not Mohe, but Connutsee was." He let some moments pass. The wind swirled around in the small clearing amidst the trees, and the large tree sheltering them from the blowing snow dropped a few petals of snow on them. She shivered in his arms. "Mohe went looking for a fight," Wahali said. "He was angry at all that is happening and was caught at the wrong time around the wrong people. I'm proud of him for trying to fight, but I would much rather have him here now." She nodded in understanding.

"Kanua wanted us to marry in the old way and to

make this trip together," she said. "But influenza took him before we departed. He went to help a relative, and, before he could do anything at all, the fever took him. I did not know until word reached us from family. He was a good man."

Wahali let that information churn around in his mind for a moment. If she recently lost someone, she might not want to take a chance on him. But he wouldn't know if he didn't ask.

"Do you think someday you could be with me?" he asked. She looked up at him. She was tall at about 6 feet, but he was about the same. She looked into his eyes. He was capable of providing for her and any children that might come to them. But everything was so unsettled.

"How can we say what will happen?" Hummingbird asked. "Whether we will make it to the new territory? Whether we will survive the journey? How do you know this?"

"I know," he said. "You will make it, and so will I. We are young and we know some of the old ways, the healing ways. If the Great Spirit smiles upon us, we will do well." What Wahali did not say is that he had seen in a vision many children gathered around him and Hummingbird. She would be a well-fed woman. She would bear him children, and they would give him grandchildren.

"Can we stay here a while?" she asked. He didn't answer her but got to work with a large branch. He dug a deep hole near the hollowed tree and placed his blanket in it. He then gathered many branches to make a covering for the hole. They sat down inside and backed up and into the hollow oak tree. He made a small fire at the base of the hole using stones he gathered. The warmth from the fire warmed them. Before long, they held each other close and promised to stay with one another.

"We must tell my mother and father," she said.

"I will ask properly when we return to camp," he said. They lay in each other arms, caressing and holding each other, warming each other.

CHAPTER SIXTEEN
Winter 1837

John Burns had been assigned the duty of helping to
get many of the Cherokee from their homesteads to
the western area that was Oklahoma. He was heart-
broken at the suffering. Though many of the
Cherokee traveled in wagons, most left their homes
with little in the way of protection from the elements.
As they traveled, he noticed that some of the able-
bodied offered furs and wool blankets. He wondered
where these things came from. There, of course, was
not enough to go around, and many of the people
died of exposure. They were buried in graves along
the road. When the pass was blocked by snow,
Captain McCullen ordered the men to begin digging.
But the fierce wind, ice and snow were too much
even for the many soldiers who were assigned the
arduous duty of transporting the Cherokee. Everyone
was ordered to hunker down until the worst of the
weather passed and the soldiers could get to work
clearing the pass.

John had been recruited by the army because he
spoke fluent Cherokee. He had grown up in the

backwoods and had spent many days hunting with various groups of Cherokees. He'd saved the life of a young hunter once and had been rewarded with acceptance into the young man's family and tribe. When it became apparent what was happening to the Cherokee, he hung his head in shame. This all came about because gold was discovered on Cherokee land. When that happened, Andrew Jackson, who had once accepted the help of the Cherokee during war, turned his back on them. Many people made an effort to provide blankets and other protection from the elements. When the snowstorm began, those who were unable to endure sickened and died.

Galilani, the sister of the young man John had saved years ago, had become a good friend to him. Fortunately for her, she had some thick clothing on. She walked in boots that had fur on the inside. Much of the time, she was allowed to ride in a wagon, but when it began to snow, the clothing did not help her overcome the elements. When John saw her shivering when the procession stopped for the storm, he offered her his blanket and his body heat. The people in the wagon where she rode looked distrusting of him, but they did not seem to mind that he helped this young woman. He was surprised to see that she recovered quickly. He shared his rations with her but quickly decided that she needed more help to survive. John helped those he could, but the suffering was enormous. He heard that there was a young Cherokee man who was helping those who were ill, along with one of the doctors assigned to assist them. He walked to the back of the line and found the young man, Wahali.

When John arrived at the camp where people directed him, he saw the young man tending to his horse, which had the signs of medicine man on it. This was unusual for one so young, but John was not going to turn this gift away. He walked up to him and spoke to Wahali in his native language.

"Osiyo," John said. This was the "hello" greeting most used for addressing someone held in high esteem. He knew that the young man was surprised by his greeting, but John stood for a moment in a position of humility. He wanted help for Galilani. Wahali nodded at him.

"Otahitsa," John continued. "How are you? "

"Nina," Wahali answered. "I'm fine and you?"

John explained that a friend of his, a young woman, was not doing well and asked whether Wahali would see her. Wahali nodded and grabbed a couple of bags. When they arrived at the space where John made camp, Galilani was being harassed by an old woman and a soldier. When they saw John coming, they scampered off. Wahali frowned at them and went to the woman named Galilani. He checked her hands and feet and then motioned for them to go to a more secluded area.

Wahali noticed that her hands and feet seemed to be suffering, so he coated them in fat and covered them with the skins that she had been using to protect her hands. He showed her how to warm her hands but to not thaw them completely. He said sacred words to her and then made a fire and heated some of the meat and tubers he'd found. John offered him a cup; Wahali scooped out some of the broth and fed that to the woman. She drank it greedily and smiled gratefully at him. Wahali told John to continue to get as much of the broth in her as possible. Then he gave her some of his goldenseal tincture for strengthening her body. When he finished with Galilani, he went to the wagon where she rode with a family. Wahali fed them similarly. The family members were huddled under their wagon, pulled to the side of the road, like other travelers. Some were clearly close to the end of their days.

John motioned to Wahali that he wished to speak to him again. John pulled a map from the pocket of his coat. He had been given more than one by his superiors. He could share one with Wahali. He pointed to a place on the map that said, Hopkinsvile, in Kentucky, which was some distance from Nashville. They had traveled several days from those places. The trip would take more than 180 days, he told Wahali. He pointed north to John's Ferry, in Illinois, and to Jackson. Next, they would travel further west and north to Rolla, near Missouri, and then south to Springfield. They would travel further south to Fitzgerald Station and then arrive in Westville and later Tallequah. Wahali noted the rivers and other bodies of water they would cross as they traveled and thanked John for the map. It would help Wahali to plan for what was to come.

When Wahali returned to the camp of Hummingbird and her family, he noticed that everyone was huddled in her father's hut. He asked permission to enter and was invited in. He sat beside Hummingbird, and her father handed him a pipe. Wahali coughed as he realized that her father must have gathered some herbs for the pipe. But he appreciated the gesture and returned it by placing some chicory root into the pipe. He showed Austenaco the map that had been given to him by the soldier, John Burns. He explained their route and the challenges ahead.

Wahali and Austenaco were surprised to learn that the northern route that they were traversing was one of many. Some Cherokees and others would be traveling a southern route through Arkansas, a more direct path which took less time. Others would be taking a route through Tennesee, also a more direct path. He wondered why they were being forced to take such a long circuitous route. Perhaps it had something to do with what hunting could be done along the way.

A particularly harsh wind blew outside the little hut, as they sat there partly sheltered from the wind. The soldiers who were camped nearby looked on their little gathering with envy and had tried to replicate the shelters that Wahali and Hummingbird's father built. The conversation began with Hummingbird's mother, who played the prominent role in the matter of family unions, as was customary in Cherokee families.

"My daughter tells me that you wish to marry her," Trahlyth said in the Cherokee language. Wahali answered in the affirmative.

"What can you do for my daughter? How will you care for her? This is a bad time to pledge your care for her when many of us are not surviving this ordeal," Trahlyth said.

"I understand this," Wahali said. "I plan to be a medicine man in the ways of our people and those of the whites too." Austenaco, Hummingbird's father, frowned.

"I do not think the ways of the white man will be a good way for healing," her father said.

"It is true that the white man's method of healing is not as advanced as our own," Wahali said. "But we can learn from one another. This is what I wish to do." Trahlyth nodded her head and reached under her wool dress.

"I have already seen that you are a good hunter; you use your weapons well and seem to know how to use the snare and other methods for capturing game," Austenaco said. "What will you do when we arrive at the new lands?"

"Likely, I will be given land. I will build a

temporary home for Hummingbird and provide food for her until I can gather the means for a better home."

"What if your plans include travel back east?" her mother asked.

"As you know, your daughter also is educated in the healing arts," Wahali said. "She will go where I go. We will learn together and help our people. We will be dedicated to healing together."

Austenaco nodded and looked at his wife, Trahlyth. They whispered to each other and then looked at their daughter. Trahlyth spoke.

"Since there will not be time nor the traditional seven sacred days for the waiting period, the two of you will exchange the required gifts and then Wahali will share our home." Hummingbird rummaged in a sack she had at her back and pulled out a cob of corn. Dustu, her brother, gasped as there was no such food available to most of the people. His mother looked at him sharply, and he looked down. It would be Dustu's job to educate Wahali and Hummingbird's children in the religion and ways of their people. While most of the Cherokee had embraced the Christian religion, they kept the customs of their people alive. Hummingbird held the corn gingerly, and Wahali took a cut of meat from his sack. Hummingbird handed him the dried corn to symbolize that she would be a good wife and care for the crops. Wahali handed her the meat to represent that he would be a good provider of meat for their home. When it was done, her mother pulled a blue blanket over the couple.

Wahali could see Hummingbird through the tiny holes in the blanket. He grinned at her. She smiled back demurely. Then her mother removed the blue blanket and covered them with a white blanket, which symbolized the beginning of their new life together. Then she removed it. And the ceremony was considered complete. Her mother began to sing a wedding song and the couple joined in with her mother and father. They ate more of the food Wahali had brought and invited in one or two others who were made aware of the small celebration. This was a time to be flexible. And so, the couple were married and retired after an evening of feasting and singing.

When the pass was clear and the people began moving again, they came to a fork in the road that would take them west. It had been a long trek north. Now they were headed toward the land that was to be a reservation for the Cherokees and many other peoples. But, as Wahali contemplated the long journey, he wondered how many would make it. He and a soldier buried three more people this day. One of them was a young girl. He had helped dig the shallow grave while the child's mother wailed. His chest clinched as he watched the mother fall to the ground in agony. The soldier who helped him dig the grave pulled the woman to her feet and put her in the wagon with other women, but she did not stop wailing. Soon, she was embraced by the other women. Wahali rode ahead to find that Hummingbird was concerned with her grandmother. The old woman had been riding one of the horses with Hummingbird's brother. But she wasn't able to stay on the horse so she slid to the ground. Hummingbird walked swiftly to help her grandmother stand.

"I am fine," she said to Hummingbird in Cherokee. "I wish to walk."

"But grandmother," Hummingbird said. "It is very cold and you might. ..."

"I know what I'm doing, Hummingbird," her grandmother said. "If the limbs do not move, one can have trouble with them later, so I wish to move." Her grandmother fished around in a pouch she carried on her side and put a clump of herbs in her mouth. She chewed on it a bit and then spat. Hummingbird nodded, knowing that her grandmother had wisdom for survival that many women did not have. She had learned much of her skills for healing from her grandmother. She tried to help her grandmother assume a walking rhythm, but the old woman flapped her hands as if to say "I do not need help." She then moved slowly behind her daughter and her daughter's husband using a gnarled, heavy stick to help her balance. Hummingbird's mother looked back and shook her head at Hummingbird as though to say, "Let her do as she pleases." The family kept moving.

Hummingbird learned the wisdom of using herbs and other aids for healing at her grandmother's side. From time to time, she rode in a wagon with friends who were from her village. Though it was bitterly cold, she ran to the wagon of her friends, Kamama Lowry, Te-ta-hah and Falling Blossom. They were cousins who were friends and who had a strong connection to one another. Their wagon had a canvas covering over it, which gave the women some protection from the wind. Kamama had been married, but her husband had died in the camp that had been used as a holding area for Cherokee. Te-ta-hah's husband was injured but riding a horse alongside the wagon. He had availed himself of the healing skills of Falling Blossom. Falling Blossom's husband drove the wagon. Her father sat beside him. Her mother had died in childbirth. Kamama's long, dark hair and bronze skin were striking. She sat in the wagon nearest the large iron pot her father and Te-ta-hah's husband kept warm with wood, droppings from the livestock and large smooth stones.

Te-ta-hah was short and fair skinned. She always had a pleasant appearance and took care to ask about others. She had met her husband while out on a chore for her family. He was from the Choctaw tribe and had fought with Dragging Canoe. But those days had long passed, and he was now content to stay near his wife and to help with the move west. All three women were pleased to see Hummingbird when she wrapped herself tightly in her blanket and sat down on the wagon floor. The women had padded the wagon with blankets and straw to make the journey less jarring.

"How is the newlywed?" Falling Blossom said, smiling and taking a bite of a corn patty the women had made. All three women had visited Hummingbird's father's hut after the wedding ceremony. They had given her small gifts, a comb for her hair, a leather pouch of fragrant herbs and sweet smelling soap. They offered some of the corn patty to Hummingbird with a cup of warm tea. She thanked them, nibbled on her corn patty and drank deeply of the warm brew.

"Enjoying it very much," Hummingbird said, smiling shyly.

"Are we to expect a new addition to your mother's hut soon?" asked Te-ta-hah.

"Too soon to tell," Hummingbird said, drinking more of the tea to hide her embarrassment. The women exchanged conversation about the cold, the long journey and the delay, remarking that the soldiers were pushing the people too hard. They talked also of the many people who'd died along the way and of the sickness some people suffered.

"I think we should try to help the women who are having troubles," Falling Blossom said.

"Not everyone had time to pack goods and prepare for this journey," Kamama said. "Some were rushed from their homes in the clothes they had on their backs. Others were taken from their fields and forced to walk to Fort Cass. So many died before they even arrived at the fort."

"What can we do now?" Hummingbird asked. "We are here now. What do we do to help those we can help?" The women were quiet for a moment.

"We can't help everyone," Falling Blossom said. "But we can help those who are traveling nearest to us."

"But how?" Kamama asked. "Everyone is using the goods they have as well as they can. The idea is to make it stretch."

"One of the things we can do is to help with the shortage of meat and tubers," Hummingbird said.

"Who are the best hunters among the men?" Te-ta-hah asked.

"What about the women?" Falling Blossom asked. "We are some formidable hunters. I caught two rabbits by sneaking off the trail."

"The soldiers did not stop you?" Hummingbird asked.

"They might if they noticed," Falling Blossom said. "But some of them are so cold and so ill, too, that they are barely staying on their horses. Also, the ones who are watching us need a little of the goods we gather; they might allow us to come and go without notice." The women sat there for a while thinking about Falling Blossom's proposal.

"I think it is a good idea," Te-ta-hah said. "I am better at finding food from the ground than using a snare or bow. So, I will collect nuts, tubers and any dried grasses and ramps that are good for boiling into a soup. We need to collect as many bowls as possible so we can take the food where it is needed the most."

"We should gather grasses for the animals, too," Kamama said. "They will not be able to carry their burdens if we do not care for them." The women nodded in agreement.

Hummingbird's face brightened as they seemed to be developing a sense of purpose on this awful journey. This would take their minds off the suffering and give them some way to help people who needed it. "But we should focus first on the people. What do we have that can be spared?" Hummingbird asked.

"That's a good question," Kamama said. "We can ask various families if they have beans, corn, squash or anything else that we can use as extras for feeding people. Then we can add to that as we go along."

"Let's start with a rabbit stew," Hummingbird said. "I will catch the first one." She grinned and climbed from the wagon. When she saw most of the soldiers hanging their heads against the wind, she knew she could find what she needed and get back to the wagon of her friends in no time. She went to her horse and removed her bow and arrows and crouched to run to the woods.

The day was cold and sunny. The trees were a mix of tall dark green and thin naked branches. In the distance, she could see a small pond in the woods. It was difficult to see as there were many trees between it and the path the travelers were taking. However, Hummingbird spotted it. Where there was a source of water, there would be wildlife. No one would question her if she left the trail temporarily. After all, relieving oneself in the woods was expected. When she arrived at an area that appeared to be good hunting territory, her luck was good. She spotted a large rabbit. It was trying to hide at the base of a spruce tree and had been nibbling on some greens. It blended in so well that had she not been looking carefully, she would not have noticed it. It sat very still while she looked at it. She slowly pulled her arrow out, notched it and aimed. She let it fly, and the rabbit was caught. She apologized to it for taking its life and put it in her pouch.

She saw a small stream in the distance and wondered whether she might catch fish. She crunched through the snow and noticed that the stream was shallow but had some large fish in it. She fashioned a scoop from tree branches and dried grass, leaned over the water and scooped a fish onto the shore. It flopped and twisted in the snow, but she was able to catch it before it got back to the water. Pleased with herself, she made her way back to the trail. Before she arrived, there was movement in the trees. A soldier had spotted her and was following her tracks. She ducked behind a large tree and held her breath. It was dangerous to be caught out in the woods by one of the soldiers; some of them were known to rape women who were found alone. Just as she feared he had found her, she sensed Wahali behind her.

He motioned to her to be quiet and turned her around to face him. He pulled him to her in an embrace. When the soldier arrived near them, he stopped his horse and stared for a moment.

"It's time to get back to the trail," the soldier said impatiently. He smirked and huffed. "Come on now." Wahali looked at the soldier and frowned.

"My woman has a habit of going too far in the woods," Wahali said.

"Make sure she don't get too far again," the soldier said. He wore a big hat with a bandana around his neck, a thick wool coat and black boots.

What some of the people wouldn't give for those boots, Hummingbird thought. Wahali dragged her away to his pony and helped her up, then nudged the pony so that they rejoined the trail.

"What were you doing out here so far from the trail?" he asked.

"Catching dinner," she said. He laughed and looked back at her. "My new wife has many talents." He could smell the fish and the rabbit in her bag.

The sun was out, and the snow was melting, but it was still cold — too cold for the elderly and the young. Wahali watched Hummingbird carefully as she sat atop his paint. He smiled as he thought of their first night together — the best he had had in his life. Hummingbird was warm and loving and held him close. When he loved her the first time, she inhaled sharply, but said nothing. He held her close and caressed her lovingly. She was so beautiful; he could not wait to be with her again. He felt a little guilty that there was death all around them, so much misery and suffering. But some of the people were enduring. He did not want to express this hope as it seemed unfair. He was happy with Hummingbird, hopeful that though they were being forced to a new place and a new life, they would thrive and have many children. He looked forward to finding food and helping Hummingbird care for their children. All they needed to do was get through this part of their new lives.

Hummingbird's parents had promised when the journey was finished that they would have one more horse if the animal made it west. They had traveled many days over hills and through some small bodies of water when they arrived at Berry's Ferry. The river was large and intimidating. People were being ferried across at a cost. The ferry owner was charging the people more than they could afford to give. Some of the people had nothing and attempted the crossing without help. A few did not make it and were washed downstream.

When it was time for Hummingbird and her family to cross, Wahali went to negotiate with the ferry owner. He managed to arrange for two crossings with coins he had stashed away for just this purpose. Hummingbird's mother, Trahlyth, father, Austenaco, and grandmother, would cross first with their possessions. Then, he would cross with Hummingbird and her brother, Cutsu. He had dug out what he intended to pay and had it ready when they arrived. He kept half the money and agreed to give the other half when Hummingbird and her family were across.

Sibu, Wahali's horse, and Coyote, Hummingbird's horse, were hesitant as they stepped on the raft to join them. However, he had had to struggle to get Austenaco's horse on the raft. Hummingbird craned her neck looking to the other side, trying to find her parents and grandmother on the bank. She hardly seemed to notice the rocking and pitching of the raft as they crossed.

"Do you swim?" Wahali asked.

"Yes," Hummingbird said. "But I have not done so in many days. This river is strong and wants to eat us, I fear." Cutsu held on to the rails of the raft. Though it was made of sturdy wood, the raft seemed swamped by the rushing water. Wahali placed a protective hand on Cutsu's shoulder.

"It will do so only if you give up," Wahali said. "Hold on to your horse if something happens; he will carry you over."

The raft took a deep dip and before they knew what happened, Cutsu had fallen in. Wahali jumped into the churning waters to reach Cutsu before he was swept away. Hummingbird was not a screamer, but her mother was. Wahali could hear her screaming in Cherokee for her son. Wahali whistled for Sibu to join him in the water. The horse rose on his hind legs and leaped into the water, swimming toward Wahali. When Sibu reached them, Wahali held on to the horse, who swam the remaining distance to the shore. Sibu sliced powerfully through the water as though it were a trickle from a stream.

Wahali had reached the other side before the overwhelmed raft. He pulled Cutsu out of the water and began pressing on his back so that the water the boy had swallowed would come out. Cutsu coughed and sputtered and was sitting up when his mother arrived. She hugged him and spoke nonsense, running a hand down his head.

Cutsu's father pushed his wife aside and picked up his son, carrying him to their horse. He turned and signed his thanks to Wahali for saving his son's life and walked to the ferry dock to receive his daughter.

The waves that were being created by the river's swirling waters still threatened to swamp the raft. Wahali stood at the ready in case Hummingbird was forced to swim for the shore. The man poling the craft across the water seemed to be struggling to keep it on course. But finally, Hummingbird was across, and the family, as well as Wahali, sighed in relief. He helped Hummingbird and her family dry off from the frigid water by quickly building a fire and helping her out of her wet clothing. They huddled together using what dry clothes they could find until they were able to move about freely.

The day was long and hard, but, as the sun set, the soldiers ordered a halt to the procession. Wahali watered the ponies at a nearby stream. He then went about finding grazing food by digging up the melting snow. His paint was not fussy and used his hooves to paw the ground until he was able to get to the dried grasses below. Wahali found a stream that flowed swiftly. He hauled some water back to camp and hoped it would be safe, as many people still were not boiling water. Since it was cold, the Cherokees thought it was safe. He saw, though, that Hummingbird, her mother and grandmother were boiling a great deal of water in a large pot. He nodded to them and they smiled as though to say, we know what to do.

He had helped a man, Long Foot, who had flux that evening. Long Foot was one of the lucky ones. Wahali gave the man some of the herb that helped with such conditions and urged him not to drink anything but boiled water. Wahali saw Long Foot sit down on the side of the trail a few times, but the soldiers did not bother him. It was clear the soldiers thought Long Foot would not make it. But Long Foot was unable to understand all of what Wahali wanted him to do. The man sometimes bent down to scrape up snow and ate it as though he were dying of thirst. Of course, he probably was. He lost so much. Wahali saw Long Foot go into the woods many times. What surprised Wahali is that Long Foot was still in the general vicinity of the wagons and people walking along the trail. Wahali expected him to give up and to give out, but Long Foot kept going. When Long Foot came to Wahali for more help, Wahali gave him boiled water and an herbal brew. That seemed to keep Long Foot well for a while.

Wahali went to Jason's wagon to see how his patients were doing and was surprised to see that two more had left and had been replaced by two new people. He mixed some goldenseal in a pot and left it for Jason to administer. It was time for him to hunt before anyone could ask him to do anything. He had to see whether he could range far and still get back to

the camp before sundown. He set a snare in the
woods so that he could catch a rabbit and found his
way to a river. It was full of ice, but he was able to
catch two fish and placed them in his pouch. He was
headed back to camp when he spotted a deer. He
noticed some movement on the far side of a meadow
and realized that he was not the only one who
hunted the deer. Both hunters crouched to be certain
the deer was not spooked by their presence. The
hunter appeared to be someone from the camp.
Wahali had noticed a strong young boy who
appeared not to need help traveling and who was
part of a large family.

They waited for a while and crept closer to the
deer. As they both neared, Wahali leveled his bow
and arrow and aimed. At the same time, the boy let
fly his arrow, too. One arrow hit the deer in the left
rump, another in the neck. The large deer struggled
to get to its feet, but Wahali hit it again near its heart,
and the animal stopped struggling. When they
neared, Wahali apologized for taking its life. The boy
came near and stood back while Wahali checked the
deer for life. When Wahali was certain the deer was
ready, he began to skin it. He asked the boy for his
name.

"Young Panther," the boy said in their language.

"I am Wahali," he said. "You can help with the
skinning. We will share the meat." The boy nodded
and commenced the help Wahali skin the deer. They
left the sinews in the deer's legs as it was their
custom not to take that part of the animal. After
dividing the meat into portions that they could take
back to the camp, they pulled what was left of the
carcass to a safe area, buried it and returned to the
camp. Wahali heard Young Panther's family praise
him quietly as they went about preparing the meat.
Wahali took his portion to Hummingbird's mother

and grandmother, who began to prepare a rich meal. They added tubers, sweet potatoes and other dried vegetables to the pot and prepared a rich stew. He then took some of the meat to Jason Roberts to feed his patients. When the excess meat was stored and hidden from predators, the family cleaned the clearing. Wahali checked the horses and fed them a little extra grain. He settled them in a lean-too near the hut and went to attend to his own needs. He found Hummingbird doing the same.

The night was cold and dark. The sky was covered in clouds so the moon was muted and the stars well hidden. His eyes had adjusted to the darkness. He saw her washing herself and cleaning some clothing in the stream. "Don't be alarmed; it's me, Wahali," he said. She wrung out the cloth she'd been using to wash and placed it in her pouch.

"You startled me," she said.

"You shouldn't be here alone, Hummingbird," he said.

"I planned to be quick and knew you would be nearby," she said quietly.

"You're right," he said, walking up to her and using his arms to circle her from behind.

"What is to become of us?" she asked. "So many people are suffering and dying on the way to this new territory. It seems that our numbers are being cut in half."

"Yes, there will be many who can't make it," Wahali said. "But we will continue on and do our best to help those who are struggling."

"I wish I could help them all," she said. He said nothing for a while. They stood still and listened to the water as it trickled across stones. An owl hooted in the distance; wolves howled. But it was safe here. He sensed the animals feared the great numbers of humans who would hunt them.

He turned her around. "Let's go back," he said. "While I'm certain most predators are trying their best to avoid this mass of people, there could be some who are looking for an opportunity. I need to be certain the horses are safe, too. We are near the end of the travels, so we don't want to be here too long." They returned to the camp. While Wahali made certain the horses were taken care of, Hummingbird hung clothing on a branch. While the sky was cloudy, it appeared there would be no rain or snow. She crawled into the hut that was built onto her parents' dwelling. It served as a wing to the structure built by her father. Inside, to her left, her brother and grandmother lay near each other. Her father and mother snuggled. She waited eagerly for Wahali. The days were full of the work of travel, but the nights were theirs. When he came into their hut, she opened her arms to him.

CHAPTER SEVENTEEN

Hummingbird had taken the rabbit to her friends and had given the fish to Wahali to give to her mother. Her friends, Kamama, Te-ta-hah and Falling Blossom were excited when she arrived with the food. It was Falling Blossom's turn to go out next; one of the men in her family accompanied her. Hummingbird had explained to Wahali that the women were going to ask those who had plenty to contribute to a store of food for those who had little. The women were going to feed those who were too weak or ill to hunt for their own food. Wahali had agreed to help her but urged her to take her horse with her and to let him know when she planned to hunt so that he could go with her. Together they could help keep each other safe and catch up with the trail a little faster.

So, the game became steady with five young people making a concerted effort to find food for

those who needed it. The travelers were so many and
the line of people so long that the women were able
to help those nearest them only. However, that help
resulted in a number of people who were strong
enough and well enough to endure the harsh weather
and the long journey. When the people arrived in
that part of the country that was known as southern
Illinois, they stopped and the soldiers were met by
groups of whites who offered blankets, clothing,
food and other necessities. The donations helped
people continue on the journey. But some of those
gathering were not friendly. Some whites spat at the
Cherokee, and others scolded the soldiers. It was a
confusing time.

Te-tah-hah and Kamama visited the wagon of
their friend, Gola. She was called Gola by her family
and sometimes Golda. It was said that she was born
in winter near gold. But what was more important
for the women was that Gola was about to have a
baby. Hummingbird, Kamama, Te-tah-hah and
Falling Blossom had regularly visited the wagons of
other travelers. Some of the other women had joined
them in helping those who were struggling to survive
the difficult journey. One woman had more than one
large barrel of beans that she agreed to share with the
four women. Another woman, Yona, had hidden a
great deal of dried corn. She had been removing the
kernels and storing them in several large buckets.
Fawn, whose family had little in the way of property
but who were successful farmers, had dried beans,
potatoes and carrots hidden away. The women met
together secretly when the soldiers stopped the
people for the night. The women agreed that they
would share a certain amount of their goods and
divide it among those who were destitute.

"This is a good idea," Fawn said. "I wish we had thought of it sooner. But many of the people are afraid that their food will be taken by the soldiers."

"There will be some who need it and some who will steal," Hummingbird said. "But most of the soldiers have their own food and rations, provided by the government."

"I heard that they were directed to provide some of that food to the travelers," Kamama said. Gola nodded her head, saying she had heard this too.

"I think that with so many people on this trail, everyone is hunting as much as they can," Falling Blossom said. "It's surprising that the game isn't all gone by now, that there are any animals left for us to catch."

"That's why we need to try to look for vegetables among us and on the trail," Hummingbird said. "There are some wild plants that can be harvested even in the winter that make good eating. We have to know which they are and where to find them. Acorns can be soaked in water and used as flour."

The women agreed that there were plenty of oaks in the wild and that they would look for them. They all agreed to gather as much as possible before sunset. They agreed they would do this every time the travelers stopped for the night. The soldiers stopped the Cherokee and other natives who traveled with them, but did so before night fell so that there would be enough light to water and feed the horses and to prepare food. So the women devised a plan that included going out to scout for wild edible plants.

"Watercress also makes a good meal," Falling Blossom said. "I'm not certain we will be able to find them in this area, but we can try. They have to be eaten soon after they are gathered. I can look for onions and burdock. Burdock has a heart-shaped leaf. It's very good for women." The women muttered in agreement, and Gola winced as they sat there. They all turned their heads to look at her. Was it time for her to have the baby?

"When this baby comes, I will do my share," Gola said, patting her large, round tummy. "Pine needles are good as a cleansing tea, and cattails make good eating." Hummingbird smiled and wrinkled her nose at the idea of pine needles. She liked them for grinding to make soap and for keeping her environment, person and things clean. She also knew it made a good tea for those who had grippe. She was thinking about the many pine trees she'd seen in the woods and how she'd make a greater effort to harvest their needles so that Gola could concentrate on her new baby. Just then, Gola bent over and a gush of water came from her. The women knew what was coming next.

"I'll get fresh water," Falling Blossom said.

"I have some cloth that can be used," Te-ta-hah said. The women rushed to prepare the items needed for Gola's delivery. Fawn ran off to find Gola's husband, Atohl. Hummingbird helped Gola stand and then squat as the women returned to the covered wagon to welcome a new soul into the world. As Gola panted and grunted, groaned and strained, the women took turns speaking softly to her and rubbing her back. After a few hours of soothing encouragement, Gola seemed ready to push the child out. She rose and squatted, and Hummingbird, who had washed her hands and the blade she was to use to cut the cord, caught the baby in her arms. The little girl was large and healthy. Falling Blossom helped hold the child while Hummingbird cut the cord and tied it off with string that had been put in the pine-needle liquid to clean it.

The women helped clean up the baby and placed

her in Gola's arms. Gola's husband, Atohl, came to the back of the wagon to see his new baby girl. He grinned and whispered words to his wife and child as Gola breastfed her infant.

As the days and nights passed, Wahali and Hummingbird fell into a rhythm of food gathering and preparation. She regularly went into the woods with him in search of acorns, pecans, other nuts, pine needles and wild edibles. The women had a system worked out where they shared the goods they gathered and fed those who seemed to be lacking. Their success was noticed. When the soldiers saw that the women were making stews from very little meat and a great deal of vegetative matter, they at first turned up their noses at it. But gradually, as hunger hit everyone, all of the people, Cherokee and soldiers alike, found that the resourcefulness of the women was nothing short of genius.

As they headed further west, one of the men in Te-ta-hah's family began to behave strangely. He took off his clothes and walked naked in the snow. He urinated in front of soldiers' horses. He jumped up and down and screamed war cries. He laughed and shouted, talked to himself and seemed to have long conversations with someone who was not there. The Cherokee believed in rabbit tricksters. Hummingbird thought of the story of Rabbit who wanted to catch Flint. He invited Flint to his home, and they ate. When Flint feel asleep, Rabbit struck Flint with a mallet and ran to his hole. But Flint exploded and struck Rabbit in the back of the head. Hummingbird sighed as she thought of this story that her grandmother had told her long ago. The lesson, of course, was that there are always consequences to our actions. She wondered whether,

Rayetayah, the man who was behaving like a trickster, would suffer consequences. He walked backwards and then forward and then ran into the woods screaming. Hummingbird knew that the elders would think that an evil spirit possessed the man or that he was a trickster. But she kept walking when she saw Te-ta-hah's family go after Rayetayah. Later when they settled for the night, Te-ta-hah came to tell her that Rayetayah could not be found. Apparently, he had lost his way.

CHAPTER EIGHTEEN
Fall 1837

Lucinda walked some of the way to the North Carolina mountains, but Walking Bird insisted she take the horse that he'd brought. They had arrived at the mountains in a few days and were greeted by her grandmother, Amadahy.

"Grandmother," Lucinda said, hugging her lightly. Her grandmother placed a hand on her granddaughter's head and looked affectionately at Lucinda. She placed a hand on Lucinda's belly and smiled. There would be a child soon.

"What took you so long?" Amadahy said. "We need to be together for the negotiations that are underway." She explained that Tsali had fought for the right of the western Cherokee in this place called North Carolina. The government had agreed to allow the Cherokee to remain together, but under the leadership of Chief Yonaguska. His adopted white son, William Holland Thomas, who knew the law, was also working on negotiations for the Cherokee to remain in the western territory of North Carolina.

"Those who are not part of this band will need to go west to the new territory," her grandmother said. "However, we want to stay in this part of the country. This land is partly ours. Some of it has been sold, but the only way we may be allowed to remain is if we stay together." Walking Bird was busy greeting old friends, other young men who were part of the contingent of Cherokees who were to remain in the North Carolina mountains. Some of his friends were patting him on the back and shoving him playfully. Lucinda smiled to see that they would have many friends.

"Lucinda," her grandmother said. "This is very important. You and Walking Bird will go with us to Birdtown. From there, we will listen to the words of Thomas. He is trying to help us remain on our land." Lucinda frowned.

"But I thought it was already our land," she said. "How can he help us to remain when the land belongs to us?"

"Changes have come, Lucinda. This is beyond our ability to negotiate. It is time for us to listen and find a way to remain here. There is no other way." Lucinda nodded but secretly she wondered whether there would ever be a time when they were not being pushed from one place to another.

"Enough of that, now," her grandmother said. "First, we must see if this young man of yours is adequate." Lucinda looked at her grandmother with surprise. She saw a smirk on her grandmother's face and knew then that her grandmother was teasing her. Lucinda had met Walking Bird during a gathering of her mother's people. Walking Bird had come the long distance with cousins — one man and two young women. Walking Bird and his cousins were related to Cherokee who by now had probably walked away to the Western territory. The cousins had married into the Tennessee-area Cherokee tribes. He had met Lucinda after a wedding celebration that included much dancing and singing. He was one of the most attractive men she'd seen. He smiled at her and approached her after she danced and asked her to walk with him.

When they were a distance away from the celebration, he pulled her into a cove and held her close. He smoothed his hands down her waist and and confusing things began to happen. She breathed heavily and leaned back, stepping away from him. He pulled him to her and kissed her. After that, she knew that they would be together.

The problem, though, was that her grandmother did not trust the Cherokee tribe from which Walking Bird came. The Qualla group of the Cherokee were a crafty and clever group. They were tricksters of the best kind. They could find a way around the most difficult of challenges and, if they had to adapt to make things happen, they would do so. Her grandmother warned her of this. When Lucinda's mother was still alive, Lucinda had gone to her mother to ask what she thought. Sitting Deer did not approve of Amadahy's advice but didn't contradict her.

"Why do you think this matters?" her mother asked.

"Because grandmother is usually right," Lucinda said.

"What does your heart tell you to do?" her mother asked.

"I'm not certain."

"Then, you must do nothing until you are certain what you feel for Walking Bird," Sitting Deer said.

"What if no other man asks for me?" Lucinda asked.

"You will have no end of attention," her mother said.

She remembered her mother smiling when she said those words. Sitting Deer was sometimes more wise than her own mother. She often said things that calmed Lucinda or Easter. Her mother made certain the two girls were educated in more than one way. Both girls were encouraged to seek education with the missionaries. At one time, Lucinda thought she might want to be a teacher herself. But there were too many things to do on the farm. Her sister mostly ran everything, but she spent time studying and dreaming of a time when she might do something else with her life. It appeared that now that she was with Walking Bird, she might not have the time she would like to pursue more education. She pressed a hand to her stomach, wondering whether they would have children.

When the visiting with friends and relatives came to a close, Walking Bird came to her at her grandmother's cabin. They were on the edge of the forest that led into the Great Smokey Mountains. Walking Bird knocked quietly at the door and entered upon hearing Amadahy's invitation.

"Osiyo," Walking Bird said, entering the cabin and nodding to show respect to Lucinda's grandmother. Amadahy stood at a little wood-burning stove, stirring a pot of stew. It was cold out and time for a nourishing meal. Amadahy made corn cakes and served both young people and herself. They sat at a small, round table. Amadahy was one of the fortunate women to have been given Walking Bird's cabin when she arrived months ago. Her family wealth made this possible.

"What is the news, grandson-to-be?" she asked. Walking Bird swallowed his mouthful and rested his spoon by the bowl he'd been given by Amadahy.

"Because of the war with Tsali, our people may be able to stay on this land," he said. "Chief Yonaguska's adopted son, William Holland, is trying to negotiate on our behalf."

"But so many have already been removed," Amadahy said.

"Yes, but many are hiding in the mountains, so that they may remain on our ancestral lands," Walking Bird said.

"Who is this man, Holland?" Lucinda asked.

"He owns trading posts in this area and has lived among our people for many years. The Chief and Holland became good friends, and Chief Yonaguska adopted Holland as a son," Walking Bird said. Amadahy grunted as though she did not approve.

"How is this man able to help us? He has no power with the U.S. government," Grandmother said. "He is only one puny white man."

"But grandmother," Lucinda said, looking pointedly at Amadahy, "it is not unusual for Cherokees to adopt foreigners. It is done all the time. Why should you be suspicious?"

"I'm not suspicious," Amadahy said. "But how does one so interested in doing well come to care for us?"

"That's simple," Walking Bird said. "People come to care for one another under the most odd circumstances." Some minutes passed as they contemplated the ideas.

"These are odd times," Amadahy said. "So many people have been forced from their land and marched west, even from this area. Only those who appear to be with Tsali, Yonaguska and Holland seem to have protection. Still many of our people hide like scared rabbits in the mountains. It is outrageous. It is sad." Her voice trailed off.

"We will need to be vigilant," Amadahy said. "We

don't know which way the wind will blow, whether we, too, will be forced to flee to the hills or go west with other Children of the Sun. We need to be aware of what is going to happen to us. It is clear that so many are being forced to do as they do not wish." She took the bowls and spoons from Walking Bird and Lucinda and cleaned them in hot water. She dried them with a cloth and put them on a shelf near the little stove. The cabin was stocked with tubers and sweet potatoes, grain and other goods that Amadahy used to make food for not only her own family, but any of those Principal People, the Cherokee, who came to her from the mountains in need of food. She taught her daughter, Sitting Deer, and her grandchildren to be resourceful.

Whenever she could, Amahady traded with those who were passing through, westward-heading settlers, other tribal peoples who were also heading west. Many people seemed downhearted, but she forced herself to be cheerful. This was necessary if the next generation was to survive. She realized that her skepticism regarding Thomas was influenced by the roiling unrest among the people. Things were changing fast, and the people were being pushed to the edges of their tolerance. Still, it was necessary to be calm to wait and see what would happen. She prayed for good fortune to come to the Principal People.

William Holland Thomas was a small man. When he was just a boy, his father died, so he was forced to work for Congressman Felix Walker, who had interests in Cherokee territory. Little Will, as he had become known to the Cherokee, learned their language and quickly became endeared to the Cherokee people and to Yonaguska, who later adopted him. This period in the friendship between Will and the Cherokee was sometimes strained and fraught with tension. Chief Yonaguska was not well. Some said he would not live long. Yonaguska had asked Little Will if he would take over the responsibility of being chief of the Cherokee, but the thought of it made Will uncomfortable. Yes, he spoke their language and was friendly with many of the people, but he was not certain he could bring about the changes needed for the Cherokee to live on their lands. He had one good friend in the territory, a friend of Felix Walker's, Charles Davis.

Davis had been a friend to him when Walker, who could not pay William when he worked for him, gave him law books. Felix knew all about the law; there being no school for him to attend, Will studied the books and learned of many ways he could help the Cherokee. He learned of other things as well — how land disputes were settled, how slaves were retained, how wills were written and how property was divided among heirs.

Though Davis was not a schooled attorney, he knew more about law and things that went on in the legislature and government than most people. Like Will, Davis was a self-made man. He read and studied and knew many things. Often when a problem was too difficult for Will to solve, he talked to Davis when it concerned the white man's world. When it concerned Indians, he went to his adopted father, Yonaguska. So Will saddled a horse and went to Davis' cabin in the north part of Haywood County. When he arrived, he saw smoke coming from the chimney of the small cabin that Davis called home. Davis came out on the porch with a pipe in his mouth.

"So there must be a very good reason for you to come all the way to my little cabin in the woods," he said, smiling, holding the pipe away from his mouth and tapping it on the side of his boot. Will sat on his horse for a while looking at Davis.

"You are right, sir," he said. "I have come for some of that precious wisdom you have thrown about from time to time. I wish to ask for some of it." Davis motioned for him to come into the cabin. He made Will a hot drink and settled down in a rocking chair, one of the two chairs he kept in his cabin. Davis knew better than to offer Will strong drink or tobacco. Will was reared by his mother, Temperance, and as her name suggested, she was a firm believer in being the best person one could be.

She drummed in the virtues of abstinence of all kinds, along with the habit of prayer. The woman had constantly reminded Will that it was important to have a sterling character. His father had died shortly after he was born, and his mother struggled to provide for them. When Felix Walker offered him work as a teenager, Will quickly took advantage of it. Davis was there when Will arrived and tutored him through the worst of his adjustments. He had gradually prospered and acquired stores of his own. That meant that Will never really learned to be rowdy, to indulge in alcohol or the vices that other men took for granted. He'd been too busy trying to run three businesses and adhering to the principles taught to him by his mother.

"What's on your mind, Will?" Davis asked, rocking in his chair. The man seemed to be content to live on his own on the edge of the woods with the mountains as a background. Will wondered how he did it. There were no people around. Davis sometimes interacted with the Cherokee, but rarely left his little cabin. The two of them never lost touch, however. Will felt comfortable dropping in on Davis from time to time.

"I am in a bit of a fix," Will said, holding his hat in one hand. Davis said nothing but kept rocking in his chair. The thing squeaked as he rocked back and forth. Will wanted to tell the man to stop that confounded rocking. But when you were coming to someone for advice, it was best not to be unpleasant. As his mother said, you catch more flies with honey than with vinegar.

"It's like this," Will began, clearing his throat. "I have, as you know, been quite friendly with the Cherokee." Davis lit his pipe and pulled on it. He nodded as though to say he was aware of this.

"I am trying to help some of them, about 60 families, stay on their land, here in North Carolina, in the mountains," he said. "I have studied the law books that Felix gave me, but nowhere is there a case like this." Davis pulled on his pipe.

"Sure there is," Davis said.

"What do you mean?"

"This is a property dispute, plain and simple," Davis said.

"It seems more than a simple property dispute to me," Will said.

"It may seem that way, if you think about it too hard. But try not to do that. Think of it all as a simple property dispute. Someone wants the property of a group of people. That group of people don't want to give up that property."

"I don't think you're understanding exactly what I mean," Will said.

"I do," Davis said. Will took a deep breath and got up from his chair and paced a while; he looked out the window of Davis's cabin. The glass was not clear, and you really could not see much, but it at least alerted Davis to predators if there were any.

"Let's make this a little simpler," Davis said. "Imagine for a moment that there are two white families fighting over land. Let's say one family is the Smith family; the other is the Jones family. The Smith family was on the land first. But the Jones family comes along and says that because there are more of them and they have a relative in the Smith family, that the land belongs to them too. Now I know that most whites are not saying they are related to the Indians, but bear with me for a moment. What would solve the problem between the two families?"

Will looked down at his feet in frustration and walked back to his chair and sat down. "I suppose that one family member could marry someone in the other family and they could share the land."

"That's one way," Davis said. "And that's the opportunity that is partly before you. Didn't you say some time ago that the old Chief cared deeply for you? That he adopted you?"

"Yes," Will said, his voice trailing off. "But what does that have. . ." Will stood up and paced again and then sat down again. He got up again and paced. "So, you're saying that because the chief and I are related, that I can somehow sue for protection for the tribe?"

Davis nodded, puffing on his pipe. "But don't leave it at that, Will. You have means now; you've made lots of money on trading as a merchant. Use those wits of yours. There's nothing stopping you from buying the land where the Cherokees are located and calling it your own." He smiled at Will, coughed and tapped his pipe on a small dish he kept on a nearby table.

"This is about ownership, so make it about ownership," Davis said. "The government can't say that a white man can't own property. They might say that to a Cherokee, but they are not going to say that to you."

"It's a sad sign of our times that we must go to

these extremes," Will said, muttering under his breath. "I have not heard of anyone else doing such a thing." He thought perhaps Davis did not hear him, but the man had hearing as sharp as a wolf's. Davis nodded again and pulled on his pipe.

"That's what the law is about," Davis said. "Creating new precedents where none was before. You will only know whether it will work when you try."

The two men spent more time together and went fishing in a nearby river. Will spent the night at Davis's cabin and headed out in the morning for home. He had a great deal to think about. He had earned some money as a merchant. It seemed like he was a trader for some time and then the Cherokees and settlers came to him with more and more demands. As they brought goods to trade and money, such as gold and silver to pay for goods, he was able to save quite a bit. His mother cautioned him to always give back to those who gave to him. He remembered the early days of his work with Felix Walker. The man threw him into the business and gave him little in the way of directions. If it hadn't been for Yonaguska and his people, he might have failed completely. But Yonaguska, now chief, took him under his wing and sent people to him that had goods to trade.

Women made interestingly decorated clay dishes and wooden dishes, baskets and blankets. Men and women brought furs and skins for trade. Yonaguska told him where to send his agents for the best goods and how to negotiate with people for the best prices. As the seasons and years passed, he traded in meat, fish, corn, grains, and any other produce that could be kept in a barrel. It didn't take long to sell those goods because people were always in the market for something that they didn't have at home. There was plenty of produce because everyone was a farmer. But sometimes a farmer's crops went bad, or there was a fire or there was sickness that kept a family from prospering. When that happened, people sold things that were hard to get: needles, thread, cloth, furniture, gadgets and stoves. The list went on and on.

He imagined that there would come a day when outposts like his would become obsolete. But for now, his stores were the only resources for many people for miles around. Felix Walker really did him a favor by throwing him into the merchant business. If the man hadn't done that, Will would never have learned to be the merchant he was. He would never have become the son of Yonaguska and he would never have befriended the Cherokee people. Yonaguska said many times that he wanted Will to take over as chief when he died. But Will just couldn't see himself doing that.

Yonaguska was a large man, with dark skin, and kind brown eyes. He wasn't that old; Will guessed maybe he was nearing 50. But the man looked much younger. He did not cut his hair as many Cherokees did, but he tried to maintain some of the tribal customs. Yonaguska taught those ways to Will, impressed that Will quickly learned, as a 13-year-old, to speak the language of the people. Soon, Will was trading with many of the Cherokee people, but with Choctaw, Creek and others as well. When Will sensed the violent changes that were underway for the Cherokee people, he was invited to many gatherings where women and men sat around speaking of what was coming and how to cope with it. When it was clear that Cherokees would be forced west, many came to him for advice. Will did what he could to advise them, but most fled to the

mountains. Now it would be up to him to find a way
for them to live in peace with their neighbors. He
wanted that for both groups, but he felt caught
between the warring forces. No, it was not violent
now, as it had been when he was younger. The
people had mostly given up fighting, but the fight
was emotional. People loved their homes and land
and wanted to continue as they had been for
generations. He understood this but felt powerless to
do anything about it.

He had arrived home at noon, having left Davis
on his little porch, puffing away at his pipe. Maybe
what the man said was right. Maybe what he needed
to do was simply to buy the land that the Cherokees
had been occupying. After a long rest, the next day,
he went to visit his adopted father.

Yonaguska had been a friend of Tsali's for some
time. But the man was rash in his judgment. He had
fought the soldiers in the interest of remaining on his
land. Will had helped in the escorting of some of the
Cherokee who were being forced to go west.
Oconaluftee Cherokee of the Qualla territory had
attempted to reach an agreement to remain on their
lands. They were in the western part of North
Carolina near the Oconaluftee River Valley. The fight
that Tslai waged last year was bloody. In return for
the honored treaty allowing them to remain on their
lands, his people agreed to help capture those who
were responsible for mortally wounding two soldiers.
The hunt for Tslai was brutal. When the Cherokee
finally found him, he was willing to make the
sacrifice for the entire tribe. With his death, the
Oconaluftee Citizens were permitted to remain on
their lands. But that agreement seemed tenuous at
best. Sometimes, Yonaguska wondered whether his
people would ever find peace. When Yonaguska's

adopted son knocked on the door, the chief bid him to enter.

"Osiyo," Will said.

"Greetings, my son," Yonaguska said. "Come in, come in." Yonaguska was ill and had been bed-ridden for some time. However, he was upright for his adopted son's visit. After they spent time on preliminary conversation and the sharing of a drink, they got down to the business of Will's visit.

"I have been studying the law, father," Will said.

"I know you will find a way, Little Will," Yonaguska said. "For many years you have lived as one of us. I know you feel for the Principal People. Many of our people are saying that when I am gone you should become chief." Will swallowed hard. He had heard the same, but was not convinced he was up to the challenge. There were mixed feelings about his role among the Cherokee.

"You must fight in the way that makes sense to the people that are opposing our existence here," Yonaguska said. He took a moment to breathe deeply, coughing a bit as he settled himself on the floor among some bedding and blankets. Will sat across from him and reached his hand out to his father. Will's own father had died when he was quite young, and Will admitted to himself that when he was thrown into the trading business, he was completely unprepared.

But Yonaguska, seeing a frightened young boy doing the best he could, showed him how to sell and how to talk to the people. Yonaguska's nephew and Will's best friend among the Cherokee, Gawonii, who was about his age, taught him to speak Cherokee. Gawonii and his sister, Ayita, made up games so that Will learned fast. They were his family now. Will's mother would always be important, and he always checked on her. She had done her best for him. She reminded him that it was important to be a good man and that the definition of being a good man would change as the times changed. He had to look into himself to decide what being good meant.

Yonaguska looked at Will again and nodded, drinking more of the brew that the medicine man said would help ease Yanaguska's ailments. Will took a deep breath. He was nervous about this decision, but before he could change his mind, he said it.

"I plan to buy this land that we are on and more acres around this area to have someplace for the Cherokee to remain," he said. There, he'd said it. He waited for Yonaguska's reaction. The chief said nothing at first.

"Can you afford to do this thing, Little Will?" Yonaguska asked.

"I have saved much in the many years of my trading," Will said. "I am able to do so because the government is selling the land cheaply. So, I will be one of the people buying the land. But," he paused. "It will be your land."

"No, it will be your land and the land of our people, if you decided to help them," Yonaguska said.

"That is part of my plan," he said. "If the government wants most Cherokee to go west, some will — some already have gone. But I will petition the government for the rights of 60 families to remain on the land that I buy." Yonaguska was quiet for several minutes while he thought of the consequences of this act of generosity by Little Will. He had named the boy Little Will years ago when he saw how slight the boy was but also how smart he was. Will had become wealthy enough to do this thing for the Cherokee. He wondered whether a Cherokee man could do the same. No, he thought. The government was determined to push the

Cherokee from their lands. This might be the only way for some of them to hold on to their ancestral land.

"I would recommend that you take on the responsibility of being chief then," Yonaguska said. "It is the only way." Will sat there for a moment, dreading the weight of that responsibility. He knew that Yonaguska wanted it; his father had said so many times. But Will was not ready to accept so great a responsibility. How could he? There was no one he could turn to for help. This thing he was proposing to do for the Cherokee was unlike any he had ever heard. He knew there would be hostility. He sometimes had had to do things that were shameful and not in the interest of the people. But, like Davis said, he might be creating a new precedent where there had been none.

"There is one problem that we might encounter," Will said. Yonaguska looked away as though he were not listening, but Will knew that his father was listening to every word he said.

"Our people might need to claim U.S. citizenship in order to stay on the land," Will said. After a few minutes, Yonaguska responded.

"That will not make them less Cherokee," Yonaguska said. "They will always remember who they are. That will not keep them from being who they truly are. If it means that they survive and that they remain on their ancestral land, it is the way it must be done." Will exhaled in relief. He knew that such a thing would be difficult for the people to accept. But it might be the only way. He would run for Congress eventually, but soon all would know that he was defending the Cherokee. First, he would go about the business of buying up as much land as cheaply as possible in the Qualla area. Then, he would be able to negotiate for better circumstances.

He left a gift of healing bark for his father and reassured him that the people would prosper.

Dale Marie Taylor

CHAPTER NINETEEN
Winter 1837

Lucinda made the cornbread and stew that would be their meal for the day. Walking Bird and his friends had encountered a troop of soldiers in the mountains, but had been able to outrun them. Things were becoming tense in the mountains. Lucinda wanted to ask her grandmother when they would have a traditional wedding ceremony, but things were a little unsettled, and she wanted things to go well. She finished off the stew with some salt she had traded for with one of the villagers and put the lid on the pot.

When she walked out of the cabin in her long wool skirt and thick jacket, the snow had begun to fall. The wind began to blow and the temperature was dropping fast. She went to the barn that held not only her and Walking Bird's horses but those of other villagers. She prepared feed for the animals and gathered eggs. She put blankets on each of the horses and made certain they were securely in their stalls. She filled their water troughs with water from the well and secured the big wide doors to the barn. One of the doors flew from her hands as a gust of wind hit, accompanied by fast-falling snow. Where was everyone? Just then, she saw grandmother walking back to their cabin. Walking Bird followed behind her, accompanied by three men. They were talking excitedly about a meeting they had just attended.

"He wants us to become citizens of the U.S.," Salal said of the talk Little Will had had with the people. Yonaguska was there, too, though he wasn't well. The meeting was in Yonaguska's cabin so that he would not need to travel. But it was widely accepted that Yonaguska would not be long for this world and that he would pass on the mantle of leadership to Little Will. Diwali did not like this. He thought he should be the one to lead the tribe. Diwali was mixed and had gone to the missionary schools. He was certain that Yonaguska was making a big mistake by allowing Little Will to lead them.

"I could do anything that Little Will can do," Diwali said. "It just takes some know how. I could get elected to office too and could buy land for the tribe."

"No, you could not," Walking Bird said. "You would need to be a citizen of the U.S before they would recognize you as having a right to the land." Diwali grimaced at that. He did not want Walking Bird to be right, but he knew it was true. The soldiers were hunting the people like they were animals — forcing them to go west. Walking Bird knew that Diwali and his family had some wealth but it would not be enough to cover the expense of all that land. Even if they had enough money, the government would likely not allow Diwali or any other Cherokee, for that matter, to buy the land as cheap as it was selling to the settlers.

Andrew Jackson and other leaders were making certain that the land would not go to the Cherokee. Anyone who was left behind in the mountains was being hunted and dragged away. But Tsali had fought them. He had resisted, and the soldiers were a little more reluctant to hunt for families who hid in the hills. Just then, Walking Bird saw Lucinda. He hadn't noticed the falling snow and gusting wind. But now that he saw Lucinda wrapped tightly against the wind, he realized they were in for bad weather. He looked at the sky and turned to gesture goodbye to his friends. They lived at other shelters in the village; Salal's cabin was hidden in the mountains. He took his horse from the barn and jumped on, and rode the pony into the woods. Walking Bird knew that Salal would probably be safer than he and the other villagers.

When Walking Bird arrived at the cabin, the snow was coming down so swiftly that it was beginning to sting his face. He walked around to the back of the cabin to check their store of wood. There was plenty to last through this storm. He piled some wood in his arms and took it into the cabin. He was now sharing it with Lucinda and her grandmother. It had been his family's cabin, but most of his people had been driven elsewhere or had died in conflicts or of disease. He had a sister who lived in the village with her husband and a son. She was expecting another child soon. His sister's cabin was not far away. So, when he finished bringing in the wood for their cabin, he jogged to his sister's cabin to be certain she and her husband had enough for the winter. Big Bear was a good husband to his sister and did more than most. He was a large man with broad shoulders and strong muscles. Rumor had it that Big Bear had fought with Tsali, but it was just a rumor. Big Bear was quiet and unassuming.

When Walking Bird arrived at his sister's cabin, Big Bear was doing the same thing Walking Bird had been doing — piling wood into the cabin. Big Bear

was also tying a rope from the back of the cabin to
their outhouse and to their barn. Walking Bird waved
at Big Bear and returned to his cabin. The wind was
howling, and when Walking Bird shut the door
behind him, he noticed that the women had the fire
going in the fireplace and the cabin smelled of good,
rich food. They sat at their small table and ate the
rich stew and corn patties. When they finished,
Lucinda and her grandmother cleaned up the
wooden bowls and spoons and put them up.

There was more than one room in the little cabin.
It was larger than that of most Cherokees. Walking
Bird and his family had done well before the removal
talks. His family had been large, so his father had
built this cabin with four rooms and a loft. The
kitchen and living area were one large room, but
behind it were three bedrooms and between them a
hallway that led to the back of the house. The rooms
were small. Each had a rough-hewn door. In the loft
over the bedrooms, there was space for three more
beds — all of which had been used by his siblings.
His two sisters and two brothers were hardworking
and well-educated in the ways of the people. His
sisters cooperated with getting education from the
missionaries, but his brothers did not participate.
They hunted and fished and helped with the heavy
crop planting, but otherwise showed little interest in
the ways of the whites.

Walking Bird thought that his brothers had likely
gone far north into Canada to escape the ever-
encroaching settlers. But his older sister had died of
the grippe, and his younger sister had married Big
Bear. His parents had been caught by a group of
soldiers who had insisted that his parents had no
right to be on the land and had forced them to travel
west. His brothers had already left, and he had been
urged by his mother to hide. His sister had been

taken by Big Bear into the mountains. They'd hidden out there for quite some time until it seemed safe for them to return. When negotiations seemed to be in favor of their staying on the land that was held by Will, they ventured back, but with anxiety and fear that they would be removed.

They tried to stay ready for anything, with foodstuffs and hunting gear handy, in case they were removed suddenly from their land. Fortunately, his parents had expected something like that and had a wagon loaded with goods that was prepared for the journey. Walking Bird wondered whether he would ever see them again. It was such an uncertain time. He wanted to write his parents a letter so that they might know that they were all safe and well, but there was no way to get the letter to them. He would think of that later. Now, he wanted to retire to the room that was his parents'.

Lucinda took the room next to his, by her grandmother's request. Her grandmother took the room on the other side of the hall. Before the winter weather had set in, Walking Bird had gathered clay from the creek banks and filled all the cracks in the cabin. The hardened muck seemed to keep the cold air out. He was certain that there was more to do to the little cabin, and to the barn, but he did not want to invest any more time in improving the property until he knew whether they would be able to remain on the land.

The Qualla area had a rich assortment of wildlife and plentiful streams and rivers that were the source of good fishing. He hoped this plan of Will Thomas's resulted in their being able to stay. Other leaders were helping Thomas, but they stayed mostly in the background. Standing Bear and some of the other leaders encouraged the Cherokee in the East to help Thomas buy the land on behalf of the people. The people hoped that the negotiations would result in 60 or more families being able to stay on the 50,000 acres requested.

Walking Bird was thinking about all of this and the other questions regarding their existence in the eastern portion of Cherokee lands when he heard Lucinda open the adjoining door. He grinned as she came to him. He embraced her and they fell into the bed, exhausted from the day's work.

CHAPTER TWENTY

The next morning, the snow was so deep and so thick that Walking Bird was unable to open the door. Wooden shutters covered most of the windows. One window contained glass, a precious commodity. Walking Bird looked out that window and could see nothing but white. The snow had risen to cover much of the window, and the land was quiet and cold. The sky was gray, and it appeared that this would not be the last of the snow. Walking Bird grabbed his coat, blanket and boots and put them on. He grabbed leather mittens too. He struggled to get the door to the cabin open, but finally did and closed the door behind him so the women would stay warm.

Fortunately, the cabin had a small porch with a roof that sheltered the house from the snow. Still the door was difficult to open. He pushed the snow away from the door and grabbed a wooden shovel to clear away some of the snow from the porch. Climbing on a crude ladder, he then cleared some snow from the roof. He walked to the outhouse, took care of his needs and returned to create a path to the barn. He shoveled the snow, making a path to the barn. When he got there, he provided feed for the horses, cleaned their stalls and watered them and the other livestock.

When he returned to the house, it had begun to snow again, and he heard the women stirring inside. They had cleaned up and were preparing a morning meal. His mouth watered as he considered what they had prepared. Both women were excellent cooks. He stomped the snow from his boots and walked inside. He sat in a chair that looked out at the cold snow as it came down in heavier drifts. They put food on the table, and he got up to join them. They ate sweet potatoes and eggs, with meat grandmother had dried in the summer.

When they finished, he helped Lucinda clean up and found his flute. He began to play a haunting melody. As the snow fell, creating deeper drifts, they wrapped in their blankets and dozed before the fire. A long bench with a comfortable back and cushion made a space for the two women, and he took a cushioned chair. The women had made quilts that they shared not only with him but with other villagers. Each family member had his or her own. They were quiet as they listened to the sound of the wind and the occasional faint muttering of the horses or clucking of the chickens.

The storm lasted for more than a week, increasing in intensity and then pausing for a while. Then the wind picked up again. Trees were upended; those who did not clear their cabin roofs suffered cave-ins. Lucinda, Amadahy and Walking Bird played games when they could not get outside. They played a hiding game where each had to guess which of them had a small object. They also played a game that allowed them to pitch a small bag of beans between one another using a stick. When they tired of the games, they went out between snowfalls.

Walking Bird hunted, sometimes taking Lucinda

with him. Amadahy mostly stayed near the cabin but
dug in the woods for nuts and tubers. They gathered
what grasses they could under the thick snow to
supplement the diet of the livestock. Amadahy had
planted a substantial garden while she waited for
Lucinda and Walking Bird to settle their business of
being a couple. They thought she was hesitant to give
her approval, but she was not. She wanted Lucinda
and Walking Bird to be certain. Hard times were
ahead.

Before the snow arrived, she had harvested a great
deal of the large garden. She had squash, beans,
carrots, pumpkin and sweet potatoes. Her garden
was so prolific — since she always provided the earth
with fertilization from the livestock — that she was
able to store a great many of her root vegetables in
large barrels in the cellar of the cabin she shared with
Walking Bird. When they tired of games, she and
Lucinda went to the cellar to use the pots she had
made during the summer. Amadahy thought ahead
constantly. Though she was aware of the unease
between the whites and Cherokees over land, she
knew too that it was important for her children to
eat.

She and Sitting Deer had taught Easter to trade
with the missionaries and settlers that came through
the area where her children lived. So, of course, she
had done so herself. She went to the merchant stores
where Will Thomas sold goods and bought some of
the jars that whites sold. She exchanged baskets and
clay jars for some of them. But she held back many
of her baskets and her clay containers, knowing that
she would need to preserve some for winter.

Little did she know that it would be this difficult.
When Lucinda arrived in the dark cellar, Amadahy lit
a candle, knowing exactly where she'd put it. She
opened each of the baskets and the barrels so that

Lucinda could see the bounty she had placed there during the months that she waited for her granddaughter to arrive in the Qualla territory. Amadahy had talked to Easter about coming to the Smokey Mountains too, but Easter had her own ideas. With two men chasing her, Easter had options that she was not likely to share. But Amadahy understood. The women in her family sometimes took two men. What one man would do, the other might not do. Some of them were great hunters and fighters; some of them were good farmers. No one could say that every man was alike. Amadahy wanted Easter to have the best life possible and knew that she would find her place in the world.

"Grandmother," Lucinda said, "How did you come by all of this food?"

"I grew it while I was waiting for you to make up your mind about Walking Bird," she said.

"But I thought Walking Bird was with me only a short time and then returned to you," Lucinda said.

"No, he went to wherever his friends were. These young men, they want to fight. Walking Bird is a peaceful man, but he wanted to listen to what his friends said. He wanted to find out whether it was safe to bring you here. Everyone is so uncertain about the times. So, he went to the mountains to visit friends and to the lowlands to listen to the talk among the elders." When he had finished, considering everything he'd learned, Walking Bird came to Lucinda to encourage her to be with him.

"Why did he invite you to stay here first?" Lucinda asked.

"Because he is a smart man and had no other female from his family to prepare the way for you. He asked me to do this since I was not far from his family and had lived in his family's village for a short time as a girl. I knew people here and had always kept in touch with cousins and other relatives that I had here. So, it was natural for me to come. If I had not, there would be no food for you and Walking Bird."

The two women looked through the spacious cellar, speaking of what they could do to preserve those vegetables that might not keep through the winter. They hung some up to dry and also took dried meat from a barrel where it had been prepared for later consumption. The women took squash and beans, closed all of the containers tightly and returned to the large room where they began to prepare a stew of squash, beans and meat. Amadahy added herbs to the brew, along with onions and garlic. From the merchants she had bartered for salt. She used it sparingly and seasoned the stew. When it was ready, the three sat down to a hearty meal.

The days passed this way, Lucinda and Amadahy working on baskets and quilts and Walking Bird going out to hunt and fish when he could. Finally, the snow stopped falling, and the women wrapped themselves in layers of wool clothing and skins and went outside. Word spread quickly that day that Yonaguska had died and passed on the mantle of leadership to Will Thomas. Yonaguska had recited the traditions of the Cherokee and reminded Will of his promise to the people. The villagers grieved Yonaguska's passing. The funeral was full of ceremony. Will Thomas was considered one of the relatives. However, only the priest of the village was to go into the cabin where Yonaguska had lived. The body was washed and then taken to a burial area not far from the council house. They buried him in a traditional mound and put tokens of his accomplishments with his body: his favored bow and arrow, a rifle, a set of beads, feathers that he wore as part of his headdress, some gold trinkets and other items that demonstrated what a powerful and good leader he was.

When the burial ceremony was complete, the priest said sacred words and went to the house of Yonaguska to purify its environs with cedar. He burned all furniture and other items in the house and then purified the cabin. He made a tea for the family to drink. After that, their baths were prepared for them using herbs, and the family bathed in the herbal mixture. Following this, the relatives of Yonaguska, including, Will Thomas, Yonaguska's adopted son, were to observe seven days of mourning. They were taken to the river; they removed their clothes; their clothes were burned, and they were immersed in the river seven times. They were then given new clothing and were to engage in no bitterness or unpleasantness. Yonaguska had taken a young wife late in life; she was to mourn differently by letting her hair hang loose and by dressing poorly. After seven days of mourning, the family and relatives celebrated with food and dancing. The celebration was subdued, as many of the villagers were uncertain of what would happen as Will Thomas took leadership.

However, Yonaguska had instructed his relatives and close family members to accept Will's leadership, for this was the only way for the Qualla group to overcome the current circumstances.

Lucinda played with other women in the snow. They were passing a ball about and chasing one another. They then went to a large hall that was used as a gathering place for the villagers. Those who were nervously staying behind to see whether the purchase of land would result in the eastern Cherokees being able to stay in the area were gathered around a fire and talking quietly among themselves about the coming changes.

"I think Will Thomas can buy the land on our behalf," said Running Fox. "It is likely we will need to be prepared to claim citizenship with the government of the whites." Murmurs arose from the crowd of people. They said things like, "How could this be?" "They would not want us," "Does that mean we will no longer be Cherokee?" The idea created quite a bit of tension in the crowd. Running Fox asked for silence.

"The idea is for us to survive this time, to stay on our land. No matter what they say we are, we know in our hearts we are the Principal People. The Great Spirit watches for us as he watches for others. If we keep our traditions alive in our hearts, no one can take that away from us," Running Fox said. The women talked among themselves, murmuring that Running Fox was wise but maybe foolish too. The men scowled at him and looked away as though they did not want Running Fox to speak for the entire group. Running Fox took a deep draw on his pipe.

"This is the way it will be," he said. "Those who don't want to do this can go to the place called Oklahoma where there will be land reserved for us."

"What about the land that was stolen from us?" Henry Beaver said. "If we go to this new place, those who sold our land for a pittance, who actually stole our land from us, should die." A gasp came from some of the crowd, and the people began to talk excitedly among themselves. Running Fox was quiet for a moment to allow the crowd to settle down.

"Violence is not the answer if you go to this new place," Running Fox said. "We are faced with a reality that we must accept. Through no fault of our own, those of us who are farmers have had their land taken. But we are a strong people, a people with belief in the next generation and in the survival of our people. If we wish to keep some of the land, this is the option open to us here."

"I would prefer to stay here," said Walking Bird. "This land belongs to my family's people. It does not matter that for now it does not belong to us. But I believe my son's son will buy it back. It is not for us to give up now. The answer is to wait to see what can be done to keep what we have."

Some members of the gathered group uttered agreement; others disagreed, hotly saying they should continue to fight. But most of the Principal People knew that fighting was futile. Every day, more people were dying or disappearing, whether they were being captured by the soldiers and being forced west or killed was anyone's guess. Still, most of those at the Qualla area were certain to offer resistance, even if it meant hiding.

One day after the snow had melted and the village was quiet, soldiers rode into the encampment. They looked around, asked for food and then rode off. Lucinda was out hanging wash over branches near the woods when the soldiers returned. She watched in horror as the soldiers began dragging people from their homes and forcing them out of the village. She dropped the clothing she held and was backing away into the woods when one of the soldiers saw her and rode his horse toward her. He grabbed her around the waist and hoisted her across his horse. Her heart pounded and she lost consciousness. Before long, she felt herself thrown to the ground.

"Put this one in the wagon," the soldier said. "She's not dead, just fainted." Lucinda remained very still while someone lifted her up and threw her in a wagon among some other women and children. The wagon pulled away, and the soldiers began moving out of the village. She panicked, thinking of her grandmother and Walking Bird. Would he come for her?

Walking Bird felt something strange affect him as he was out hunting. He'd caught two rabbits and fish while he was out. When he walked into the cabin, Amadahy jumped from her chair, tears staining her cheeks.

"You must go for her," she said. He frowned and listened. "The soldiers came and took many people from the village. You must get her back."

"Why did they not take you?" he asked.

"I hid in the cellar among the barrels of goods. They did not come into the house. But they saw Lucinda hanging wash and took her."

"How long ago was she taken?" he asked.

"Not long, maybe as far as Red Clay," she twisted her hands. "You must go quickly." Walking Bird gathered up his weapons, some he kept well hidden, a knife and a long rifle. Amadahy had already prepared food for his journey. He attired himself warmly and went to his sister's cabin. She had not been taken, and Big Bear had just returned from hunting himself. Walking Bird explained what happened and Big Bear prepared to go with him.

They took off on their swift ponies and rode until dark. It was not difficult to follow the trail of the wagons and horses that took the village people. Most of those taken, Big Bear had been told by his wife, were women and children. Walking Bird thought how lacking in honor those soldiers were. They had to know that the Qualla area was full of people who would become U.S. citizens and who were being protected by Chief Will Thomas. But it would not be surprising if the soldiers had not heard or simply did not care. Their orders were to gather up as many Cherokee as they could, and they did so, sometimes without regard to negotiations or agreements.

Walking Bird and Big Bear stopped to water the horses and considered whether they should continue.

"I wish to continue," Walking Bird said. "I think the full moon will light our way. It is clear that they are taking this path to the northwest. Let us continue to track as long as we can."

They rode slowly, being careful not to lose the tracks in the moonlight, which occasionally hid behind clouds. But they were able to get within visual distance of the camp. The soldiers had lit fires and were sitting about, some on watch and some sitting about eating. Their horses were tethered in one place. Walking Bird thought how foolish they were. Did they not care for their animals? Perhaps this carelessness would be an advantage.

Lucinda knew she was headed west but stayed down as well as she could while the wagon moved over holes and bumps in the road. She wondered whether Walking Bird would come for her and immediately put that thought from her mind. He would be here. She knew it; somehow she could feel him nearby. She sat with the other women and children who had been given water and a little dried meat. They huddled together on the cold ground trying to stay warm.

One of the soldiers walked toward them, swaying as though he were drunk. He went to the edge of the woods and urinated and then walked back toward the other men. He stared at the women and focused on Lucinda. He bent down and fingered her hair and then pulled her up by one arm. He said nothing to her as he pulled her into the woods and threw her to the ground. He was on top of her before she could roll away and had her clothing pulled up. He was fumbling around when she felt a rock to her side and hit him in the head. He went limp and she rolled him off. She gasped in terror. Then she felt someone put a hand over her mouth and drag her away.

"Shhh. It's me, Walking Bird," he said. He pulled her into the brush and uncovered her mouth. Her heart pounded and she breathed deeply. "Did he hurt you?" She said nothing.

"Stay here," he said. He went back to the camp and sat near the horses. He counted five women and six children in the group that had been with Lucinda. He let the horses get accustomed to his smell and then began to untie each one. He quietly took two at a time to Big Bear, telling him that there were women and children who needed the horses.

Big Bear crawled on his belly to the women and spoke softly to each woman. They all knew him to be the gentle giant of the village and, by twos, followed him into the brush. The soldiers had been drinking, and the one soldier on guard was on the other side of the camp. When Big Bear had gotten all of the women and children to the horses where Walking Bird waited in the woods, Lucinda was waiting with him. They helped the women and children mount and cautioned everyone to be quiet. He put Lucinda on his horse in front of him. They walked the horses quietly away. There were only four soldiers. One was unconscious in the woods. When they were out of hearing of the soldiers, Walking Bird and Big Bear jumped on their ponies and rode into the night.

Walking Bird thought it was likely that the soldiers would try to come after them, but they had stolen their horses. If the soldiers arrived for their mounts, they would find the lost horses were not there. When they arrived in the village, Big Bear returned the women and children to their families and they were advised to hide in the hills until the chief could intercede. Walking Bird slapped the rear of each horse and hoped they would make their way back to their owners, but not anytime soon. Knowing that Amadahy would want to console Lucinda, Walking Bird went to his sister's cabin.

Lucinda walked into the cabin with her head down and her shoulders hunched. Her grandmother came to her and held her close, patting her head. She whispered words of encouragement as Lucinda sobbed. Finally, when Lucinda appeared to have calmed, Amadahy asked her that important question. Lucinda, in her confusion, did not know what to say. So, Amadahy prepared a cleansing bath for Lucinda. She boiled water in a large kettle and made a hip bath for her in a large wooden tub. She then prepared a sweat lodge for Lucinda near the cabin. She allowed Lucinda to wrap in blankets and wait for her to finish the work on the lodge. It had been used in the past, so Amadahy did not need to start from scratch. But she did need to place animal skins over the top of the structure and heat the stones that would be used to create the steam for the sweat.

When she was finished preparing the sweat, she went to Lucinda and guided her into the small sweat lodge. She sat with her for a while, pouring water over the hot stones to make steam and opening the animal skins from time to time. When they had remained in the sweat lodge for a time, she took Lucinda back into the cabin and put her back in the wooden tub. She washed her with another purifying herb mixture. Then she washed Lucinda's hair and sat her on some blankets near the fire to dry her hair by brushing it.

When Walking Bird came back from his sister's home, he walked to his room and closed the door quietly. Lucinda was in her room. He got undressed and went to her bed and slipped under the covers with her. He pulled her to him and he held her tight. Her tears wet his chest but he kept holding her. "You will be fine, Lucinda," he said. "I love you. Never forget that. My love for you will not change."

Dale Marie Taylor

CHAPTER TWENTY-ONE
Winter 1837

Easter woke early one morning, seven days into their occupation of the cave. She had had a nightmare about Ezra Poe and was restless and disturbed. She placed a hand on her growing middle. The child was active. She did not want to upset the child, but the journey was annoying. All of the bumps and pits in the trail seemed to upset her stomach and made her feel nauseous. Arter had warned her that since the cougar had raced past them a few days ago, it would be better to stay in the outer part of the cave. They had heard nothing of the big cat. The dogs had gone deep into the cave, exploring and seeking the cougar.

Easter was reluctant to allow Awinta to accompany the dogs, since the cougar might be protecting her cubs. However, eventually, she relaxed, remembering the values of her clan. In their creation story, Cherokee believed that the cougar was sacred. There were seven clans of the Cherokee — Paint, Wolf, Blue, Deer, Long Hair, Wild Potato and Bird. Each group was known for special talents, and clan membership was held by the female. Her maternal grandmother was of the Deer clan; they were known for being messengers. Her paternal grandmother was of the Wolf and Bird clans; strong on protection, self-sacrifice and interpretation of dreams. They had other clan connections through the years, but Easter thought about the Wolf clan to which her friend, Ninovan had been born. Ninovan had been sympathetic to the cougar or wildcat. She and Ninovan spent time together before the burdens of farming became too demanding.

Ninovan invited Easter to her family's cabin one sunny winter day. They sat around the fire as Ninovan's grandmother told the story of creation. It went something like this: "Someone created the earth. No one knows who. Maybe it was the eagles or the great vultures." Ninovan's grandmother stopped to add sound effects and motions to suggest what happened when the earth was created. She rattled beads and waved feathers as she talked. Ninovan's eight sisters and brothers all sat still, entranced by their grandmother. "All the animals were told that they were to stay awake for seven days. But of all the animals, only the cougar and the owl were awake when the seven days were up. All of the other animals feel asleep. And that is why the owl and the cougar are our sacred friends."

Easter thought back to that day wistfully. She snuggled up to Arter to keep warm. Her feelings for Arter were deepening, perhaps into love. The dogs were barking. But it was a playful bark. No urgency seemed to be expressed. She rose and walked to the wagon to see if Awinta was there. She was not. She walked back to Arter and touched his shoulder. His eyes sprang open, and he sat up suddenly.

"Awinta is not here," she said. "She has gone back into the cave with the dogs." He lay back down and exhaled, then sat up.

"Can you hear her?" he asked. "I can. She is singing. If she were in trouble, I don't think she would sing."

"Maybe that is why she is singing," Easter said.

Arter arose from his bed of furs and blankets and grabbed his long rifle. He motioned for Easter to remain behind him and walked softly into the depth of the cave. He allowed his eyes to adjust to the light. There below them was a pool of water that had sparkling lights coming from it. They were surprised to see bits of light trickling through holes in the cave walls. The effect of the water and the light seemed to make it sparkle. They followed a path down to the inviting water and saw Awinta swimming.

"Awinta," Easter said. "You know how to swim."

"Of course," the girl said, pushing across the water. "The water is warm here. Come join me."

"What about the cat?" Easter asked.

"It has not come out," Awinta said. "I think it is hiding. It might be afraid of the dogs."

"No, if it wanted to come out, it would," Arter said.

Ama and Waya were sitting sentinel at the other end of the pool. Every now and then the two would look up into the dark recesses of the cave. Water dripped in many places. Perhaps the dogs smelled or saw the cougar. Neither seemed overly concerned.

"I could use a bath," Easter said. Arter agreed to watch her and Awinta while they bathed and then Easter would guard while Arter bathed. It took a while for Easter to get out of the warm water. She marveled at how magnificent it was to have a warm spring in a cave on a cold winter's day. She wanted to leave the cave and thought that soon they would be getting back to their travels.

As she swam to Awinta, she felt the baby kick and smiled. She let Awinta feel the baby; the child was active. Her sister grinned. She turned to look at Arter and told him. He smiled warmly as she neared to let him feel the baby's kick. Awinta climbed out and used a cloth Easter had brought. Awinta changed into clean undergarments and walked back to the front of the cave with Ama.

"Do you think it will be a boy?" Arter asked.

"No, it will be a girl," Easter said.

"Why do you think this?"

"She is very active and sitting high. She can only be a girl since you boys are so lazy." She laughed, splashed water in his face and took off to the other end of the pool. When she got out, she dried off and dressed in clean clothes. Then it was Arter's turn.

She sat near the pool with his long rifle. When Arter finished, he dressed and they walked back to the front of the cave with Waya. They looked out of the cave entrance. The snow was melting, and the sun was out. It would be muddy in some places, but they could leave soon.

Arter took the horses out to graze first and then the cows. The dogs went out with him to protect the cattle. When the animals were watered and had grazed enough from areas that had melted snow, Arter brought them back to the cave, but he left Poe's horse near the stream. He went back to the stream and slapped the stallion on its flanks. It took off like a frightened rabbit, running deep into the woods. Arter nodded to himself. Tomorrow they would leave.

That night, Easter dreamed fitfully. First, images of Ezra Poe kept invading her thoughts. She twisted and turned. Arter woke when she groaned in agony. He put an arm over her and brought her to him. She settled down for a while. Then she dreamed of the cougar. It spoke to her, sharing its fear and concern. "I must feed my children," the cougar said. She had babies and wanted to get out of the cave so she could hunt. It was time for them to go, to leave the cougar in peace. When Easter woke the next morning, she knew there would be no further delay.

The day was sunny, and the earth was quickly drying out. It was cold, but there was plenty of water. Arter prepared the horses and cattle for their departure. They replenished their supply of water from the cave and checked their stores. They had not used much of their stored goods. Easter had quite a bit left of the harvest she'd brought with them. The two sisters wrapped up tightly, and they continued their journey. As they traveled, Arter occasionally dismounted to help the horses pull one wagon or another from the mud. Their journey to the Giles area was uneventful, but full of the sights and sound of wildlife. At one point, Arter and Easter thought they might have passed an area where the Cherokees were being driven west to Oklahoma. The trail was torn up; the vegetation was stripped bare. There was not much in the way of grazing, so they kept going west toward the land where Arter's friend Joe Rhea had promised they could settle.

It took them three days of further travel up and down steep hills and over streams before they arrived at the little town of Pulaski, where settlers looked strangely at them and considered whether they should get their weapons. Arter steered them to the merchant's store where he knew he would find Joe. He left Awinta and Easter in the wagon, but they quickly got down and let the blood flow back into their nether parts. Easter stretched and smoothed Awinta's hair while Arter walked into the store. John McNabb, Joe's partner, stood behind the counter of the little store.

"What can I do for you?" McNabb asked.

"I'm looking for Joe Rhea," Arter said. "He and I are good friends. He . . ." Just then, Joe walked in from behind the store and stared at Arter, then he walked quickly toward him.

"Arter?" Joe asked. "Is that you?" Arter laughed.

"Unless you know another Arter, it's me," Arter said.

"I expected you days ago," Joe said.

"The snow storm," Arter said. "Plus we had a little trouble on the way." Arter looked down. Arter wasn't going to say he had to kill a man, but he was certain it was in self-defense and he couldn't turn the hands of time back to get rid of the problem in a different way. The man had intended to hurt Easter. He knew that she suffered nightmares from the incident but he did not lose a night's sleep over it.

"Of the animal or human variety?" Joe asked, chuckling.

"Both," Arter huffed. McNabb walked to the back of the store to give the two men time together.

"Have you come a long distance?" Joe asked.

"From the Red Clay area," Arter said. Joe whistled.

"Long way," he said. "You're ready to get off the road, I reckon."

Arter nodded. They walked out the front door. When Joe saw Easter and Awinta, he looked at Arter as though to ask if Arter knew what he was doing. Arter had written that he was bringing his woman, but he did not say he was bringing an Indian woman. But Joe, himself had had Icho, and his family were known for not wanting to exploit people. They believed in not poisoning the Indians with spirits or with bad habits. It appeared that the woman and child could easily blend in. Arter introduced them.

"Would you like to see your cabin?" Joe asked Easter, noting that she was pregnant. She nodded, but didn't say anything. Joe went to the back to get his mount, and they headed out of town. They wound their way through hills and up and down small mountains to get to the area where Joe owned property. Easter looked sadly at the area. She would have inherited this land if things had been different. Because this land was part of the lands that settlers wanted, her family had to forfeit it. There was no way to prove that these were ancestral lands. She gave herself a mental shake and came back to the present. When they arrived where Joe said they could occupy a cabin, she let Arter help her down. Her back ached, and her buttocks were sore. She was ready to bring this journey to an end.

The cabin was to the north of the road. Tall trees, seemly standing sentinel over the people who lived there, surrounded the area. Many of the trees were bare of leaves. But some thrived in spite of the cold. To the west, someone had cleared the land, and the fields were being worked by blacks and a few whites. Easter squinted to try to see who they were, but they were too far away. Someone looked up and waved.

Joe, Arter, Easter and Awinta walked up to the little porch and went inside. The cabin was more spacious than Easter had imagined. From the outside it looked small, but the cabin reached into the woods. Windows, an unusual luxury, were throughout the cabin. The rough-hewn floors were solid, with a braided rug on the floor of the first room.

The first room was for cooking and for eating and receiving guests. There was a small table there. But Easter knew that she'd have another made. There were crude frames for beds that allowed for some straw ticking.

Another small table with a large washing bowl sat on the opposite side of the room on a small table. A hip tub was in the corner. There were two bedrooms, one on the left, the other on the right. A loft served as extra sleeping area. Small tables were in the

bedrooms. Each table had a small kerosene lamp. A
third large room in the back of the cabin appeared to
be a workroom. It opened into a clearing behind the
cabin. A barn was in back of the cabin. It appeared
large enough to accommodate the livestock. A
closed-in pasture was available for the animals. An
outhouse was some distance from the little cottage.
Easter was pleased with the space.

"There is space for you to have a small garden, if
you wish," Joe said. "The other tenants are preparing
the fields for planting, but they will be in come
sundown and will introduce themselves. Of course,
there is no need to pay anything for it. You can pay
for it with any labor you contribute to the farm.
There are three families of blacks living here. The
Bufords belonged to my wife's family and have been
passed on to me. I have told them that they will not
be required to stay. Some have left, but most have
remained on the property. We plan to sell the land to
those who can afford it as time passes."

"Will we be required to share this space with
anyone?" Easter asked.

"No, not at this time, but if the need arises, I hope
you will be generous," Joe said. "It will likely be
temporary if someone needs the space. I am usually
informed regarding the needs of the tenants as they
go along. Everyone is mostly self-sufficient, since my
family is not wealthy. Hunting is permitted on the
property, which includes about five square miles. I'll
have one of the men show you, Arter." Arter nodded
as he looked out the window of the cabin. He looked
worn out from the long trip.

"Thank you, Joe," Arter said. "I'm certain we'll be
comfortable here." He did not refer to Easter as his
wife or define anything else about their relationship
as it might be necessary to change their circumstances. Awinta came in from outside, smiling as

though she had discovered a secret. Joe frowned slightly and then smiled at the dark-skinned girl. He was likely trying to figure out her relationship to Easter and Arter.

"I found a spring," Awinta said. "The horses are ready for a drink." Arter smiled at her.

"So they are, Awinta," Arter said. He shook hands with Joe and promised to visit in town after they were settled. With that, Joe Rhea walked out of the little cabin, which he seemed to dwarf. He was more than six feet, with broad shoulders — a large man. Arter watched as Joe put a foot in the stirrup and sat in the saddle. The horse moved a bit as Joe found his seat.

"There's a well not far from the cabin," Joe said. "And one of our family homes is just up the road. If you need anything, don't hesitate to call on us. Introduce yourselves to the other families here. You'll find they're a friendly lot." He tipped his hat at Easter and rode away.

Arter led the horses with the wagons behind to the barn and then unhooked them from their traces. Awinta helped him get a few of the chicken cages in the barn. Then, he led the horses to water, following Awinta as she led the way to the stream. Arter allowed the horses to drink; Ama, Waya and Awinta stayed with the horses and mules while he returned for the goats, cows and other creatures. He then unloaded Lucinda's precious birds into the barn. He was pleased to see how clean the barn was. He then began to unload the wagons. There were barrels and boxes of goods. He placed planks against the edge of the wagon, with its gate lowered, and rolled the barrels down the planks. Then he rolled each one to its place in the barn. He took a break, spotting the well near the cabin. He noticed that there were about five other cabins a distance away. It seemed that Joe had made certain that each family had adequate space for raising animals and growing food. Arter walked to the well and lowered a bucket. The water he brought up was clean, cold and sweet. He took a long drink and went back to unloading the wagons. Easter had brought a great deal of produce that was still good and would help them survive winter in their new home.

Easter came out to the barn to help Arter. They moved sacks of corn, beans, potatoes, squash, onions and assorted other vegetables. At some point, Arter stopped her. "The baby," he said, looking at her growing middle. Easter took light boxes of dining and cooking ware into the cabin and began planning a meal. She heated a large pan of water in a fireplace that included a crane with hooks on it. She marveled at this. Someone in this compound was a blacksmith and knew how to create convenient tools for cooking. She gathered some of the produce from the barn and killed a chicken for dinner. She wanted to be certain they had enough to last through the winter, so she was careful to allow her hens to hatch some of the chicks. For now, she had plenty. She plucked the chicken and cut it up. She then used it to make a dish that included squash, onions and other vegetables. She made bread with flour she'd bartered for before leaving the old compound.

Arter, after having brushed down the horses and cows and settled them in the barn, brought in more fresh water. Awinta had helped him take care of the animals and was excited when she walked in with Arter. She peered longingly at the large kettle of food made by Easter.

"Looks like you're a little hungry," Easter said, looking at Awinta. Awinta smiled and licked her lips. She stood there away from the table as though she was not certain whether she was invited to sit down.

"Go wash your hands in that bowl," Easter said to both Arter and Awinta. They readily complied and dried their hands on a towel near the bowl. Arter sat down at the small table and hit his knees on the underside of it. The chairs were comfortable, but the table seemed as though it was made for a child. Easter thought she could probably find a better solution. She began to think about the possibility of having a table made that would accommodate her new family. She ladled the food into large bowls and sat three on the table. Awinta still held back. Easter turned to look at the child. She realized then that the girl might not have been invited at some other places. She knew her father would certainly have Awinta at his table if his wife allowed it. She knew her mother would not have objected, even if she were annoyed with her husband for taking Awinta's mother. Still, the girl should be assured that she was family.

"Awinta," she said softly. "Your place is with us. You are my sister." She pointed to the chair. Awinta looked at Easter then at Arter, swallowed and then slowly approached the table. Easter thought back to the times they ate on the trail. Each time, Awinta seemed to eat apart from her and Arter. She had not thought of it before.

"Awinta," Easter said. "Tell us about your mother." It took a few minutes for Awinta to respond. She ate quickly and with relish. She seemed grateful for the meal and expressed her appreciation. Awinta could cook, but she was not as good as Easter. She swallowed her last bite, drank a little water and wiped her mouth with a cloth Easter had given her.

"My mother was Inola, or Black Fox, as they called her. She was a good mother; she was very beautiful. She liked to sing to me and tell me stories before time to sleep. She cooked too. When she cooked, people liked to join us. Her food was very good. Everyone thinks she ran away or lost her mind, but I know what happened to her."

Easter tensed and held her breath. She knew that women were especially vulnerable while the removal was occurring, but just what happened to Inola was unclear. Could Awinta have witnessed something violent that happened to her mother? Arter placed a hand over Easter's and shook his head slightly to let her know to relax and not make this any more traumatic for the girl.

"We were out gathering some of her plants for the meal that day when a man came riding up," Awinta whispered. "We were a distance from the village in the woods, so no one heard us when my mother screamed. She saw the man before he came upon us and told me to hide in the hollow of a tree. She ran and ran. I looked out and saw the man pick her up and take her on his horse. She fought him. I think she bit him because he slapped her and knocked her from his horse. She got up and began running again, away from me. Then he caught her again. This time, he did not let her go. I have not seen her since."

Easter and Arter were quiet for some time. They looked at one another. Easter's eyes were full, brimming with tears. Easter had met Inola a few times and had friendly conversations with her. Easter was aware that her mother was cordial, but not friendly, with Inola, but that did not mean that the two women did not care about one another. She was lost in thought as she watched Arter get up to give a second helping to Awinta. She wiped away her tears quickly so that Awinta could not see. She took a deep breath and plastered a smile on her face. It was tremulous.

"We will send word out through our brothers and sister that we wish to know what happened to her,"

Easter said. "Perhaps we will learn something of her soon."

"I think she is on her way back," Awinta said confidently. "I had a dream that she was calling to me and looking for me. I am certain she will find us." Easter smiled at Awinta and offered her sister a hug. The child got up from her chair and stepped into Easter's embrace. Easter thought, Awinta has the gift of dreams too.

"We will find her," Easter whispered as she held Awinta. "We will find her."

The community of blacks who lived on the Rhea property was large. The black residents had prospered in their limited ways. Anderson and Margaret lived in the cabin not far from Arter and Easter. Margaret was slim and dark-skinned, while Anderson was heavy-set and lighter than his petite wife. They came knocking Saturday evening. Not much field work was required in winter. Margaret held a pie and smiled genially when Easter opened the door.

"Good evening," Anderson said. "We're your neighbors down the way. Wanted to come by to say hello and welcome you to the neighborhood." Anderson dressed in overalls and a sweater. Easter was surprised that both husband and wife were nicely attired. She smiled and welcomed them. There were only the dining chairs. But Anderson said he had brought a welcome gift. Easter had not noticed. She followed Anderson to the door as he went out and picked up a bench that had an attractive back to it. Easter covered her mouth in surprise. The man had made a gift for them without meeting them. Arter placed an arm around her shoulders, and they backed up to let Anderson in with the bench.

"If you don't like it, we can certainly take it away," Anderson said. "I make furniture for people round these parts and can easily give it to someone else." There was a moment of silence as Easter ran a hand over the back of the bench where Anderson had carved intricate patterns of swirls, petals, flowers and other designs. He used small crosses and suns as well. It seemed his design was hinting at nature but also Cherokee values.

"Thank you," Easter said. "Thank you so much. This is beautiful, Mr. Anderson. How ever did you know we needed this?"

"Just Anderson, m'am. The cabin has been empty for some time," he said. "It was used by another couple, but the man died, and the woman remarried someone on the other side of town. She took most of her furnishings with her. Her husband had made them for her. We helped her load her furniture in a wagon, and I drove her across the valley. So, I pretty much knew what was here and what wasn't. Hope you don't mind."

"Of course not," Easter said. "Again, this is too generous of you. Can we pay you for it?"

"I'd be insulted to take a penny," Anderson said. "It's a gift." Anderson put out his hand, and Easter and Arter shook it warmly. They then invited the couple to sit on the new bench, and Easter went about making tea for the visitors. She had some bean bread that went well with the tea.

"Does everyone work sun up to sun down six days a week?" Arter asked.

"Not always," Anderson said. "The Rheas are good people. They're religious folk and don't believe in bondage. They allow us to work out a schedule that fits us and we work our own plots in between. It all works out. We plant seeds in the spring and help harvest the crops in the fall, and they leave us alone between planting and harvesting. In the winter, we tend the fields for pests and care for the earth. But in our free time, we can do what needs to be done at our own homesteads. We call the place Apple Hill."

Easter was stunned silent for a moment. This was similar to the way many Cherokee treated their slaves. Slaves were treated as equals in many clans. She was surprised that there were whites who were not believers in extreme exploitation of captives.

"How did they come by the people living here?" Easter asked.

"Some of us were owned by Matthew Rhea's wife's family, the Bufords," Margaret said. "She wanted to hold us, sell some of us, but Matthew would not hear of it. He granted some of us our freedom — those of us who were not legally owned by someone else in his wife's family."

"Why did you stay?" Easter asked.

"Some of us did not stay," Margaret said. "I have a brother who left. He'd been used badly by the Buford family. But my two sisters are still here. I have two half brothers who remained here too."

"The treatment is good?" Easter asked. Both Margaret and Anderson laughed.

"We wouldn't say it's good," Anderson said. "It's better than some people have it. We stay for the promise of owning the land we work some day, and because it could be worse elsewhere. We get plenty to eat, make our own clothing, furniture and such and trade with one another in this little community. No one is beaten. There are problems with outsiders from time to time, but we cope with it."

Easter thought that "coping" with the circumstances of the people who lived there probably meant hiding someone who was being subjected to abusive behavior. But she didn't say anything about that. She smiled. It could be worse. Maybe she could stay here.

"I traded at my village," Easter said. "I know it's not unusual to do that, but we lived at a junction where people passed by all the time."

"We get a little traffic up here in the hills from time to time," Anderson said. Easter shrank back in the little chair. If there were soldiers looking for Cherokee fugitives, she might be taken from this place.

"Are you Cherokee?" Anderson asked. Easter looked at Arter and then down at her lap. Awinta came in just then. She nodded to the company and Easter introduced her.

"This is my sister, Awinta," she said, without further explanation. The couple greeted the little girl and left the question unanswered. Anderson and Margaret knew full well that the Cherokee were being driven to reservations in the West. Easter was a refugee. They would not sell her out. The test of that community loyalty would come sooner than Easter thought.

Easter helped Arter repair fences near the fields. There wasn't much to do yet as it was winter still. She felt the baby move occasionally. It was a girl; she sat high and small within Easter. The earth was being turned and enriched. Arter had been given tasks by Anderson, who served as an informal foreman. Arter worked in the west fields for most of the morning. In the evening, he worked at making a bed for Easter's baby, who was fast getting ready to make its appearance. He made other items that would be useful, a rattle, a table to use for the baby's belongings and care, a small tub for bathing the baby and small toys. Midday, Easter brought him food, and they returned to their own plot to prepare their own large garden for cultivation. The days passed peacefully, with Easter and Arter tending the animals in their barn, feeding them and taking them out to pasture. As February arrived, the weather fluctuated, mild some days and freezing with snow at others. They had put up food, and Arter had gone hunting and fishing to round out their diet. Awinta helped by snaring a few rabbits.

Late one evening, they had new visitors, Elizabeth and Jethro Smith. Elizabeth wore a bright blue wool dress, and Jethro wore a gray wool shirt and pantaloons. They were smartly put together. Jethro was tall and dark as the bark of the oak tree. Elizabeth was light like the leaves of turning ash trees. Both had the glow of health and were pleasant and welcoming. They had white teeth and well-groomed hair. Their smiles were warm and friendly.

"Welcome to the neighborhood," Jethro said in greeting. Elizabeth beamed at Easter.

"Yes, we've been looking forward to meeting you. Anderson and Margaret said you were all settled in and doing well. We wanted to welcome you too. Elizabeth held out a bundle of wool fabric in bright blue colors. Easter gasped.

"Oh," she said. "This is so beautiful. Thank you. Come in. Come in." It was a cold winter day. Easter wondered if they had trouble getting to the cabin as there was snow on the road. They had a horse and little wagon that they tied to the hitching post. Easter had a pot of hot water and tea in clay pots. She made the tea, added a little honey on request from Elizabeth and sat down to visit.

"We wanted you to know that there is no reason to fear being here," Elizabeth said. "We all look out for one another around here," she said, taking a sip of her tea.

"Yes," Jethro said. "We have ways of letting each other know what's going on around here. So, if you want to stay safe, it's important to stay in touch. We ring a bell that serves as a warning. Four loud rings means there are strangers that are a threat — danger. There is a whole system. You have a bell on your porch too; we'll teach you the various rings. We make it a habit." Arter and Easter looked at one another in surprise and smiled, giving their attention back to the couple.

Elizabeth also held up a cloth bag that had baked goods in it. Easter's cabin had a brick oven, but she had not used it for baking. Easter thanked Elizabeth for the baked goods. She still did not comment on her status. She realized that Elizabeth and Jethro were trying to be friendly, but it made her nervous that so many knew her secret.

"I like to bake and share some of my goods with people around here," Elizabeth said. "I also make cloth; it's something of a community project. All the women join in to help."

"How do you do that?" Easter asked.

"I have a spinning wheel and a loom. I think Mabel might have left one of each in your loft. The man she married had his own. People in town send away for their fabric or get it from the town's general store. But we don't always have the means to do that. So we make our own clothing."

"Where do you get the wool or cotton?" Easter asked.

"Different farmers have excess. We have one among us, Caleb, who raises sheep. He works for a farmer, but does so well that the farmer gives him a portion of the wool from the sheep. Sheep do well here, but there are predators, other hands have to watch them. Caleb cuts the wool for the farmer, and we are given a portion for our use. He spreads it around in return for goods we can trade. We live too far out in the country to get fabric from the general store, and it is too expensive for us. So we make our own. A couple of families have their own sheep too."

Easter was beginning to understand that the little community was self-contained. The people exchanged food, raw materials for clothing, made their own furniture and handled their own smithing. Everyone had a purpose, and no one was undervalued. She wondered whether the people in the community might accept her own trades. This was a little different from her Cherokee village but not by much. People worked together at her village. The difference here seemed to be that the men and women worked together in the fields. Whereas, in her village, the women took care of the fields, and the men hunted for game.

"I've been taught how to use the spinning wheel and loom," Easter said. "But it has been a long time since I've tried it."

"Oh, I'd be happy to help you with that," Elizabeth said, grinning. "You can come to my place, or we can see what you have here. I see you have a workroom where you can set out your supplies and your equipment. Let's see what Mabel left you in the hayloft." The two women walked out to the barn, exchanging pleasantries and sharing recipes. The horses, cows and goats were put up for the day and were happily munching on hay. The animals turned their heads to look at the two women. Easter gave them an affectionate pat as she passed by. When they came to the ladder leading to the loft, Easter went up first, holding her skirts out of the way.

"I don't remember seeing anything up here," Easter said. "So I would be surprised. But I admit I didn't' look carefully." Elizabeth climbed up behind her, clutching her skirts in one hand. She pointed to the corner where there was fabric and wood covering a spinning wheel and a loom. Easter walked over to the items and lifted the fabric.

"I didn't realize this was here," she said. "I guess I was so busy trying to get everything organized that I did not notice it." Elizabeth helped her uncover the wooden devices, and they began to dust them off with an old cloth they found in the hayloft.

"These are in excellent shape," Elizabeth said. "I suppose we can review the use of them and then you can help us if you want."

"On my farm, I mostly concentrated on planting and harvesting," Easter said. "I'd trade since I was so near places where people needed goods. But we had some merchants who were able to get cloth from Virginia too. I'd like to help if you could use it."

"Good. We'll start with the basics, and later, I'll bring over some wool for you to work into thread for making cloth. It takes us about a year to make what we need but working together makes the work go quicker. We try to work on it in the winter since by spring we're needed to help with seeding, tending the crops and then harvesting. In between, we get together to make cloth. Sometimes the cloth becomes so popular that it is sought by women in town. So don't be surprised if you get some sales as we continue. Do you sew?"

"Of course," Easter said. "Once I have the fabric, I can make anything we need. I'll add to our store of clothing." Elizabeth smiled.

"You'll fit right in," Elizabeth said. Arter lowered the wheel and loom from the loft and moved it to the workroom in the cabin. The women got to work on the spinning wheel and the loom. Elizabeth demonstrated some of the methods for using the spinning wheel and loom by using some old wool that had been left in the corner of the barn's loft. She spoke of carding the wool, cleaning it, stretching it and feeding it into the spindle to twist it into thread. Then she demonstrated the weaving process. It all began to come back to Easter. These were skills taught to her by the missionaries. The missionary women did this work with determination and skill.

"We've done our dying of the wool already, so we can bring some to you if you want to work on the loom," Elizabeth said.

"I'd like to do that," Easter said. The two women promised to be in touch."

The next day, Jethro dropped off a bunch of wool and some clay containers with preserved fruit and other goods. Easter in turn sent Elizabeth some of her dried corn and beans. Easter went to work that day, having Arter bring the spinning wheel and loom into the back room of the cabin where she got to work. The back room and the other rooms were furnished with crude but functional fireplaces. The weather got cold up in the hills. Easter added her blanket to her attire and worked for several hours. When she looked up, it was getting dark and she had nothing prepared for a meal. She rushed into the kitchen to find that Arter had prepared a meal. He grinned at her.

"I thought you could use a hand," he said. "Also, it's Christmas" This was unusual. Her brothers and father never prepared a meal unless it was something that they made while out hunting. They normally did not observe Christmas either. Arter gave her and Awinta small trinkets. She smiled at his generosity.

"I suppose you have hidden talents," she said. He invited her to sit down, and Awinta followed her. He served up their bowls, and Easter's brows rose in surprise. Arter's food was excellent. She grinned. Later, she and Awinta gave him mittens and sweets.

Dale Marie Taylor

CHAPTER TWENTY-TWO
Winter 1837

The snow came again and again, keeping everyone inside and preventing the workers from adding fertilizer to the soil in preparation for the spring planting. It was cold, the wind blew fiercely and Arter went out several times to be certain the animals were well nourished. He had cut dried grass before the snow fell, being careful to select the right kind so that the horses and cattle would not get colic. Arter also cut plenty of firewood each day. Now there was a large pile by the back door. He came in the back door, the wind blowing snow inside with a gust of freezing air. He stomped his feet on the back landing to get the snow off. Easter shivered. She was using the loom to make cloth. He stood there for a while and watched her quick hands.

"Where did you learn to do this?" he asked.

"The missionaries taught us," she said. "They wanted to help us continue to embrace Western ways. Of course, we had long given up our skins by trading for cloth, but the mission schools thought it was important for the women to learn skills that would help them adapt better."

"What else did you learn?" he asked.

"A great deal of Bible lessons," she said,

chuckling. "And various ways to cook in the manner of the whites. Some of it was useful, baking and such. We did not do so much of that in our village. But we also learned simple ciphering, reading in English. We learned about civilizations in other parts of the world too. Some of them wanted to help us understand what was happening to us and why some many Europeans were coming to our land." Her hands flew over the loom, threading the wooden needle through the threads, using the pedals, harnesses and bringing the wooden frame down with a thwack. The fabric was turning into a beautiful lavender mosaic-like piece with symbols and shapes. Arter marveled at her skill. But he felt she must be working too hard.

"When you get a chance, after this snow blows over, let's take a walk," he said. "There is so much to explore here, and we should know where we are and get familiar with the territory." She nodded in agreement.

A few days later, the snow stopped falling and the sun came out bright and intense. The snow began to melt, and the ground began to dry out. Arter and Easter wrapped up some bean bread in a kerchief and told Awinta to stay near the house to care for the animals while they were gone. She really didn't need to be told. They knew that she understood the dangers of straying.

They walked far up a trail that skirted a shelf of rocks and boulders. The land rose and fell as they followed the trail deep into the woods. They found a pond not far from the Rhea's homestead. They kept walking until they ran into thick woods. Arter carried his long gun in case they encountered any hostile animals, and Easter carried her knife. However, all was quiet as they walked along, deeper into the woods.

"We're traveling north," Arter said. "I think I see some structures to the west of here. Shall we investigate?" Easter nodded, and they went off the trail to see what was hidden deep in the woods. Easter noticed some movement and saw a young boy running toward a small cabin. Arter rested his weapon against a tree and approached the boy. He noticed the boy was actually a teenager. He was thin, but had a healthy look to him.

"We mean you no harm," Arter said in English. The boy looked at him as though he understood nothing. Then Easter spoke to him in Cherokee. The boy's eyes brightened and he spoke to Easter in his language.

"Are you here alone?" she asked.

"No," the boy said. "My grandmother is here with me. She is too old to go anywhere so I take care of her."

"What is your name?" she asked.

"Atsadi," he said. She nodded, saying to Arter that the boy's name was Fish.

"Can we meet your grandmother?" she asked.

Atsadi hesitated, watching cautiously and looking between Easter and Arter.

"We mean no harm," Easter repeated in her language. The boy led them slowly into the cabin where an old woman sat in a chair. She was wrapped in a blanket. The boy had lit a fire in a crude fireplace and on the grill a large fish was cooking. He also had tubers he'd dug from the earth cooking in the fire. The woman tried to stand but could not. Easter rushed to her and motioned to her not to rise from her chair. She introduced herself and Arter to the woman, whose name was Star. The old woman welcomed them to share her meager fare. They sat on the floor cross-legged as there were no other chairs in the one-room cabin. The old woman offered a story to the visitors and her grandson.

Star began the story of the wolves and the rabbit. "One day the rabbit was surrounded by the wolves. The rabbit said to them, 'If you will dance with me, I will show you something special.' The wolves agreed, and the rabbit began to dance. The rabbit said, 'Now, when I dance to the right, stamp your feet. When I dance to the left, stamp your feet hard.' So the rabbit began to dance to the right and to the left. When the rabbit neared a field, the wolves stamped their feet. When the rabbit was near enough to the field, he ran into the woods. The wolves were after him right away. The rabbit ran into the hollow of a tree, and one of the wolves stuck his head inside. The rabbit spit in the wolf's eye. The others were afraid to come after him, and the rabbit got away."

Atsadi grinned. He said something low and quiet to his grandmother and walked out of the cabin. It appeared Star had an arsenal of stories she told her grandson. "How did you come to be here alone?" Easter asked. Star drank her tea.

"Our village was rounded up and marched west, but we escaped because we were away at the time. When my grandson and I saw what was happening, we hid in the woods and ran as far as we could. We found this cabin and have been hiding for many moons. Easter took a deep breath. Arter understood what was being said but allowed Easter to speak for them both.

"We are living not far from here on the road west," Easter said.

"You will want to be careful there," Star said. "The soldiers have been known to come through here looking for us. Be certain to hide when they come. There is no need to bring trouble to yourself." Easter nodded in agreement. Easter and Arter shared their bean cakes and other food with the boy and woman and promised to return later with more food. They continued their walk and on the way home saw a large oak tree. They stopped under it for a while to rest. Easter placed her hands on the bark of the oak and looked into its branches. It was thick and had several large branches. She asked if she could borrow its bounty. Assured that the oak agreed, she looked at Arter, who was staring out into the distance.

"This is it," she said.

"What?"

"This is the tree I wish you to use to make a table for me," Easter said. "A large table that has the wisdom of this magnificent tree." He smiled at her and looked around to mark where the tree was.

"I will begin tomorrow," he said. "If I'm careful, the tree will not suffer." They continued on their return and eventually found a trail that led them back toward their cabin.

When they arrived at their cabin there was a surprise. John Hester was there. His sable mustang was tied to the hitching post.

Arter winced inwardly when he saw his half brother sitting on the front porch. The man was like a grass burr in his boot. Awinta opened the door to the cabin and looked out. She'd stayed nearby as she was told, but had not come out to visit with John. She had met him long ago but did not remember him.

"So brother," Arter said. "What brings you our way and how did you find us?"

"Easter told me where you would be," John said, getting up from his squatting position on the porch. It was no big mystery. You can't hide from someone who is as good a tracker as I am." He laughed and pounded Arter on the back. Arter inhaled and looked back at Easter. This was going to be a test of his patience. He knew that Easter and John had been married. But he was

hoping he would not need to share her. His brother
swaggered as he walked his horse to the barn where he
watered and fed the animal and then brushed him down.
When John returned from the barn, Arter invited him
inside and shut the door. Arter's rage was simmering
beneath the surface.

CHAPTER TWENTY-THREE

Degataga and his wife, Ruth, lived in a large house near Coosawattee Village that was once owned by his parents. The house was part of a large compound that included farmland, slaves, cows, horses, goats, sheep, and chickens. The land was rich for planting. But there was so much of it that the areas that included silver and gold mines were some distance away. Degataga's parents had been descendants of warriors and that had made it possible for them to claim land in the many conflicts the Cherokee had had with other tribes. They were a proud family and had spread their wealth and goods among the children and among those who worked for them. They were generous in their rewards. When his parents died, Degataga had promised his mother that he would find a way to save the property. His mother and his father died of the flu. But he thought it was likely their spirits were broken because of the encroachment of settlers. Still, his parents were optimistic when it came to their children. They urged each of them to take advantage of the education offered by the missionaries. However, they were cautious too.

When it was apparent that their holdings were being chipped away, little by little, Degataga's parents sent their children to various parts of their property to hold the land. They thought that possession of the land would prove their rights to it. But possession did not always prove strong enough to keep the land. The family had papers that proved to the courts that they legally owned the land. This was one of the arguments used against the Ward family to take what was theirs. First, it was the land where there were gold and silver mines. Then, slowly, it was the land where the best crops were cultivated. Degataga knew that things would get worse. However, he was powerless to stop it. His father was friends with Chief John Ross and appealed to him to help. But even Ross could not keep his assets. In the end, every Cherokee who could be driven away, was.

Degataga met Ruth when they were youngsters; her father was a missionary, and her brother was a businessman. They played together as children, but when they came of age, their parents prevented Ruth from visiting his family so often. Degataga saw her at a village dance one summer evening, and her beauty nearly took his breath away. She was slim and short, but her auburn hair shone in the light of the outdoor gathering. Her waist was so small that he could span it with one hand. Her brown eyes sparkled with mischief. She loved to play practical jokes on him and his brothers when they were children. Once, she gathered a sack of frogs and when he and his brothers were swimming in a nearby pond, she put the frogs in their pants. Another time, they were swimming at the same pond, and she hid their clothes. The boys were not shy about walking around without clothing, but the villagers laughed at them for letting Ruth play tricks on them.

She was full of humor and enjoyed playing with them when she could escape the critical eyes of her father. Her mother had died from the complications of childbirth when Ruth was a baby. Her father devoted his time to serving the needs of his daughter and son, the missionaries and the Cherokees. He was a selfless man who did not believe in drink — no surprise there. But he did believe in education. He insisted that his daughter and son be educated and sent Ruth back east to a fancy school. When she came home, she joined her father in educating the people around Coosawattee Village. Her brother, Charles Stevens, much to the disappointment of his father, was not interested in becoming a missionary. Instead, he became a railroad investor. Though the family appeared to have little in the way of wealth, Charles had inherited money from one of his uncles and used it to invest and to create opportunities in this land that was full of possibilities for development. He was gone for long periods but was devoted to his sister.

Charles came to Coosawattee Village from Baltimore after plans for a South Carolina railroad had been established. His father had died, and he had come to Coosawattee Village to put their affairs in order. When the sad details of his father's death were put to rest, Charles turned his attention to his sister. Unfortunately, it had taken a little over four months to put everything in order. He was sitting in the room his father used as a study when his sister knocked. He stood to greet her and offered her a seat.

"Charles, I know that this is a bad time to broach the subject," Ruth said. "Father was not one to discuss such things. But I know he would not have objected."

"Yes, he would," Charles said. "Don't fool yourself, Ruth. You know as well as I do that Father cared what people thought. Times are such that there is much prejudice against the Indians." Ruth and Degataga had been friends for some time; she had hinted.

"There is another thing I wish you to consider, Charles," she said. "Would you buy Degataga's family land?"

Charles rubbed his jaw, frowned and put down his quill. She was asking him to invest. He was dressed in a fitted dark coat with tails, vest, dark pantaloons and calf-high leather boots. He was surprised that Ruth had not left by now. Many Cherokees and missionaries were being urged to move on. He had heard that Degataga's family land might have silver or gold on it. It might make for a good investment. Still, with the politics of removing the Indians, he was hesitant to leave his sister here.

"Why do you want to stay here, Ruth? This is not a good time for a white woman to be in love with a Cherokee man. This is something you must face." There was a moment of silence between them. Ruth was dressed in the black of mourning. It would be a year before she stopped wearing her mourning clothes. Still she wanted to ask this of Charles because time was running out. Degataga had been told that he must leave his land and his mother and father's home. She had to convince Charles to do this for her.

"I understand this, Charles," she said. "But I do not want anything else for my life. I have always loved Degataga since we were young. I have waited for the right time. He has waited too. He is not aware that I am asking you to do this. In fact, he would be insulted if he knew that I was asking you. I think he is trying to hold onto the land in as many ways as he can think of without help from anyone. But, Charles, I want Degataga to marry me and for his family's land to remain his — if not now, at least in the future. Surely things will not be hostile toward the Cherokee, for that matter all Indians, forever." Charles exhaled and ran a hand down his face. He got up from his chair and walked to a window where he paced back and forth, looking down and thinking.

"It will go hard on you, Ruth," he said. "What if there are children? They will be considered half-breeds. Do you want that?"

"The child of a good family will not be affected by such evil language, Charles," she said. "All children are God's children and that's all that matters. I know that this is a sensitive subject for you." She fidgeted with the folds of her dress as she waited for his response. Charles himself had fallen in love with a woman whose Boston parents were very wealthy. They had not approved of Charles because his family did not have the wealth or social standing that they wanted their daughter to have. He was miserable when he had to give Priscilla up. Priscilla herself was devastated. He hated that he had caused her such grief. He did not want his sister to suffer so.

He looked out the window of their father's home and pondered the circumstances. There were more cases of white men marrying Indian women than the opposite. He had a good friend who was an attorney. He would speak to his friend, Daniel, about this. Daniel was not far away and had a family who was settling in the area. They had become friends when they were children. When Daniel went back east for an education, so did Charles.

"Let me think about this," he said. "I need to consult a friend of mine who knows the law." Ruth looked crestfallen but agreed to wait for her brother to find out more about the circumstances. Later that night, he knocked on her door and asked her to join him in the parlor.

"I have spoken to Daniel," Charles said. "Daniel suggests two things to make your lives easier. He says that Degataga should make haste to become a U.S. citizen. That may not be possible here, but we will go to a different state to take care of that. Also, you will need to marry him elsewhere. We can handle that at the same time he becomes a citizen. It does not mean that he gives up his citizenship in the Cherokee Nation. But the issue is unclear as yet.

"Before those things happen, I will purchase his land and make it possible for your descendants to inherit it. I will also set aside some of it to remain in his name secretly. We should try to change his name and be certain his appearance is as Western as possible. He has one thing working in his favor and that is his light skin. With that, he will be able to do these things that will make it possible for you to live together. I would suggest that the two of you not make it apparent that you are married or that you live together."

"But Charles," she said, exasperated by his seemingly rigid approach to their problem, "I don't wish to hide. That is not the way our Lord would behave." Charles shook his head.

"I appreciate your understanding and adherence to our faith," Charles said. "But we must face facts. Things are quite unstable now. I have spoken to Daniel about this, and he has agreed to seek out people who will be sympathetic to your cause, God-fearing people who are sincere in their efforts to do no harm to the Cherokee people."

Before the plan could be put to work, Ruth had to invite Degataga to her home. When he arrived, she invited him in the parlor. He was dressed similarly to Charles — black pantaloons, a vest and coat. He wore riding boots as well. His hair was cut short and styled in the way of a European man. Degataga's black, tall, top hat gave his 6-foot height added inches. He carried a pipe that he hid away when in her presence. When he walked into the parlor, she was there waiting for him. She twisted her hands nervously and invited him to sit. He gave her a polite hug and bussed her cheeks. The fireplace crackled with a newly lit fire, warming a cool fall day. It was sparsely furnished with modest Victorian pieces.

"Degataga, I've invited you here for an unusual request," she sat down on the parlor sofa, and in the manner of Western men, he sat after her. They had seen one another secretly for more than a year but had decided that their affection might cause complications.

"I have spoken to my brother about your land and your family's issues," she said, waiting to see whether he wanted to intercede. "He has. . . he has offered to. . . Well, first things first. Degataga, do you think you might consider marriage?"

"Marriage," he said. "That is the right of every Cherokee man. I have not considered taking a wife from the Cherokee Nation. It would not be wise at this time." She suspected that he knew very well what she was suggesting but was teasing her. Her lips twitched in an effort to keep from laughing. She sat for a moment. The clock that sat on the fireplace mantel clicked loudly in the room.

"What I mean by that ... what I mean is, would you consider marrying *me?*" There was silence in the room. His warm brown eyes stared into hers. He smiled and stood, walking to the window and looking out. He turned suddenly.

"And what does your brother have to say about this?"

"Degataga, first I want to know. Do you love me? Do you want to share a life with me?"

"Of course," he said. "Of course, I love you. But we have had many quiet discussions about this, Ruth." She stood and walked to him. He turned to be certain the curtains on the window were closed and stood away from it. He embraced her and pulled her tightly to him. He lowered his mouth to her lips and kissed her, first tenderly and then, eagerly. She returned his affection. When they parted, both were panting.

"I think we'd better stop while we can," he said quietly. He adjusted his clothing.

"I know that this is not a good time," Ruth said. "But we can't give up on what we have. I can't. Can you?" He looked down and then peered into her eyes. His eyes narrowed.

"Do you realize what this will mean?" he asked. "Life is likely to be difficult for us. It will not be simple. There will be many challenges."

She nodded her head in agreement. Ruth had given

the idea much thought. She considered who she could trust among her friends to hide her secret and who she could trust among Degataga's friends. Her love for Degataga far outweighed the risks they were taking. She was willing to live through the difficult times in relative obscurity. She knew it meant not making her relationship with Degataga obvious, but she could hardly consider doing otherwise. She loved him so much her heart hurt.

"I know love is not the only answer," she said. "But I do love you so much. I would rather live my life with caution as your wife than live without you." He held her again, stroking her hair and running his hands down her back. She trembled in his arms. She whispered, "Your people will be my people."

"I feel the same for you. Gvgeyu, I love you. We will have hard times ahead, but this too will pass," he said.

That was the beginning of their journey to become husband and wife. Charles helped Degataga become a U.S. citizen. They went elsewhere to do that. Degataga's name became Degan. And he married Ruth in a brief ceremony witnessed by Charles and his friend Daniel. When Degataga and Ruth returned home, it was clear that they would live on his family's land. Charles arranged for the sale of her father's home. It was a modest home so it did not garner much in the way of profit. But they were able to use the money to take care of problems with the Ward family land.

When Ruth found that she was pregnant some months after the wedding, they both celebrated quietly. Degataga's land was not part of the main town of Spring Place, where his parents had lost one of their many holdings, so they were hidden without trying. People who remained with the farm were sworn to secrecy. Degataga picked them carefully. Slaves were set free; those who wanted to remain worked for wages. Degataga left the financial end of the farm business to Ruth and Charles. So when the crops were negotiated for sale during the fall harvest, Charles made it a point to be in the vicinity to act as a sort of proctor. When they needed to negotiate a price for livestock or for land, Charles asked for Degataga's recommendation and the price was agreed.

Degataga hated that he had to remain mostly out of sight — not obviously the owner of his family's property. But with the child that was his and Ruth's the land would come to their firstborn. The child would be a citizen of both the Cherokee Nation and the United States.

When he and Ruth married in the Cherokee tradition, his grandmother, Amadahy, made the trip from her family land to Coosawattee Village to perform the ceremony. It was to be a quiet affair.

The family celebrated with dignity but only allowed those who could be trusted to keep their secret. Now, many months later, with his family scattered abut the country — Lucinda in the Smokey Mountains of North Carolina, Easter in Middle Tennesee, and Wahali headed for Oklahoma — keeping the land for them as well seemed futile. But, he tried to look ahead, not back.

He thought of the silly pigeons Lucinda had trained to fly to her in North Carolina and went to one of his barns to see how they were doing.

Four of his dogs were milling around. He sent Koko and Nanye to guard the sheep along with his other farm dogs. Outa and Yansa usually stayed near him. They had followed him to the barn and were looking curiously at the birds, wagging their tales as though they might enjoy a snack.

Outa and Yansa were his companions when he was in the fields and going about his work. They were close to him, two large dogs that enjoyed the outdoors. They followed him everywhere. Yansa barked as though he had sensed some animal or person in the area who should not be there. Outa took off running as though he were chasing something. Degataga peered into the distance and checked around, but found nothing.

He wrote to his sisters, Lucinda and Easter, as time went by, but he didn't know whether they received his letters. They all had easily learned to write in the new alphabet of the Cherokee people that Sequoyah had developed. So, it was only a matter of putting pen to paper to stay in touch. There were some Cherokee who could be relied upon to take letters from one village to another. But with so many being pressed into removal, Degataga wasn't certain that he could find a reliable delivery rider.

Degataga believed that the ghosts of his parents still lingered on the farm. As he went about his daily chores, he noticed evidence of their presence. Or perhaps it was one of the little people who the Cherokee believe inhabited this world too. One day, he was in the barn checking the hooves of the cows, and the door to the doves' cage kept opening. The doves were sitting back well away from the cage door. He went to the doves' cage and closed it. He walked over to the cow whose hooves he was tending. He dug into the hoof, removing pebbles that were stuck and making certain the cow was not hobbled. The dove cage popped open again. This time, it made a loud clanking noise. Degataga looked up from his work with the cow and stared at the cage. He walked over to it and closed it again. He stood there for a moment and watched the cage to be sure that it wasn't a malfunction. He pushed on it a few times to make certain the latch was secure. When he was certain it was, he walked to one of the goats and began to check its health.

He was walking to the horses to brush them down when the door to the dove cage popped open again. He sighed. Someone must be trying to communicate with me, he thought. This cage continues to open. Maybe it is a sign that I should use those silly doves that Lucinda trained. He sighed again and stood before the cage. He reached inside and placed a hand gently over one of the doves. The one with white and grey streaks seemed calm and strong. He placed it in a small box and walked over to a small table in the corner of the barn where there was a bit of parchment. He sat down and wrote a brief note, using the Cherokee alphabet, to Lucinda. "Things are fine here. Ruth will have the baby soon. Farm doing well. Write of news about Easter and Wahali please. Degataga." He fastened the note around the bird's leg as Lucinda had shown him and walked out of the barn. He hung his head for a moment.

"This is silly," he said out loud. But he held up his hands and opened them so that the dove could fly. It seemed stunned for a moment that it was being offered its freedom. But it stood, fluffed its feathers and took off toward North Carolina.

"Well, I'll be," Degataga whispered. He would believe Lucinda had something of a good system worked out if he received a message back from her soon. He went back into the barn and noticed that the doves' cage door was closed. He shook his head and laughed. His mother and father or the little people were likely letting him know that it was time to check with his siblings.

CHAPTER TWENTY-FOUR

Fall 1837

Ruth managed to handle the finances of the farm while Degataga managed the day-to-day running of it. They had more than 5,000 acres, which they used to grow corn, peas, hay, cotton, and peanuts. They also kept several chicken houses, where they harvested eggs and sold some of the chickens, especially in winter when the meat could be frozen. They also raised some sheep, which they used for wool. With the promise of a railroad coming soon, there might be an opportunity to expand the market for their crops. Ruth wondered whether Degataga would agree that this would be a good decision.

The house on Degataga's family farm had five bedrooms — three upstairs and two downstairs. The kitchen was large and had conveniences in it that her father would never have spent money to obtain. The water was pumped straight into the kitchen using a well pump.

Water was collected at the back of the house in a large cistern. The outhouses were far enough away as to not smell up the house. Several outbuildings had been used to house slaves and workers. Ruth's father did not approve of slaves, and neither did she or her brother,

Charles. Degataga had long given the slaves their freedom. The freed workers who remained by choice were paid in crops and housing.

There were four large barns where Degataga kept hens, sheep, horses and cows. Her father would not approve of Ruth taking such an active role in running the farm, but she did it not only for Degataga but for the child they would soon have. She touched her large belly. It would be soon now. She was nine months pregnant and had been waiting patiently for the child to come, but it seemed to want to take its time. She could not see her ankles or bend over without toppling. She wished that Easter or her sister Lucinda could be here to help her with the birth. Both women were competent at those things that women did when it was time for children to be born. Ruth was friends with Sarah, who was close to Easter. Sarah had come to visit her several times since Easter left. Sarah's husband had bought Easter's small farm. Easter probably did not get what the farm was worth, but many people were selling out, rather than risk having their land taken. The Cherokee Nation was supposed to have paid people for the land through the money that was given it, but many people received nothing.

Sarah was certain that Easter had arrived at her new home safely. Lucinda had received a note from Easter using one of the birds that she had trained to fly back to her at Walking Bird's village. From there, Lucinda sent a letter by some traveling settlers. That was some consolation. It had been a long day. Though she felt better when she stayed off her feet, Ruth wanted to be certain everything was ready. The baby's room included a small rocking bed, a table with towels and cloth diapers. Sarah had tatted a small gown for the child. Lucinda had made several gowns and sent them to Ruth.

The farm's ample supply of cotton made it possible for Ruth to make diapers, sleeping and day gowns for the child. She knitted socks. She'd made clothes as soon as she found that she was pregnant. Four of the other missionary women who remained in the area also made clothes for the baby and gave them as gifts. Ruth had invited them over for tea one afternoon, and they had surprised her with baby clothes, homemade rattles, small balls, carved animals, baby lotion and such, and an assortment of other toys that the child could use later in life. They all knew her secret, but no one dared speak a word of it. They knew her husband was Degataga. But they also knew how dangerous it was to speak of it. So each woman held tight to the secret.

Ruth had walked out to the nearest barn to check on the eggs and was pleased to see that one of the workers had placed several within easy reach. She put some in a basket and was returning to the house when her stomach cramped and she bent over with a sharp pain. Then, she felt water dripping down her legs. She lifted her gown slightly and saw that her ankles were wet. Realizing that things could proceed quickly, she called one of the hands to ask whether Viola could come to help her. Viola had worked for the Ward family for some time. She was an experienced midwife and knew exactly what to do. Ruth walked around the house a few times to see whether the baby was coming fast or slow. It seemed that she would be lucky. The baby was eager to arrive.

Viola was milking one of the cows in the barn some distance from the house when Ely came to get her. Viola knew why she was being called and ran to her little cabin to get what tools she had gathered in a small bag. She took off at a fast walk toward the house where Degataga lived with Ruth. Viola had brought each of the Ward children into the world. She was clever and had a good sense for what was prudent when it came to caring for people. Some said she was better than a doctor. But she never wanted that to get out. Viola's dark brown skin was smooth and unwrinkled. She was much older than people assumed because she took good care of herself and never let a day go by without doing something healthy. Unlike some of the other hands, she ate only vegetables, eggs, fish and bread that she could make herself. She remembered some of the old recipes her family had passed down to her of peanut-butter soup with spinach.

When she arrived at the house, Viola walked straight to Ruth's bedroom and set up her tools. She had sparkling clean scissors, cloths and a pulling tool. She hoped she didn't have to use the pulling tool as it sometimes made the baby's head look misshapen. Ruth was lying on the bed that had been covered with cloth. Ruth had stripped it and covered it with straw and then with layers of cloth. She wanted her new mattress not to get spoiled. Viola marveled at the way Ruth thought. The girl had asked for as much spare cotton as she could get and used it and wool combed from the sheep to make fluffy mattresses. Viola had been sleeping on straw for as long as she could remember. But Ruth was always thinking of some way to make their lives better. When Ruth had figured out how to make mattresses, she had had one made for everyone on the property. The problem with that was that the new mattress made Viola sneeze so violently that she had to hide it away and pretend gratitude.

"How are you doing, Miss Ruth?" Viola asked. Viola called her that though Ruth had asked her time and again to call her simply "Ruth." Ruth sat up in the bed and put several pillows behind her.

"I think this baby wants to come right away," she said. "I thought the baby was going to take its time coming, but I think. . ." She stopped to wince and push. Her brow began to sweat. Viola had called her niece to help. She pointed to the table nearby and asked Nelly to bring it near.

"Go boil some water and clean your hands first.

Bring it up and place it at the back of this table. Pour some in three bowls there. We'll use it to clean the things we'll need. While you're down there, tell Jeremiah to go find Mr. Dega. And tell him to hurry." The people on his farm called him Mr. Dega for short. Nelly nodded and rushed off to do as her aunt asked. Nelly wanted to learn everything her aunt knew about healing and birthing, so she was eager to get the water boiled so she could return to see what was happening next.

"Let's see what we have here," Viola said, pulling up the hem of Ruth's dress. Ruth had removed her underthings and pulled the dress up in the back so that it would not get soiled.

"I think we can take this off," Viola said, removing Ruth's dress. Ruth had on just a chemise. Viola could see that Ruth was clearly aware of where she was in the birthing process. Viola could see much of the baby's head. She helped Ruth get in a better position to push at the end of the bed, fixing pillows and what not so that Ruth could scoot down to use a birthing chair. It had a hole in it so you could catch the baby and required squatting if need be. But it didn't appear that Ruth would need any additional assistance. She was pushing again, and the baby's head was coming out. Just then, Nelly returned with the boiling water, poured it in one of the bowls on the table. Nelly put the instruments in it. She used another bowl for washing her hands. Viola got up calmly from her seat at the end of Ruth's bed and washed her hands in a bowl of hot water too. Both women dried their hands on a cloth and returned to Ruth. Nelly began to place the instruments on the little table beside her aunt — scissors, and a tool for pulling the baby out. Nelly looked nervously at her aunt.

"Light more candles, Nelly," Viola said. "We need to see better." No sooner than that was done but that the baby's head was out, but it was turned oddly. Viola could see that the baby was in trouble; the umbilical cord was wrapped around the baby's neck. Viola gently pulled the cord away and unwrapped it. The baby was blue. She hoped that it would begin to breath, but it was not breathing yet.

"Ahhhhh," Ruth screamed as she gave another mighty push. The baby came rushing out in all its squishy glory — bloody and wet. Viola went to work on the baby. She cleaned out its mouth and then, pinching its nose, breathed gently into its mouth. The baby coughed and hacked and gasped. Then he let out a loud cry. Viola smiled. She had Nelly hold the baby while she massaged Ruth's stomach to encourage the placenta to come out. When it came seconds later, Viola cut the umbilical cord with the clean scissors and then tied the cord off at both ends. Nelly and Viola used a soft cloth to clean the baby off. Then they wrapped it in a soft cloth and then a blanket. They laid the baby in Ruth's arms.

"It's a boy," Ruth whispered.

"Don't be disappointed, Miss Ruth," Viola said.

"Oh, I'm fine with it," Ruth said, beaming. She opened the blanket and examined the baby's toes and fingers. "He's perfect." Just then, Degataga stood at the door. All three women turned to look at him.

"Is she all right?" he asked of Ruth. "Is the baby?"

"Come look, Degataga," Ruth said. He stepped slowly and quietly into the room. Viola and Nelly began cleaning up their tools. Viola motioned to Nelly to dump the water and return the bag of tools to her cabin.

"Come back here when you're finished," Viola said. "We'll take turns watching the baby so Miss Ruth can rest."

"No need," Degataga said. "I can watch him." He quietly pulled a cot into the room so that he could be near both mother and baby. Viola looked at Nelly and shrugged. They both grinned and gathered everything so they could leave the family to bond.

Later that day, Degataga released another dove from
Lucinda's batch of messengers. He marveled at the way
his sister's mind worked. The woman was not the oldest
or even the cleverest. You were deemed to be so if you
could hunt, fish, plant crops and get a good yield. Did
Lucinda do these things? No. The girl spent too much
time dreaming. But this time, he was glad she did.
Because Lucinda planned ahead and spent time thinking
about ways to keep the family in touch with one another,
they could all write letters and also have the advantage of
the dove express. He grinned as he thought about it. He
had gone to the south side of the farm to check on a bull
that had taken a dislike to one of his workers. The bull
had gotten tangled up in some fencing in his effort to
separate the worker from his harem of cows. Degataga
had helped repair the damaged fence, but had been
forced to get out of the bull's way by jumping over the
fence himself. It wouldn't do to get in the bull's way.

Degataga thought about the dove he'd released and
wondered if Lucinda could get it to come back to him.
No, he thought. She had spent time training them but
had not figured that part out yet. He decided to cut
through the pasture and take a shortcut through the
woods to get to the house quicker when he saw two
white men wandering on his property. He tried to hide
and then outrun them, but they were clever and quick.

"Well, well, lookie what we have here," the one with
black teeth said. "One of them injuns got away. Been
hiding out here on somebody's property, have ya, boy,"
Black Teeth said.

"I live here," Degataga said. "I'm a U.S. citizen."

"Them northern folks might not recognize an injun
when they see him, but I do," Black Teeth said, grinning.
The other one, who looked to be a teenage boy, looked
nervously at his friend and licked his lips. He seemed
reluctant to join in his friend's bullying.

"Look now, Jesse," he said. "I ain't gonna help you

267

do nothin bad to nobody, injun or not," the boy said. "I was just along for finding some food. I ain't interested." With that the boy turned and fled.

Degataga thought this evened things up a bit. He took a chance and punched Black Teeth in the stomach. Black Teeth stumbled and landed on the branch of a tree but he jumped up quicker than Degataga expected. He hit Degataga in the head. Degataga could not see clearly.

When Degataga's vision cleared, he was standing on the stump of a dead tree, his hands tied, and a rope was around his neck. Black Teeth had pulled the rope taut around Degataga's neck, and he was standing on his toes, trying not to fall. He thought about his new son, Bali. He wanted his son to get to know him. He wanted to teach him to hunt, to swim, to provide for his family. It looked like he wasn't going to do any of that. He stood there as still as he could knowing that Black Teeth was nearby, engaging in his insane machinations. He could smell Black Teeth. The man did not bathe. But this was no time to consider the man's poor qualities. He had to think of a way to survive this. He had to distract Black Teeth to buy some time. The opportunity came sooner than he thought. Black Teeth grinned at him, a large tree branch in his hand, which he used to poke at the unstable stump.

"Any last words?" Black Teeth asked, jumping up and down as though he were a crazed fice.

"Yes," Degataga said. "I only regret burying that money I found yesterday." Black Teeth dropped the large tree branch and stared at Degataga, mouth agape and head tilted. Then he showed off his black teeth again with a huge grin.

Ely was passing by the south pasture when he saw Mr. Dega take a shortcut through the woods. That wasn't odd. But he wished Mr. Dega hadn't done that. Rumor was there were a couple of ne'er-do-wells hanging around these parts, and he did not want Mr. Dega to tangle with them. He followed Degataga into the woods and saw the confrontation with the two men. Then he saw Mr. Dega go down, and the man string him up with a rope. Ely was not much of a fighter, and the man who had attacked Mr. Dega looked big. Ely ran to get help.

Degataga heard Outa and Yansa growling. He was certain if he said where the money was buried, Black Teeth would kick the stump from under him. Black Teeth looked around for the dogs but did not see them. Black Teeth stood near Degataga and was about to push the stump over when he was attacked by the two dogs. Black Teeth fell to the ground. Jeremiah arrived at that moment, having been alerted by Ely that Degataga was in trouble in the woods. Jeremiah lifted the rope from Degataga's neck, untied his hands and helped him down from the stump. They both looked at Black Teeth, who was screaming and trying to hold the dogs off. He was attempting to scramble up a tree when Yansa took a bite of Black Teeth's leg. Blood spurted from the man's calf as he screamed but was able to get further up the tree.

"You all right, Mr. Dega?" Jeremiah asked. Degataga nodded, but he was having trouble seeing. Jeremiah helped get him to the house, deciding that he'd come back for Black Teeth after getting Degataga to safety.

Ruth was visiting with Charles so he could spend time with the baby. Charles was proud of his little nephew. Since it was unlikely he would ever have children of his own, he was grateful that Degataga and Ruth were prolific. The child was large: nine pounds. How such a little woman had given such quick birth to this healthy baby, Charles did not know. Ruth handed him his nephew, and he was walking the floor with the little fellow when Ely came into the house, out of breath and looking frantic.

"Mr. Charles, Mr. Dega. Someone got him strung up," Ely said. "They got him in the woods." Charles hurried over to his sister who had grown pale.

"Stay here with Bali, Ruth," Charles said, handing her the baby. "I'll take care of this." Charles ran to his room on the first floor and grabbed a handgun. It only fired one shot, so he had to make it count. Ely ran, leading him into the woods. He motioned for Charles to slow down and be quiet. When they reached a small clearing the sight before him made his heart squeeze. A large white man was treed by Degataga's dog, Yansa. Charles saw Jeremiah helping Degataga get to the house and told Jeremiah he'd help Degataga get home. Jeremiah turned back to deal with Black Teeth.

Black Teeth continued laughing though he was clearly hurt. Jeremiah looked at Black Teeth and shook his head. The man was clearly insane. Jeremiah called off the dogs.

Charles helped get Degataga into the back of the house and called for Viola's help. He was certain Degataga had some kind of head injury. He asked Viola not to alert Ruth until she could get Degataga cleaned up a bit. Charles sent Ely to the village to get the constable. Charles rushed back to the woods to see whether he could subdue Black Teeth. When he got there, Black Teeth was lying on the ground, motionless. Jeremiah was gone, and the dogs were panting. He could see no other evidence of injury on the man, other than the large bite delivered by one or both of the dogs. He scratched his head and looked around. Could Jeremiah have killed the man? No, Jeremiah would not do that.

The constable met him half way to town. Charles told most of the story. However, when he explained, he said the man was harassing his workers when he stumbled and fell, hitting his head and doing himself in. He mentioned that his dogs bit the man. Since Charles had a good deal of credibility, no one questioned his version of events and there was no more said about it.

When Degataga walked into the parlor, Ruth was pacing the floor with Bali in her arms. The baby was fussy and had been crying. Degataga stood there for a moment taking in the sight of her. His heart swelled with love for them both. If it hadn't been for Charles, Jeremiah and Ely, he would not be able to embrace his wife, hold his child. She looked up at him from the corner of the room.

"Dega," she said, with tears in her eyes. "Dega." She ran to him, and he embraced them both. Bali settled down immediately. Degataga took Bali from Ruth and kissed his forehead. He held the boy in the crook of his left arm and encircled his wife with the other. She sobbed into his shoulder. He walked her over to the sofa and they sat down. She hiccupped as she tried to catch her breath.

"What happened?" she asked, touching the rope burn on his neck. "Who did this?" Degataga took a deep breath and looked down at his son. The baby was sleeping. He walked over to the baby's crib and placed him on his back. The child had beds all over the house. He bent over again and kissed his son on the forehead. He covered Bali with a light blanket and walked quietly over to Ruth.

"Let's try to stay quiet so that Bali will sleep," he said. He took her hand in his and looked her in the eye.

"First, let me say how very much I love you," he said. "If the worst had come about, I would expect you to carry on without me. I would want you to take care of Bali and this farm so that Bali has something when he becomes a man." He paused to kiss her deeply. He pulled back and wiped the tears from her eyes with his thumbs.

"There were two of them," he said, whispering. She gasped and held a hand to her chest. Her eyes brimmed again with tears. "They caught me cutting through that patch of woods that is on our property. One of them ran off, but the other one decided to fight. I fought back and leveled him. But he surprised me with a blow from behind. When I woke, I was incapacitated. I'm not going to tell you more than that. The man was insane. But there are lots around here. Let me say this, my love. My thoughts were at every moment on you and Bali. I wanted to survive because I knew you and Bali needed me. I stopped resenting the circumstances that caused your brother to have to buy the farm for us. Instead, I began to consider all that was good in my life." He pulled her to him and kissed her deeply again. His kisses were desperate. Ruth could feel herself responding to him. When he pulled away, she could see what was in his heart. They took the baby to his room and then snuggled together, hugging one another close.

Bali gibbered and made noises with his mouth that morning. He was quietly playing with some of the hanging toys in his crib. Degataga heard him first and rose to take care of his son. He changed him and picked him up. Ruth stirred in their bed, so he took Bali to her to breastfeed.

When Bali was sated, Degataga kissed his wife and scooped up his son again. He carried the boy around the upstairs of the house. Soon, Bali seemed to want a nap. So Degataga changed him and sat down in a rocking chair. He began quietly to tell his son a story.

His grandmother, Haialeah, had told him and his siblings stories, but each time she told the stories, the stories changed. He wanted Bali to know who he was through the stories that were told to him.

This one was about the importance of cooperation and walking in the shoes of another. He began quietly: "There was a green hunter who could not find deer," he said. "He searched and searched but the deer could not be found. A vulture came to him and said, 'I can fly up high in the sky and see where the deer are. We should change places.' So the vulture took the form of a man, and the man took the form of a vulture. The vulture went home to the man's wife, and the man flew high in the sky and saw where all the deer were hiding. When the vulture returned, he said, 'Did you find the deer you needed?' The man in the form of the vulture said, 'Yes, thank you. I found many deer. The man showed the vulture where he was eating some of his catch. 'We should change back,' the vulture said. So the man became his human form and the vulture as a man became a vulture again. Four days later, the vulture was pierced with an arrow from a white hunter; the green hunter removed the arrow and helped the vulture heal. " Degataga placed his son back in his bed and went to his room to slide between the covers with his wife.

Dale Marie Taylor

CHAPTER TWENTY-FIVE
Winter 1838

Easter cooked a welcoming meal for John Hester. It did not escape her notice that the brothers were at odds with one another. John had made it clear that he still had feelings for Easter. He had given her a warm hug and kissed her tenderly in front of his brother. John pulled back from her with his arms still around her and touched her growing belly. "Mine?" he asked. She did not answer, but walked away from him and continued tending the food. She stirred the large pot over the fire without looking at either brother. Arter glared at John but did nothing. Awinta had gone to her room but when she came back she looked at the three adults as though she were trying to figure out what was going on among them. She ate quickly and went out to check on the goats, one of which was about to give birth. "Let me know when her time is near," Easter said to Awinta. "I will come help you." Easter put wooden bowls and spoons on the table and served the food.

"So, you found a place to call home," John said, looking at Easter. "Do you plan to stay here for the rest of your life, or will you go west to the reservation?"

"I heard that many people suffered on the trail," Arter said. "Why would I want to take Easter there? There is nothing for her there."

"I asked Easter, not you," John said. Arter balled his fists and looked away. He was close to exploding. Easter wanted to escape.

"I have been made welcome here," she said. "This land was in my mother's family, so I plan to stay here for the time being."

"And what will you do if the soldiers come to take you away?" John asked. Arter stood up so fast that he knocked over the chair he was sitting on.

"That's enough, John," Arter said. "You are welcome to stay here as long as you don't say things to upset Easter."

"I only asked about her plans," John said. "It seems to me she will want to be prepared."

"She's staying here with me," Arter said.

"As a Negro?" John asked. Arter grabbed his brother by the shirt and drug him out of the cabin. John was so surprised he did not have time to react. But as soon as they were outside, John had recovered his wits and was ready for the punch Arter threw. John shook his head and ran a hand over his jaw. John stepped into Arter and swung his fist into Arter's jaw. The force of the blow knocked Arter back a few steps. Easter was standing at the door, anxiously watching. She shouted at them to stop a few times, but they ignored her. Awinta, having heard the grunts and shouting, came out of the barn to watch.

Arter grew angrier by the minute. He took a run at John and used his shoulder to knock the wind out of him. The two landed on the ground and rolled around, getting on top of each other and swinging their fists in turn. When Easter had had enough, she went to the well, drew some water in the bucket and walked it to the fighting men. She threw it on them and stood back. "I said, 'Stop!'" she shouted. "If you don't, neither of you will ever sit at my table." That got their attention. They both stood, staggering to get their balance. John walked to the well. Arter grabbed the well bucket from Easter and walked to the well to draw water up. They both rinsed the dirt and muck from their clothing, faces and hands and sat on a bench outside the house.

"See what you did?" Arter said. "Now she's angry at both of us."

"I didn't do this," John shouted. "You started it."

"I meant what I said," Easter said. "You can talk all you want, but I will have no fighting around here." Both men looked contrite. "Now, I want you to shake hands in the white way and apologize," she said. They grumbled resentful apologies, shook hands and stood. Later, they followed Easter into the cabin. Awinta went back into the barn.

Easter prepared a bed for John in the loft. He looked at her when she did that as though he wanted to say something about sharing her bed, but she shook her head. "No," she said. John sighed. He remembered how soft and loving Easter could be, but he knew she could also be hard when she wanted. He knew that if he pushed her too much, she would find a way to retaliate. Her version of retaliation could be painful.

He recalled when they had lived together as man and wife. He had enjoyed her warmth and her cooking for many days. But he did not listen to her when she said things were changing between the Cherokee men and women. The western ways were influencing the way they lived their lives. She expected him to do more than hunt and fish. John was a man who loved the outdoors. He was not interested in farming. But that was all Easter wanted to do. She could hunt if she wanted to, but she preferred to plant vegetables and fruit. He enjoyed her cooking and appreciated it, but he was a meat eater and did not mind spending hours outdoors to find it.

The last argument they had was about how much time he spent hunting and fishing. He was a good hunter, and brought home everything he caught. But Easter argued that she needed help on the farm.

"I need your help, John," she had said. "Why is that so hard to understand? There are some things that are overwhelming."

"I don't plan to be a farmer," he had said. "I hunt. I fish. I protect you. I'm a descendant of warriors, not a farmer."

"Warrior," she said. "The fighting has been over a long time, and you know it. You've been listening to the elders talk of concessions for years now. There is nothing more we can do."

John hung his head and looked down, then up at her. "There is something we can do," he had said, grinning at her. He had enveloped her in his arms and they made passionate love that night. Loving her was always a way to take her mind off things. That was when they were a couple. But now, he was contending with his brother for Easter. Could they share? It would be up to her.

After Easter broke up the fight, she went first to the barn to see how Awinta was coming with the goat. The barn smelled of hay and droppings, but the odor was not strong, as Arter had kept the barn clean. Easter's eyes adjusted to the dim light, and she walked over to Awinta, who sat on the floor of one of the stalls with the goat who was pushing out her kid. The goat struggled and struggled, but finally the little one came out. The mother licked and chewed at her baby, and then Easter and Awinta went to work cleaning up the kid.

"She's a fine little goat," Easter said. "She will bring more goats into the world. She is strong. Look how she stands so fast. She is ready to feed." The two let the kid suckle her mother. Awinta looked up at Easter.

"Why were they fighting?" Awinta asked.

"They are both stubborn," Easter said. She missed her sister, Lucinda, and wondered whether her sister had received the message she'd sent with those doves. Easter had written of their safe arrival in Giles County and of her wish to find Inola, Awinta's mother. She wondered whether anything would come of their efforts.

"But there is no one to blame. They are brothers, and sometimes brothers fight. You will see one day. Sometime men fight over the silliest things." Awinta looked toward the cabin.

"Do you think they will always fight?"

"No," Easter said. "Arter is outraged. He thinks he owns me. But I belong to no one." Easter and Awinta sat down on a bench behind the cabin. It was cold outside, but warm enough to enjoy the evening sun. Arter had found a piece of wood and fashioned a swing out of some rope for Awinta. Easter pointed to the swing and asked Awinta if she wanted a push. Easter gave her sister's swing a gentle push every now and then as they listened to the gentle rustling of the wind and the sound of a hawk in the distance.

"That reminds me of a story my grandmother told me," Easter said. She let a moment pass, collecting her memories. "The hummingbird and the crane were in love with the same woman. She preferred the attractive hummingbird over the awkward crane, but nothing could be settled. Finally, they decided there would be a race between the crane and the hummingbird. The one who won the race would be husband to the pretty woman. The hummingbird took off and was quick. He quickly left the lumbering crane behind. The woman felt certain the hummingbird would win, since he was quick and the crane was not known for flying at night. The hummingbird flew half the night and knew he was ahead, so he stopped to roost for the night. But the crane flew steadily all night.

The hummingbird woke in the morning and flew on, thinking he was ahead in the race. But when he reached a river, he saw the crane spearing fish. The crane thought that hummingbird was far behind. The hummingbird flew on ahead. That night, the hummingbird stopped to sleep again, and the crane flew on ahead. When morning came, the hummingbird noticed that the crane was having his breakfast. The hummingbird flew on. The crane flew through the night each night and arrived at the finish near the woman's house before the hummingbird. But the woman said she would have neither the crane nor the hummingbird, so she joined her friends to celebrate her good luck."

Awinta jumped off the swing and landed in a little puddle of mud. "Why didn't she want the crane for a husband?" Awinta asked.

"Because," Easter said. "A woman does not need a man to be a woman," she said. "She only needs to be herself." She smiled at Awinta, who frowned as if trying to make sense of the tale.

As John took off his clothes and laid down on the bed Easter had prepared for him, he looked up at the ceiling of the cabin and wondered if she would ever forgive him for doing things his way. Years ago, after that argument he and Easter had had, he'd appeared at her cabin. His clothes were outside. That meant they were divorced. There was no coming back. She was finished with him. But he never gave up hope that she might take him back. In fact, he often slipped into her bed when she seemed to let down her guard. He'd bring her some select bit of deer meat or large fish. Then, he was called by Ross and the other elders to sit in on the talks with the U.S. government.

The work he did for the chief and for the other elders required him to ride long distances, sometimes taking messages back and forth among the seven clans. It was grueling work, and the news was not welcome. Sometimes the messenger was blamed for the message. When the Arkansas Cherokees heard what was happening, they almost scalped him. Ross and the others had no right to negotiate on behalf of all Cherokees.

John wanted to ask someone else to do some of this work, but he wasn't the only one asked to ferry messages and to sit in on negotiations and plans. He was also asked to prepare the people for the inevitable. It was the hardest thing he did — to try to convince his brethren that the time for compromise had passed. They were not going to remain on their ancestral lands; instead, they were headed to a reservation — someplace where Cherokees, Choctaws, Creek, and other tribes would be relegated to a parcel of land.

John thought it would be prudent to stay in one place for a while. This plan of Easter's was a good one. However, he loved being able to hunt and fish. He moved about so much, it was difficult for the soldiers to tell where he was. Now that the major exodus of Cherokee and other Sun People had arrived in the new territory, it would be an easy thing to avoid the soldiers. He settled on that for a plan. He would hunt and fish, not joining any one group of people. If he stayed out of sight long enough, he would be forgotten. He drifted off to sleep. It had been a tiring ride to find Easter.

The next morning, John joined Easter and Arter for a light breakfast and headed out to help Arter. He joined Arter in the barn, where he was collecting manure and bird waste from the stalls and cages. Arter collected the waste in a large wooden wheelbarrow that had been left on the farm by the previous tenant.

"You're collecting this for the crops?" John asked. Arter nodded but said nothing. It was obvious that Arter was still angry. The two worked silently for hours, gathering manure, ash from the fireplace and fish leavings. A river ran not far from the cabin, and Arter had added fish to their diet. He'd been saving these leavings for some time, as had the other tenants. The men took the mixture to the fields to the north of the cabins and saw other workers spreading fertilizer on the fields. Arter introduced his brother to Anderson and

Margaret and Jethro and Elizabeth. Arter and John were introduced to other workers who lived on distant parts of the land. The women stayed for a short time and returned to their cabins while the men finished the work.

Other men joined in the effort — Duncan, Edward, Beck and others, some with women, some alone. They cleared some of the brush from the fields by burning some of it and digging out roots and rocks from the soil. Anderson explained that they would be planting on the east side of the fields in an effort to give the other patches of soil a rest. John had heard of crop rotation from Easter but had not shown interest in it. For her sake, he tried to listen this time, as Anderson explained the concept of enriching the soil and letting it rest.

When Arter and John were returning to the cabin, Anderson told them of plans to have a dance in a large barn not far from the settlement. They thanked him for the invitation and headed back after a day of cultivating the earth. John wondered whether he would be able to sustain an interest in such work.

Easter prepared a hearty supper for the little family. She was stirring a pot and had placed clay bowls on the table. She had unpacked some of her possessions and was pleased with the appearance of her table. But it was a small one, and her thoughts returned to the large oak tree that she had asked for permission to harvest one of its limbs. She felt certain that the oak had agreed. She served their food and, still in a pique with the men, cleaned up after everyone and helped Awinta with her lessons. She had been trying to teach Awinta, a little at a time, to read and to cipher. The girl was extremely bright. She was surprised when Awinta told her that she had had some learning when she was at Spring Place.

Degataga had ordered that one of his servants teach Awinta the Cherokee alphabet. So the girl had a little notion of reading. She quickly learned the English alphabet and was reading simple books in no time. She enjoyed reading the books that Easter had managed to pack for the long trip; Awinta's favorite was *Tales of Shakespeare*. The two of them worked on creating new books and writing stories. Awinta was a talented artist too. She could draw anything she decided to represent on parchment. It was difficult making their own, but some of the women in the settlement exchanged paper for other goods. It could be bought in town and was precious.

Using rags and an assortment of other items he borrowed, Arter created as much crude parchment as he could for the women. They always seemed to be working on their reading and writing projects. Easter used the Bible to help Awinta become more fluent at reading and writing. John, surprisingly, had brought a gift of paper to Easter, who thanked him warmly. John and Arter settled into an uneasy truce of working on the farm. They watered and fed the horses and cows and put them out to pasture every day to find areas where they could graze. Ama and Waya guarded the animals while they grazed and helped keep predators out of the chicken coop. Easter's belly had grown large with child by February. She was in the barn helping Awinta feed the chickens when she felt a sharp pain in her lower back. She realized what was happening immediately and walked to the cabin. She readied all that was needed for the birth and asked Awinta to call the men in from the fields.

They all arrived together. Arter arrived first, out of breath and panting. John followed behind him. Awinta was the last to arrive. They all look confused and fearful. Easter took charge. "Awinta, please go to Anderson's cabin and ask Margaret if she can come help. John, go get some water from the well. We will need two buckets full. Arter, get wood to build up the fire. When you've done that, please put some water on to boil."

They all rushed to do as she asked. She settled in the

room she shared with Arter and looked around for the goods she had gathered. The small rocking bed was in the corner. The table Arter had made was to the right of the bed. Arter had begun to fashion a chest or drawers for the child. She smiled. This would be good. She fingered the cloth she'd gathered for changing the baby and small gowns that women in the settlement had given her. She was about to see whether the water was boiling when another sharp pain came and she bent over slightly. She felt water dribbling down her legs and knew the baby would come soon. She lifted up the hem of her dress to look.

"Is this your first?" Elizabeth asked from the door. Easter turned to smile at Elizabeth and shook her head, No. The contractions were getting closer together, and she felt the need to push. She did so in a standing position and Elizabeth marveled at her strength.

"Let me be certain everything is ready," Elizabeth said. Elizabeth directed Arter and John to wash their hands thoroughly and to pour hot water into the large pottery bowls on the table in Easter's room. Easter still did not sit down or lie on the bed. She paced back and forth on the left side of the bed and squatted occasionally. Arter looked at her nervously. "What can I do?" he asked. She held up her hand as if to say wait. John came into the room too, all cleaned up and ready to help. He and Easter had had a child years earlier, but the child had died. He was there for that birth and hoped that this one would go smoothly.

"I've done this before," John said. "She will not sit or lie down. This is her way." Easter paced again and grunted. Elizabeth kneeled on the floor before Easter and put a hand on her to see how far along she was in labor. Elizabeth sat back on her heels and looked up at Easter.

"Your baby is nearly here," she said. Easter nodded and pushed. Just then, Elizabeth was called away to the door of the cabin by her husband. "I'll be right back," she said. "If the baby comes, Arter and John, be there to catch it. I will help with all else."

Arter and John stood before Easter, each on one side and lowered themselves to the floor. Easter pushed again, and the baby came sliding out. Her skirts were up and both men held out their hands to catch the infant. They both looked with awe at the wiggling infant, who had come out making noise. Easter's face relaxed, and she pushed again as the placenta came out next. Elizabeth came in and helped cut and tie the birth cord and dispose of the placenta. She took the baby from Arter and helped to clean her up. John helped Easter lie on the bed and get under the covers. He took off her skirt and helped her into an undergarment that opened in the front. Her breasts began to swell with milk, and Elizabeth handed the baby to her. Easter put the little girl to her breast, and the child took to it readily.

"What will you call her?" Elizabeth asked. Easter looked at John and then at Arter.

"Hester Beasley," she said, thinking that John and Arter's last names would make a good start for her little girl. She smiled as she looked down at the child. Hester would usher in the next generation.

Elizabeth was called away from the birth for a good reason. Strangers were arriving. Four bells were ringing through the hills. Then things got quiet as the men prepared. Guns were hidden but loaded. Women and children hid. It was strange that the soldiers did not appear right away. Apparently, they were stopping at each cabin and looking for someone. Elizabeth felt a chill when her husband shared this news. That could mean only one thing.

Those strangers were looking for Easter and Arter. There was no way to tell what kind of threat these people were. She helped Jethro prepare and quickly returned. So,

Elizabeth told Arter and John about the development and asked them to hide Easter. But there would be no point in moving mother and baby. If they could just leave her where she was, it would be possible the men would move on. Elizabeth hurried to her own home where her husband and children waited for her.

Arter banked up the fire in the bedroom so that the baby and Easter could be comfortable. John had gone up to the loft to his room and was whittling at toys for Hester. Hester had been fed and was asleep in the little cradle Arter had made. He had placed it on the left side of the bed close enough to the fireplace to keep the baby warm — but not too hot. He brought a meal to Easter so that she could eat and made certain that Awinta and John had food too. An early spring snow had arrived, threatening to undo some of the work of the farmers. So Arter was staying inside. John had helped feed and care for the livestock in the barn and had brought in sufficient vegetables from the barrels in the barn. They had decided to put some of the goods in the cellar. But not everything would fit there; it was a small space. Easter woke as Arter slid in bed beside her.

"Snowing again?" she asked groggily.

"Yes, and we may have trouble soon," he said. "Strangers have been seen in the area. They are going from cabin to cabin or house to house looking for Indians. It's likely they could be looking for us." Easter sighed and turned her head toward the baby.

"Do you want to hide?" he asked.

"No, there's no point," she said. "They will either take me or not. I can't fight them if they want to drag me away."

"I won't let that happen," Arter said.

"How can you prevent it?" she said.

"There is one thing that you will need to do, Easter," he said. "Be what John suggested, a Negro. Don't behave as though you are Cherokee. If you can do that, there is no need to worry about hiding. You can hide in plain sight." Easter considered his words for a few minutes and then turned to him. Their pillows were not the best quality, but they were comfortable enough. She liked the bed they shared, but it was too small. She realized that after the table was built, Arter would need to start on a new bed.

"You're right," she said. "I only need to act like the women of this area. They have a certain way of using their bodies to suggest who they are. I will do that too. We will see what will come of it."

"Above all," Arter said. "Stay calm. Nervous behavior makes people suspicious."

"Where is John?" she asked.

"He has decided to hide," he said. "I told him of the old woman and the boy. He may go in search of them to help them remain safe from the soldiers."

It was three days before the strangers made it to their cabin as theirs was one of the last on the road to the Rhea's large house. Elizabeth and Anderson joined them in the cabin to add to their numbers and help with the ruse. There were four soldiers riding horses and checking each cabin. When they knocked on the door, Arter let them in. Two of the men were dressed in soldier's uniforms and two were dressed in civilian garb.

Arter was surprised to see Ezra Poe was one of them and realized then that he had not killed the man, as he had thought. Poe seemed to favor his shoulder. Arter was surprised Poe did not seem to recognize him. Arter had covered his face because of the snow, so that might account for Ezra's lack of recognition, but he would surely recognize Easter. The other man was Benjamin, who he recognized from the village of Red Clay. Benjamin had been recruited by the army to assist in the capture and removal of Cherokees and other natives. Benjamin did not look happy with the task that was being delegated to him. A corporal was explaining why they were searching.

"Good evening," Corporal Carlson said. "We are in search of any Indians who haven't been removed for transport to the reservation in Oklahoma. We are doing a last sweep of the area to determine whether there are any who are missing or should be headed west."

"As you can see, corporal," Arter said, "there are nothing but Negros here. We are servants to the Rhea family. I am a servant and this, he put a hand on Awinta's shoulder, is my daughter." Awinta looked up at him and grinned. He squeezed her shoulder to get her to behave. The baby began to cry. The soldier craned his neck toward the bedroom as though he wanted to look there.

"My wife has just had a baby," Arter said. "She is bedridden for some time. It was a difficult birth." Arter felt stretching the truth was necessary. Elizabeth had said that Easter's delivery was the easiest she'd ever seen, and Easter had recovered quickly. But they did not need to know that.

Ezra Poe then interceded. "Corporal, I think it's necessary to question everyone to see whether there are any possible Indians that must be removed."

The corporal nodded and gestured to the bedroom. He was a large man with dark hair and a clean-shaven face. He wore a dark uniform with a hat and a heavy wool coat. Arter waved an arm toward the corporal and said, "Only two at a time, gentlemen. My wife and the baby are fragile." Awinta smiled and moved to the fire where boiling water was waiting to make Easter a nourishing tea. Easter herself had mixed the herbs necessary to be certain her milk flow was good. Corporal Carlson stepped into the room with Ezra Poe. Easter had her hair covered in a scarf in the African style and was breastfeeding her daughter. Both men were embarrassed and looked away. She covered her baby and looked at them as though she were tired and weak. She coughed a few times and burrowed under the covers. The baby began to squirm and whimper. Then, Hester, as though on demand from her mother, let loose with a wail.

"M'am," the corporal said. Ezra looked again at Easter and frowned. He behaved as though he were struggling to remember something. However, he just could not recall what it was. He turned away and walked back into the front room. The corporal left the room next. Benjamin then stepped in the room and looked at Easter. He remembered her from the village of Red Clay. Easter had stitched up his wound. He would never forget her kind eyes and gentle hands. He had heard of her intelligence and her willingness to help anyone, no matter who it was. He looked at Easter and smiled at her, then winked.

She smiled at him and he then turned quickly into the room with the other men. The fourth soldier came into the room and quickly left as Hester still wailed for her mother's breast. The man was uncomfortable around women and babies.

"Sorry to have bothered you," Corporal Carlson said to Arter. He then tipped his hat at Elizabeth and her husband, Anderson. He waited till the other three men preceded him out the door and then turned to say something to Arter. He handed him a slip of paper.

"Give this to any other soldiers that come this way,"Corporal Carlson said. "This will affirm that you have the right to remain here without molestation."

Arter considered the paper and wondered if it was worth anything at all. If someone wanted to make a case out of their being in the area, they certainly could and no small piece of paper would make a difference. But he thanked the corporal and stood on the small porch to see them away.

When he returned inside, all was quiet. He went immediately to Easter and Hester. Easter smiled at him and reached a hand to him. He came to her and sat on the bed beside her. Hester was busy finishing her feeding. The sounds of her swallowing whispered in the room. He kissed Easter on her forehead.

"It's over," he said. She sighed.

"I think something is wrong with Ezra Poe," Easter said. "Do you think it was having been rolled down that ravine? He must have hit is head."

"I don't care what it was," Arter said. "I only care that you and Hester are safe. There is no need to dwell on the circumstances of that blessing. May I say that you did a fine job of performance?" He grinned at her and kissed her forehead again. He held her hand as she cuddled the baby with the other.

"You know that I love you," he said, almost as a whisper. She smiled at him and nodded.

"I feel this same love for you," she said. "This will be our lives for now," she said. "I will give up something of myself for you and Hester, for our family," she said. Arter sighed.

"It is the times we live in," Arter said. "But it will not always be this way. Things will change. Wait. You will see." She did not answer him. But she felt conflicting emotions — love and bitterness — rise within her. Why should she have to give up her identity as a Cherokee to survive? Why should she have to give up anything to claim the land of her ancestors? But, as Arter said, these were the times in which they lived.

"We will do our best," she said kissing Hester and then Arter.

.

Dale Marie Taylor

CHAPTER TWENTY-SIX
March 1838

Two weeks later, the women of the little community of Apple Hill prepared for a dance and little feast in the barn of Elizabeth and Anderson. Anderson had two barns. He moved some of his livestock to the larger barn and moved things about to make a dancing space. He and Elizabeth and a couple of his neighbors cleaned the barn thoroughly, and Elizabeth and her friends, Easter included, decorated with pinecones and spruce.

They found holly trees to make other attractive décor. It was apparent to Easter that the barn had been used as a gathering place before as there were decorative paintings on the walls of the barn — green and red paintings of wreaths, pineapples, crosses, checkers, willow trees and other welcoming symbols. The group pitched in with all manner of food. A roasted pig had been prepared in the early morning and by nightfall there was plenty of meat. The women prepared tubers, corn, sweet potatoes and squash as side dishes. Women baked cakes and pies.

"Taste this," Elizabeth said, holding out a fork of the most fragrant cake Easter had smelled in a while.

"Mmmmm." Easter licked her lips and smiled. "I hope you will share your recipe with me," she said, grinning. Elizabeth nodded.

"I'll do better than that," Elizabeth said. "You're invited over for a baking party next week. We will show you all of our tricks." She grinned and her pecan-colored skin shone with the look of health. Easter wondered how she was so fortunate to be with such warm and friendly people.

The dance began with the tuning of instruments. Two men had violins or fiddles, as they called them. Another man played the banjo. A woman played the guitar. An old man played a dulcimer. A young boy played a single drum and another played what looked like a bugle. A man stood in the background with a flute. Easter was pleased to see the woman had a good rapport among the men. It appeared she had been playing with them for some time. Later, Elizabeth said the young woman was the daughter of the man playing the four-string guitar. They were all related in some way, cousins, siblings and so forth.

The music began with tunes that could be danced to: the Kentucky Reel and then quadrilles. The music included "The Old Oaken Bucket," "I Know a Bank Where the Wild Thyme Grows," "My Heart and Lute," and "My Pretty Jane," along with other tunes that were adaptations of hymns. The music carried the participants away from their troubles and created a bond that was strong and true. Husbands danced with wives and children with their siblings and friends. The dancing lasted until late and when they broke for the night, the women helped clean up, and the men helped remove some of the décor and bring Anderson's livestock back into his barn.

Easter had brought Hester along, as other women did when they went to these gatherings. The children were passed around so that other women could help tend the children and they all took turns dancing. The next morning was sunny and bright. Elizabeth dropped by to invite Easter and Arter to church. They walked to a little whitewashed building that was on the road. Easter had hardly noticed it on their way to the cabin where they lived. A tall dark-skinned man named Simmons preached about the importance of forgiveness and the blessings that family and friends bring. They sang "Rock of Ages," and "On Solid Rock," both hymns Easter remembered from those days of having to go to missionary meetings when she was a girl. She also recalled that the Cherokee had their own version of spirituality. She was taught that custom by her grandmother and her parents and often prayed and cleansed herself in the Cherokee way. But, it was important to blend in with the people here who had been so kind to her and Arter and who had helped her evade the soldiers. Later that day, John came to the cabin after having been away for several days.

"I thought I had gotten rid of you, brother," Arter said. John glared at him, but smirked and looked away.

"I think I found the tree you spoke of to Arter," John said to Easter. He looked back at his brother. "Let's get started on her table." Easter's heart swelled with gratitude, but she said nothing. She gathered up Hester, put her in a sling on her back and wrapped her up tight. Awinta went with them. They walked, leading two horses, to the large oak tree in the woods. As they approached, Easter felt a strong pull to the tree. It felt as though the tree was speaking to her. Yes, she could borrow one of its strong branches for a good table. The two men got to work identifying which branch could be cut without harming the tree. Halfway between their deliberations and efforts, Easter and Awinta walked back to the cabin. Then the real work began. Arter and John had enlisted the help of Anderson for some tools they could use to do the job.

They trimmed the limb that would make the table.

They tied the heavy tree limb to the horses and drug it back to the cabin. It was a slow team effort, but they brought the wood to the backyard, where they got busy making the table. First they peeled the bark from the limb. Then they assessed which sections would make for the long cuts and which for shorter cuts. There was a sawmill not far from Apple Hill. The men loaded the wood into the wagon and took the wood to the mill to get finer cuts of wood. Rougher cuts were fine for a log cabin, but for something as fine as a table, Arter and John wanted the wood to be as smooth as possible. When they had the wood cut, they returned to the cabin and began using a plane to get it smooth and flat.

The two men worked on the table during the late afternoon hours after they had come in from working with the soil. The planting season had begun. It was now March. Arter hoped there would not be another freeze. But Anderson said if there was one, it would likely not hurt the seedlings. With their first round of seeds in the earth, Arter and John returned to the project of the table. They said little to one another, as they wanted to avoid another brutal fight. John knew that Arter was still seething under the surface and did not want to instigate another quarrel. He planned to move on sometime soon, but it gave him some satisfaction to worry his brother about his plans.

"What are you planning to do?" Arter blurted out one evening as they had finished putting together the tabletop and were working on the legs. They'd held smooth parts of the wood together with a glue that Anderson had given them. They'd reinforce the wood with tacks and let it dry. Now they were preparing it for sanding. The table legs were made. Those were fancier than anything John had ever seen. He wondered why it was important to Easter to have such a thing. He supposed that was why he should go his own way. Arter did not care why Easter wanted such a table. He only cared that it was something Easter wanted and he wanted Easter to be happy. John thought he wanted the same thing. He wanted Easter to be happy. But he could not ignore the call of freedom — the urge to hunt, to fish, to be in the outdoors free from encumbrances of any kind. He loved his family, Easter, Hester, Arter, and Awinta. But he loved being in the outdoors more, able to move about at will, to wander, to hunt and fish and be among the wild.

"I'm planning to be happy," John said, smiling at his brother. "Are you?" Arter looked at him with exasperation and went back to attaching a leg to the table. He'd been given some metal brackets to help achieve this. They'd set the tabletop face down on a bed of straw and were working on it in the bright sun. Arter was dressed in his homespun clothing of loose dark pantaloons and a grey shirt, and John was dressed in his traditional garb of leather pants and a dark wool shirt. Both men wore boots, for the ground was still muddy in places. The round table would be large enough to seat seven people. They were fortunate to have a large enough cabin to accommodate it.

When they were finished fastening the last leg on the table, they gave it a good finish with beeswax. When they'd finished, they had Awinta be certain that Easter was away. The timing was perfect. She had gone to the home of her friends where they were baking various pies and cakes. When Easter came home, they asked her to remain outside for a few moments. They placed a blindfold on her eyes, and Awinta guided her into the cabin. When they took the blindfold off, Easter gasped in pleasure. Her eyes welled up with tears of happiness as she walked around the table, running her hands across the surface of rich beautiful wood and looking at the two men in gratification. She hugged Arter first and then John. Both men looked down bashfully, but then pulled out one of the chairs they had been working on too.

They had placed some wildflowers in a clay vase. The flowers spilled over the edges making a beautiful centerpiece.

"It's beautiful," she said, her voice trembling. "You did it so quickly. How?"

"We wanted you to have it as soon as possible," John said. She looked at him intensely, fearing that this meant John would leave soon. But her thoughts were soon distracted by Awinta who sat in the other chair the two men had fashioned. It was not as sophisticated as her chair, but it was fine piece of work too.

"We will be busy making six more chairs to match the one you're sitting in," Arter said. "Then our task will be complete." She rubbed a hand on the table again and again and hugged both men.

"Thank you," she said. "Thank you. It's the best gift I've ever received. Thank you. I love you both." Both men frowned at those words, looking at one another. Then she hugged them both, and they beamed with satisfaction.

That night, John took Easter for a walk, and they talked about his plans. He wanted to share time with her alone and could think of no way for them to be alone in the cabin. Easter had Awinta take care of Hester while she was away. Hester had been fed and changed and was asleep in her bed.

"I will leave soon," John said.

"Why must you?" she asked. "There's plenty of room for you here."

"You know why Easter," he said. "I can't look at you everyday, wanting you, and not have you. It's. . . You understand."

She did. They had arrived at a small grove behind the property where there was a crude bench. They sat down, and Easter pulled a blanket around her shoulders. John took off his leather coat and put it around Easter. She shivered and leaned into him. He stroked her hair gently and kissed her. The kiss quickly became passionate, and she pulled away, looking at him. He looked back at her longingly.

"This is why," he said. "We would both share you, if you would allow it." She said nothing. "But Easter, the truth is you know what I prefer. I want to wander the land, to hunt, to fish, to be outdoors. I live for that. A wood ceiling overhead is not for me. The stars overhead, that is for me."

She did not say anything as he held her in his arms. After a time, she spoke. "Will you return from time to time?"

"Yes, I won't be far away," he said. "You only need to call me, in your mind, and I will come." They always had a close connection. Though neither could explain why, they accepted it.

She said nothing more as they held each other tightly, watching the sun go down. When they returned to the house, John gave Awinta a little carving he'd made and gave one to Easter for Hester to have when she was older. He held the baby closely to him, kissing her on the forehead. He knew the child was his. It didn't matter, though, because she belonged both to him and his brother, Arter. Arter watched in silence as John handed the baby back to Easter. John held out a hand to his brother who took it grudgingly. He said nothing to Arter. He appeared to want to say something but did not.

He'd brought his sable mustang out of the barn and had saddled him. He sat on his horse looking down at them all. "Take care of her," he said to his brother. "All of them." Arter nodded. "Remember this, if you don't, I will easily take your place because I will be nearby." Arter said nothing. John turned his horse and rode away.

CHAPTER TWENTY-SEVEN

Ezra Poe rode with the other agents who were tasked with gathering Indians to go west. Bitterness grew within him. That woman at the Beasley cabin did not look like his woman, his Easter. He seethed. She could not be that woman. She did not look like Easter. Easter did not have a baby. She was his. He parted company with the soldiers when they headed for the western part of the state. He had to get back to Georgia. But first, he needed to look for Easter. He had left her in that cave. He had to go back. He had to find her. What was she thinking? She appeared before him. He sat on his horse looking at her. She waved at him and pointed to the cave. He smiled. She was in that cave. He knew it. He rode hard back to the cave. Was this the cave where he left her? He slipped off his horse.

He frowned, struggling to remember what had happened after he had been hurt. He was dressed raggedly. His dark pantaloons were dirty and ripped. His brown shirt was torn. There was a gash on his head. When he'd climbed out of that ravine, he'd lost a lot of blood from his shoulder wound. How had he gotten that? It looked like a knife wound. Who had stabbed him? He had a large knot on the back of his head. He also had a stab wound in his thigh. He fingered it, trying to remember. He had gone into the cave and rested. He drank water that trickled from the cave walls. His horse had come back to him. He was relieved that the beast was loyal. He had dried meat and other provisions tied in small sacks on his horse. He was exhausted from the loss of blood, but had managed to build a fire and burn his wound with a knife to cleanse it and staunch any bleeding. Then, he slept. When he woke, the storm had stopped. But he saw Easter lying beside him. Smiling. He put his arms around her, but she vanished.

He looked for her in the cave, but he did not find her. So, in time, he saddled his horse and rode to the area where he thought Easter had gone. He had been watching her. She appeared to him again, as if she were a dream. Then she vanished. He went to the clearing where he had taken her. He rubbed his head trying again to remember everything that happened. Did he carry her to his cave? Did she fight him? How did he get in that ravine? Did she stab him? No, she loved him. She would not do that. He struggled to remember clearly. Things got fuzzy and he saw two of everything for a while. Then, his vision cleared.

Ezra's mind was not as it should be. He could not remember everything. After Easter had left him, he had ridden on a path that seemed to be rutted by wagon wheels. It led him to another cave. There, he was certain Easter had remained, waiting for him to come get her. He had to find her. He got off his horse and looked around. He rode until he found the soldiers, who invited him along. "Are you a guard?" they asked. He frowned. What kind of guard did they mean?

"Yes," he said. He was Easter's guard. They should know that. When he arrived at that cabin where the woman who looked like Easter was holding a baby, he realized that he'd abandoned her at the cave. He had to get back there. She was waiting for him. She would marry him and never know that he'd killed her oldest brother.

When Ezra arrived at the cave, it was much bigger than he had remembered. But he found evidence of Easter having been there. A feather rested inside the cave, as though she had left it there just for him. He picked it up and smelled it. He fingered it and sighed, smiling. She would come to him. He heard a sound deep in the cave. She was here. "I knew it! I knew you would be here!" he shouted. He ran deep into the cave and rounded a corner where there was a glittering pool of water. He threw off his dirty clothing and jumped in the warm water. It felt so good. But his head began to pound again. He pulled himself up out of the water and rested on the cool rocks.

When he opened his eyes, a large cougar hovered above him. He was too surprised to scream.

EPILOGUE

Easter missed John, though she heard through word-of-mouth and dove messengers from time to time that he'd been seen here and there, hunting or trading in villages in the area and to the west where there was less civilization. She heard from Lucinda regularly. The birds that Lucinda had trained were hearty creatures. They delivered messages among the four siblings regularly. One day when Hester was about five years old, Lucinda and Walking Bird visited. Their reunion was full of laughter, dancing, praying and celebration.

Easter heard news of Wahali and his wife, Hummingbird. They had had two children as well. Wahali went east, as he had planned, to study Western medicine. In a letter, it appeared that he would be teaching some Western doctors when he was finished with his service. He helped in a hospital and had a thriving practice. Hummingbird had gone with him, and they had adopted the Western way. Their children, Anita and James, attended schools in the city and were popular in the neighborhood. They lived in a cottage in New York city where they were quietly accepted among the many immigrants that were streaming into the country from Europe.

Wahali anglicized his name to Wally. Most people thought it was short for Walter. He did not bother to say. He managed his practice and said nothing about his origins. He was asked nothing. As long as he dressed as a Western man, no one bothered him as he went about tending the sick. Eventually, he planned to return to the Cherokee Nation in Oklahoma. But for now, his skills were needed in New York.

Degataga and Ruth were expecting another child. Their farm prospered even as the talk of war was increasing. The Georgia Guards still played a role in the state's security but played less of a role where Principal People were concerned. The neighbors were continually suspicious of outsiders and protected Degataga and Ruth. The area did not change much over the years, and they lived on their farm in peace. However, whenever they could, Degataga and Ruth helped runaway slaves and Indians who were fleeing persecutors. Ruth helped start a school in the village where they lived, and people forgot who her husband was. She was able to move about freely and so was Degataga. After a few years, he was able to engage in transactions for his family farm as any other person would.

Easter and Arter received a few more visits from John. Arter considered it odd that his brother showed up when he went to visit his other brother, Nathan, in Columbus. Nathan held slaves, and Arter and Nathan argued about that quite a bit. Arter knew that there would be a war soon about the problem of slavery, but he did not want to find himself in the middle of it. He considered moving his family elsewhere, but Easter would not consider moving away from her ancestral lands. She did not care who legally held the land. In her heart, she knew that her children would someday get the land back. They were expecting another child. Arter thought briefly that this second child would be his without a doubt. But his brother's brief visits left him wondering. He kicked a stone as he thought about it in the woods. Women in the Cherokee Nation would always hold the power. That was a given, no matter what Westerners thought.

Easter taught the children in the area how to read and write in her free time. But mostly she enjoyed creating the home that helped nurture her children. One day, as she was hanging clothes on a line in the back yard, a small horse-drawn wagon arrived with a woman in it. A man sat beside her. She was slender and dark-skinned, tall and regal in her bearing. She got out of the wagon and stretched. She looked about and walked to the area behind the cabin. Easter put down the clothing.

She squinted as she looked at the woman. She seemed familiar. "May I help. . ." She stopped and inhaled. "Inola," she whispered. Just then, Awinta came from the barn. She stood there looking at the woman. Then, she ran to her, shouting. "Iie Iie! Mother!" The two embraced and tears fell from their eyes. Inola was made welcome among the people of Apple Hill, where she became a happy inhabitant, and Easter became the mother of many generations of children to come.

Dale Marie Taylor

ACKNOWLEDGEMENTS AND AUTHOR NOTES

Thanks to my readers for reading my book and to my husband who helped edit it. Also, thanks to the many historians who have written about the Cherokee experience. If you're interested in a history of the Cherokee Nation, see Robert J. Conley's *The Cherokee Nation: A History* and Theda Perdu and Michael D. Green's *The Cherokee Nation and the Trail of Tears*. Easter was a person whose name was taken from a family history. It appears that she did not march on the Trail of Tears. Easter and her birth of Hester and her subsequent survival is true as well. I gave her siblings because this is likely, and I wanted to tell the story of how various Cherokees experienced the removal of the 1830s. The story is fictional and though some of the names might be associated with historical figures, the actual events connected to them are not extensively discussed.

Arter Beasley was likely connected in some way to the Welsh, as the story implies, but much of his story is conjecture. John Hester was an actual historical participant in the removal negotiations.

However, Arter's role in Easter's life is fictional. The Wards were an important Cherokee family, but in no way is the name used as an actual description of the family from which Easter is derived. Some of the references to historical events are true to form. For example, removal negotiations were fraught with delays and frustrations. The agreement that was finally reached was seen as unfair and cruel. Some of the negotiators paid for what was perceived as failed negotiations with their lives. Chief John Ross was indeed the figurehead for the Cherokees during negotiations with the U.S. government. He suffered many challenges during that period. Chief Yonaguska was also an actual leader for the Cherokees. Many Cherokees did not recognize one particular leader, such as Ross, as their spokesperson or as authorized to speak for all Cherokee.

The weather was indeed as unpredictable as the story suggests. However, I may have used hyperbole with that aspect of the story to demonstrate the degree to which people suffered while attempting to adjust to new and challenging circumstances. Again, my thanks to all who have helped me in the conception of this story, including my father, Joe Simmons, who asked me to write it, and his sister Clara.

Characters in *A Home for Easter*

Easter Ward--A woman of Cherokee descent who is attempting to find a new home. The pressure from settlers and the U.S. government to take land from Cherokee is persistent. She is unsure how she will find a new home. But she is a planner and is led to middle Tennessee by Arter Beasley. Easter's journey begins in the winter of 1837, two years after the Treaty of New Echota was signed. The treaty meant that many Cherokees were forcibly removed from their lands. This period is typically referred to as The Trail of Tears (occurred approximately 1838-1839 before and after this time).

Author's note on Easter's name: The name "Easter" may have been used by the Cherokee to demonstrate their adoption of Christianity. However, many Cherokees took other English names, such as John. The name Easter could have been a derivative of the biblical name Esther. The surname, Ward, is connected in Cherokee records with the name Easter, but a clear connection to the family upon which the character is based cannot be verified. Assume that all characters are fictional.

Enorle (Black Fox) Ward -- Easter's father, of the Blue Clan, died of fever. Enorle is the father of Awinta by the African woman, Inola.

Sitting Dear Ward – Easter's mother, of the Potato Clan, died of fever.

Arter Beasley – half-brother to John Hester. Arter's mother was Ahyoka, She Brought Happiness. Arter and John are both in love with Easter. Arter's father is Alun Beasley, who is an educator in Pennsylvania. Arter's race is mixed and undetermined; however, his mother is part Cherokee, and his father is white.

John Hester--the former husband of Easter. They married within the Cherokee nation and lost a child. The two broke up. John Hester is part of the Deer clan.

Nathan – Arter's half-brother who owns slaves.

Lucinda Ward--Sister to Easter, she removes to the Qalla territory with Walking Bird.

Walking Bird--is from the Qualla territory of North Carolina, the smokey mountains. He marries Lucinda, who removes with him to the Qualla territory.

Connutsee Ward – the older brother of Easter, who dies before the story opens. He was attempting to defend family property.

Degataga (Stands Firm) Ward– Easter's older brother, who marries Ruth, the daughter of a missionary. Because of his brother-in-law, Degataga retains ownership of a portion of his family's property.

Ruth Stevens Ward – Degataga's wife, whose father helped the Cherokees as part of the missionary society.

Charles Stevens – Ruth's brother, who helps Degataga keep his land by putting it in Charles' name.

Blue Clan – Easter's father's clan

Potato Clan – Easter's mother's clan

Awinta Ward – Easter's half-sister whose mother was the slave, Inola. Her father was Enorle, father to Easter too.

Hialeah--Easter's paternal grandmother, who told stories of the proposed state of Franklin, Tenn.

Wahali (Eagle) Ward--Easter's youngest brother, who wants to be a healer, but also learns the ways of western medicine. Wahali marches on the Trail of Tears.

Hummingbird – wife of Wahali who marched on the Trail of Tears. Her brother is Dustu; her mother is Trahlyth.

Kanua – Hummingbird's deceased suitor.

Benjamin--a settler who receives help from Easter.

Sarah Armstrong--Easter's white friend who is a missionary. Sarah and her fiancé are going to help Easter.

Amadahy--Easter's maternal grandmother.

Mohe Ward--one of Easter's brothers who is killed during a conflict between whites and Cherokees.

Waya--Easter's male dog. Part wolf with light colored eyes.

Ama--Easter's female dog.

Benjamin – injured neighbor who Easter helps early in the story.

Chief John Ross who was the leader of the Cherokee tribe. He attempted to negotiate on behalf of the Cherokees so that they might remain on their lands. He saw the Cherokees through the fraught period of the removal of Cherokees from their lands and was chief until the Civil War.

The Georgia Guard – a group of soldiers hired by the Georgia government to keep peace among the populace. However, some of them went rogue.

Ezra Poe – on of the members of the Georgian Guardsmen who is obsessed with Easter. The Guard sometimes raided across the border of Tennessee.

Joe Rhea – brother to Matthew Rhea who had helped to survey the state for maps.

Dutch Smith – a Cherokee outlaw who killed a U.S. Deputy Marshall.

Will Holland Thomas – helped the Eastern band Cherokee keep their lands and to settle in the Qalla territory of the Smokey Mountains. Thomas served as chief of the Eastern Band until about 1870. He assumed that role following the death of Yonaguska (1838-1839).

Dr. Jason Roberts – a doctor assigned to Cherokees moving west on the northern-most trail during the removal. He befriends Wahali.

Tisyi – Jason Roberts' driver.

Ninovan – a childhood friend of Easter's

Spring Place – a Morovian Mission; one of the places where Easter's parents owned a home.

Kay and Mico, Easter's horses

Hogan and Tom – Easter's mules

Keme – Easter's mule

Lulu – Easter's mule

Daisy – Easter's cow

Sallie – Easter's cow

Toka – Easter's cat

Alice – Easter's cat

Desa – Arter's stallion

Dates

May 1830 – Indian Removal bill ratified.

October 1832 – Chickasaws sign removal treaty.

March 1832 – Creeks sign removal treaty.

May 1832 – Seminoles sign removal treaty.

April 1833 – Chief John Ross's home taken over by lottery winners.

December 1835—Signing of the Treaty of New Echota by Cherokees, among them Major Ridge, John Ridge and Elias Boudinot. They were later assassinated. The U.S. Congress ratified the treaty in 1836 and gave the Cherokee two years to remove themselves from their land.

December 1835 – Arrest by 25 members of the Georgia Guard of Chief John Ross at Red Clay.

The Trail of Tears began in the 1830s and continued beyond that time with the forced removal of indigenous people from their lands. The Cherokee owned land in areas that include Tennessee, Georgia, North Carolina and Alabama. The Indian Removal Bill meant that more than 100,000 indigenous people were removed from their lands East of the Mississippi. The Cherokees were paid $5 million for their lands.

Books

The Cherokee Nation: A History by Robert J. Conley

Cherokee Women by Theda Perdue

The Cherokees by Grace Steels Woodward

Africans and Native Americans by Jack D. Forbes

Edible and Useful Plants of the Southwest by Dellena Tull

Cherokee Basketry by M. Ann Fariello

Black Indians by William Loren Katz

The Cherokee Full Circle by JT Garrett and Michael Tlanusta Garrett

Tennessee's Indian Peoples by Ronald N. Satz

Map of Mid South

A map of Easter, Lucinda and Wahali's journey. Easter begins in Red Clay – East Tennessee and travels to Pulaski, Tenn. Lucinda begins in Red Clay and travels to the Qualla territory. Wahali begins in Red Clay and travels on the northern most route of the Trail of Tears to what was then considered "Indian Territory" but is now Oklahoma.

ABOUT THE AUTHOR

Dale Marie Taylor lives in Georgia with her husband, her German shepherd dog and tuxedo cat. They have one adult son. Taylor has a Ph.D. in literature and writes in other venues. She enjoys piano playing, traveling and reading. Taylor enjoys hearing from her readers. Write to her at P.O. Box 70, Stone Mountain, Ga. 30086 or at ckate593@gmail.com.
See more work by Kate Ayre Campbell at narrativemagic.com.
If you enjoyed this book, please leave a review of it at an online book retailer such as Amazon.
The next book in the Apple Hill Series is
Hester's Journey –available at online retail bookstores.

Made in the USA
Columbia, SC
16 July 2023

20120654R00178